MW01616253

THE
STEPSISTER'S
SECRET

BOOKS BY KAREN KING

THE STEPSISTER'S SECRET

KAREN KING

bookouture

Published by Bookouture in 2026

An imprint of Storyfire Ltd.
Carmelite House
50 Victoria Embankment
London EC4Y 0DZ

www.bookouture.com

The authorised representative in the EEA is Hachette Ireland
8 Castlecourt Centre
Dublin 15 D15 XTP3
Ireland
(email: info@hbgi.ie)

Copyright © Karen King, 2026

Karen King has asserted her right to be identified as the author of this work.

All rights reserved. No part of this publication may be reproduced, stored in any
retrieval system, or transmitted, in any form or by any means, electronic,
mechanical, photocopying, recording or otherwise, without the prior written
permission of the publishers.

ISBN: 978-1-83618-996-1
eBook ISBN: 978-1-83618-995-4

This book is a work of fiction. Names, characters, businesses, organizations,
places and events other than those clearly in the public domain, are either the
product of the author's imagination or are used fictitiously. Any resemblance to
actual persons, living or dead, events or locales is entirely coincidental.

PROLOGUE

What the hell have I done?

I force down an avalanche of panic and bile as I stare at the body sprawled out on the floor. I will a hand to twitch, the familiar eyes to open, a groan of life to escape from the firmly closed lips. But there is nothing. I'm trembling, my eyes blinking rapidly as the enormity of the situation hits me.

Kneeling, I hold the limp wrist, feeling desperately for a pulse even though I know it's impossible. No one could survive this.

I scramble to my feet and wipe the back of my hand across my forehead, it feels cold and clammy. Sweat is pouring down my face. My heart is thumping against the walls of my chest as if it will burst out any minute. I want to scream, wail, protest that I didn't mean this to happen but there is no time, I have to get away. No one will suspect me. No one knows I'm here.

After everything that's happened they will suspect she did it.

I hope they blame her. If it wasn't for her this would never have happened. She drove me to it.

If only I could unwind time, go back to this morning. Stay at home, not answer the phone. Better still, rewind to before the wedding. No, long before that, when she came into our lives and wrecked it. But there is nothing I can do.

'I'm so sorry!' I whisper, my eyes drawn again to the body. 'I didn't mean for this to happen.'

MAY

SATURDAY

1

LIZZIE

'Nanny looks like a princess,' Grace exclaims in awe, her blue eyes wide, her hands clasped together as she stares at my mum.

My five-year-old daughter is right. Mum looks beautiful, radiant and so happy.

I just hope that she's marrying her prince. It's all happened so fast. *Too fast*, a little voice whispers in my head.

It's a warm May day, perfect weather for a wedding. Mum's dress is silver lace, knee-length, and it has a matching sheer silver voile coat, which she pairs with strappy grey kitten-heeled sandals – it's exquisite. She's wearing contacts today instead of her usual rimless glasses, and her white-blonde chin-length bob frames her face. Her simple bouquet of long-stemmed white roses wrapped in a sky-blue ribbon is stunning.

Standing beside her, George, my new stepfather, looks dapper in a light grey suit, pale blue tie and gleaming black shoes. The sun pours in through the top window, glinting on his glasses and forming a halo of light above his bald head. He and Mum turn to gaze at each other with shining eyes, their beaming smiles letting us all know how happy they are, and my doubts float away like leaves on the breeze. Mum wants this. She deserves it.

'They look good together, don't they?' Nick, my husband, whispers, placing his arm on mine.

'Yes, they do.' I can hear the quiver in my voice, and Nick's hand slides down my arm to my hand, squeezing it comfortably. He knows how difficult the past few months have been and how much it means to me to see my mum happy again. I don't know what I'd do without Nick, he's been a tower of strength.

I never thought that Mum would marry again. Dad died nine years ago, and Mum has never shown any interest in dating. Then Nick spotted the Agatha Christie Facebook group – Mum is a huge fan of Agatha Christie and has a whole shelf of her books – and encouraged her to join.

It was good to see her have an interest, and she really enjoyed chatting to her online friends. But then she started mentioning George a lot, and their online chats became video calls and then meeting up. I was a bit worried about how quickly Mum's friendship with George developed into a romance, a few weeks after they first started talking. She said they'd gelled straight away, and she seemed so happy, but I still had my reservations.

When I met George I was relieved to discover that he seemed a genuinely nice guy. He was so different to Dad though. Dad was tall and big built with a mop of ginger hair that I'd inherited, and beard. He was a workaholic, but when he was home he was funny and loving, a presence that filled the room.

George is smaller, slimmer, quietly spoken. He was a rock of support after Mum had the mini stroke. It had been such a worrying time for us all. George proposed as soon as Mum was better, saying it had made him realise how much he loved her, and he moved into Mum's house to look after her.

And now here they are, getting married, just six months

after that first meeting. They were lucky to get a Saturday, as there was a cancellation and they seized it.

Kenny and Sheila, George's son and sister, walk into the Register Office and wave to us. Kenny is tall like George, with sandy hair, but Sheila is tiny, with a mass of silver curls and pencilled arched eyebrows that make her look permanently surprised. We've met them both a couple of times at Mum's. We haven't met George's daughter Alison yet because she lives in Spain, although she's video-called George and Mum a few times and Mum seems quite taken with her.

It will be strange to have a whole new family, a stepsister and stepbrother. A step aunt too. I'm an only child of only children and always longed for a brother and sister, or an extended family. I'm hoping we will all get on, that Isaac and Grace will have the big loving family I longed for. It has only ever been me, Mum and Dad, so watching George now, putting his arm around my mum and smiling into her eyes, brings a lump to my throat. I miss my dad so much, but Mum deserves this new chance of happiness.

'Uncle Kenny and Daddy and Isaac are twins,' Grace observes, pointing to them one by one. Nick and Kenny are wearing the same silver-grey suit with a sky-blue waistcoat like George, as is our seven-year-old son Isaac.

'That's because it's a wedding, silly,' Isaac retorts.

'I'm not silly!' Grace stamps her feet. 'Mummy and Auntie Sheila and Nanny aren't twins.'

She's right, Sheila is wearing a smart navy suit with a white blouse and a navy hat, whereas I'm wearing a sky-blue dress, and matching fascinator. We're all wearing ivory rose button-holes like the men though.

Kenny overhears and walks over. 'Very observant, young lady.' He holds out his hand for a high five and first Grace then Isaac high five him. Kenny and Sheila are friendly and Kenny is great with the kids. They all seem a very close family.

I wonder what Alison will be like. Mum said that she messaged George this morning to say her flight had been delayed, and she has just messaged again to say she's on her way in a taxi.

'I hope Alison hurries up, the kids are getting restless.' I retie the sky-blue sash around Grace's ivory calf-length dress and straighten the blue bow in her dark curly hair – just like Nick's.

'I guess she can't help her flight being late, but I don't think the registrar will wait much longer.' Nick leans forward and straightens Isaac's bow tie. Isaac has my ginger hair and green eyes. The colouring looks good on him whereas I hated it when I was a kid and dyed it black as soon as I could. He has my high cheekbones too, and always looks serious, whereas Grace has blue eyes and a sweetheart-shaped face and when she smiles it lights up her whole face, just like her dad – and grandad, I remember sadly. I still miss Dad terribly.

'I can't believe we're all here to see my mum get married,' I tell Nick. 'It's been such a whirlwind romance.'

'I know, but it's good to see your mum happy again, isn't it?' He looks so handsome, the sky-blue suit brings out the deep blue of his eyes and his dark, curly hair is swept up into a quiff. 'You look gorgeous,' he whispers.

'You don't look so bad yourself,' I say, smiling at him. He's right, it is good to see Mum happy, and in love again. I was still living at home when Dad died and me and Mum were both really devasted, our world shattered into tiny Dad-less pieces, so we clung to each other for support. Then Nick came along and picked us both up. He's been beside us ever since, taking care of us, helping us whenever he can. He's our rock. I hope that Mum has found her rock in George, too.

The registrar looks anxiously at her watch. 'I'm afraid that I can't wait much longer, I've another service soon.'

George glances at the door. 'My daughter should be here any minute.'

Isaac fidgets. 'I'm hungry,' he complains.

The door opens and a tall, slim woman with short blonde hair and dangling gold earrings bursts in. She is wearing a striking red trouser suit, black stilettos and a black fascinator. 'Sorry I'm late, everyone. The traffic was awful.'

Both Mum's and George's faces crease into big smiles as the woman – obviously Alison – waves and slides into the seat next to Sheila and Kenny, her red trouser suit like a beacon amongst the sea of blue and silver-grey. She clearly wasn't told the colour scheme.

The ceremony begins and we all watch in silence as Mum and George say their vows and rings are exchanged. It's such a poignant moment tinged with sadness because it means my dad has finally been replaced, but I know he would have wanted Mum to be happy.

I hope she's always as happy as this moment, that George looks after her. They are gazing at each other so adoringly, and we all clap as they kiss. Isaac and Grace clap the loudest and keep on clapping when everyone has finished. They both adore George. And their nanny, of course.

'Now we have a granddad,' Grace says to Isaac, and my heart lifts for them. Grace and Isaac longed for a granddad, but Nick's dad died when he was young, and mine before our children were born.

Nick squeezes my hand and smiles down at me, he knows how emotional this is for me. I smile back to reassure him that I'm all right then glance over at Alison and Kenny to give them a friendly smile too. After all, we're all family now.

Kenny catches my eye and winks, but Alison is chatting to Sheila. I'll talk to them at the reception.

. . .

We all crowd around Mum and George, wanting to congratulate them. Alison hugs her dad then hugs Mum too.

'Welcome to the family, Mum,' she says.

Mum! I gasp aloud and my jaw slackens. Did she actually call my mum 'Mum'? Wow! She barely knows her. That's far too familiar.

Alison turns to me, and I wonder if she heard my gasp of surprise. I quickly compose myself.

'Hello, Alison, delighted to meet you.'

My breath catches in my throat as her eyes hold mine, a small smile curving her red painted lips. My heart pounds and a wave of dizziness sweeps over me as a memory comes pounding back.

It can't be her. It can't.

2

JUDITH

George squeezes my hand, his grey eyes twinkling adoringly through his glasses. 'Happy?' he asks when both families have finished congratulating us and are chatting to each other.

'Very,' I assure him, enjoying the warmth of his hand wrapped around mine. I am happier than I ever thought I would be after losing Arthur so tragically. I never expected to fall in love again, or for it to happen so quickly, but George is so caring and kind I know that I am making the right decision. 'It was a beautiful ceremony, wasn't it? And I'm so glad Alison got here in time.'

We were both worried when Alison messaged this morning to say her flight had been delayed. 'Look, we can postpone,' I told George. 'You can't get married without your daughter here.'

But he was adamant that we should continue with the ceremony. 'I don't want to wait a moment longer than I have to for you to be my wife. And Alison herself insists that we go ahead without her, if she's late.'

I really wanted Alison to be part of the wedding. I've spoken to her a few times when she video-called George from Spain and we got on so well. Our small family wedding wouldn't have been the same without her, so I was delighted when she rushed through the doors just in time.

'She cut it a bit short, didn't she?' George says. 'That's Alison all over, she's such a jetsetter. She might be living in Spain now, but she's worked and lived in several countries.'

I'm looking forward to getting to know Alison more, and Kenny. I envy George for having two children. If only Arthur and I could have provided a sibling for Lizzie, I'm sure she wouldn't have been such an anxious child. George's family seem so close and are very friendly. I marvel again at how lucky I am. It's just been me and Lizzie ever since Arthur died, and we've had some tough years. I was really pleased when Lizzie married Nick, I couldn't have chosen a better husband for her if I'd picked him myself, and I was so glad that Lizzie had the emotional support she needed. It had started to become quite a strain on me. The constant need to reassure her and allay her fears can be draining.

When Lizzie moved out it took me some time to get used to living alone though and I spent most of my evenings reading or watching crime and mystery dramas. Lizzie, Nick and the children often popped in but once they had gone home again the house seemed so big and quiet. Sally at work tried to persuade me to sign up to a dating app, but I didn't want to meet up with a stranger. Then Nick saw the Agatha Christie Facebook group and suggested I join. That's where I met George.

We both commented on various posts then he inboxed me to continue a discussion we'd been having about *The Mousetrap*, and we discovered to our amazement that we only lived a twenty-minute drive from each other. Soon we were messaging each other regularly, sharing bits about our day, talking about a film we'd seen, a book we'd read. I felt like I already knew him when he invited me to go to a local production of *Murder on the Orient Express*. It wasn't like meeting a stranger at all. And even though it's only been a few months since we first started chatting, I feel like we've known each other forever.

'Hey, you're miles away!' George wraps his arm around my shoulder and pulls me closer, kissing me on the cheek. 'No regrets, I hope?'

I lean into him. 'Of course not!' I gaze up at him, teasing. 'What about you?'

'Me? I'm the luckiest man alive. I can't believe I've had a second chance of happiness at my age. I bless every day that you came into my life.' He kisses me tenderly on the forehead.

'Me too,' I say softly. I miss Arthur still, but you can't live life in the past, and I know he would be pleased that I've found love again.

Kenny and Sheila join us. 'It was such a delightful cere-mony, and you look beautiful, Judith,' Sheila tells me.

'So do you. And thank you for helping with the flowers.' I kiss her on the cheek. George told me that Sheila has been a tower of strength to him over the years, and he's worried that she might feel a bit pushed out, so we've tried to involve her in the wedding as much as possible.

'I'm so pleased to see my dad happy.' Kenny envelops me in a big hug. 'You two make a fantastic couple.'

'Thank you,' I say. George's family have been so welcoming. I'm looking forward to us all having get-togethers, maybe cele-brating birthdays and Christmas together. One big happy family.

'I think Lizzie's a bit overcome with the emotion of it all though,' Kenny says.

I follow his gaze and see that Lizzie is clutching the back of the chair as if she's about to collapse, her wide eyes staring out of a paper-white face, her whole body trembling.

I instinctively go to rush over, but then Alison reaches out to support her. As I watch them a thread of unease slithers through me.

3

LIZZIE

Immediately I'm thrust back to that dreadful day, the one that I can never forget, and the intense feelings of fear and guilt are suffocating me. I swallow, my chest tightening, my head spinning as I try to regain control of my mind. I can't have a panic attack here. Not at my mum's wedding.

My head is light, as if everything is happening around me, my ears are buzzing and I'm scared my legs won't support me. I take a deep breath and reach for the chair behind me, the chair that a few minutes ago Sheila had sat on to watch Mum and George get married.

Focus, Lizzie, ground yourself. I desperately try to remember the 3-3-3 method my therapist taught me. Three things I can see. I focus on my trembling hands gripping into the chair, my nails painted sky blue to go with my dress, my shoes...

'Are you all right, Lizzie? You look terribly pale.' Alison sounds concerned, puzzled. She takes my arm. 'Is it the heat? It is rather hot in here but I'm used to it, living in Spain. Why don't you sit down for a minute.'

She holds my arm firmly, and I sink into the chair. I can't look at her, can't speak. I'm blindsided at this turn of events. I never thought that I would see her again and now she's my step-sister. I've been plunged into a nightmare and I don't know how to deal with it.

I never knew Ally's surname. I never met her father, and her brother had been so young that I didn't recognise Kenny, how could I?

It's been twenty-five years since that terrible day, but I'd know Ally anywhere. Her hair was long and a golden brown back then, scooped up in a ponytail, but I remember those blue eyes, one darker than the other, and the tiny brown mole on her right cheek just under her eye. There can't be two people with the same eyes and mole, the same name, the same age. It's got to be her.

Has she recognised me? My heart thuds so hard in my chest that I fear it might burst through my ribcage and explode.

'Lizzie.' She bends down to talk to me. 'Are you okay?'

I bite my lip and force myself to meet her concerned gaze, waiting with sick dread for the recognition in her eyes. Recognition that will turn to horror and rage when she realises who I am, what I did. My hands are sweating, my pulse racing, and I'm bracing myself for her cry of outrage. But all I see in her eyes is concern.

I draw on an inner strength, dredge down through the anxiety consuming me and reach for a thread of common sense. Even if Alison recognises me all she will remember is a seven-year-old girl she met on a school trip, I remind myself.

No one saw what I did. No one knows.

The dam of guilt bursts and a river of relief floods through me, washing away my fears when I see that Alison is smiling at me. She's speaking to me. I can't hear what she's saying but her tone sounds friendly and comforting.

I scrape through the fog in my mind to focus on her words. 'It's probably the emotion of the day. It's been such a whirlwind romance, hasn't it? But it's so good to meet you at last. Dad speaks so highly of you.'

She doesn't recognise me. Thank God.

I breathe out slowly. Of course she hasn't recognised me. I've changed a lot over the last twenty-five years. My hair is black now – tired of the taunts of 'ginger nut', I'd dyed it when I was fourteen and despite Mum and Dad's annoyance I've kept it that colour ever since. I'm slimmer too. Nothing like that dumpy red head Ally – now Alison – had met on the school outing at the amusement park. My head whirls and I start to feel faint as the memory of that day shoots into my mind. I squeeze my eyes shut to block out the awfulness of it all.

'I'll get you a glass of water,' I hear Alison say.

'Lizzie, darling, are you all right?'

Mum has noticed me and comes over to check. I flick open my eyes and see her face tight with anxiety. I don't want to spoil this day for her. The last thing she needs is to worry about me. She's done enough of that over the years.

I force a bright smile on my face. 'I'm good, Mum. Really. I forgot to have breakfast. I'll be fine in a minute. You go and mingle.'

'If you're sure?' Mum frowns, her eyes raking my face.

I force my smile wider. 'Positive.'

Alison returns with the glass of water. 'Here you are, Lizzie. Drink this.' She hands it to me then turns to Mum. 'I'll stay with her until she feels better.'

George calls, and Mum squeezes my hand. 'Sit and rest for a while, darling.' I nod and she goes off to join George.

I slowly sip the water, keeping my eyes focused on the glass. I daren't look at Alison again yet, not until I can compose myself. My head is swimming with images of her mother desperately trying to breathe, gasping, her eyes bulging, dying in front of our terrified eyes.

And it was all my fault.

4

LIZZIE

'Lizzie?' Nick is beside me now. 'What's the matter, love?'

'I think it's the heat. She seemed to go all dizzy,' Alison tells him. 'I'll leave her in your capable hands, Nick.'

She walks away to join her brother and aunt. Nick crouches down in front of me, his forehead creased. 'Are you all right, Lizzie?' Nick is always patient with my anxiety attacks, treating me with kindness and understanding. I try to keep them under control, not only because I hate them but also because I'm worried that he will get fed up with me. I know that I can be difficult to live with sometimes and I don't know what I would do without Nick. He and the kids are my world.

He's a patient listener, and is never judgemental, but I can't tell him what's caused this attack. I can't bear him to know what I did. I never told Mum or Dad either. I buried it deep down, nailed a lid on it, tried not to think about it. I told myself that I'd never see Ally or Kenny again so no one would ever find out.

How wrong I was.

The nightmare of the situation I'm in engulfs me and dizziness claims me once more.

I feel Nick squeezing my hand and hear the concern in his voice. 'What is it, Liz?'

I draw on every reserve of my strength to pull myself together and reply as calmly as I'm able. 'I'm sorry, Nick. I think it's the heat, and I was in such a rush this morning I forgot to have breakfast.' I repeat the lie I told Mum. 'I'll be fine in a moment. Honestly I will.'

'Are you sure?' He stands up now and turns around, his eyes scanning the room, and I know he's looking for Isaac and Grace.

'Yes, please go and look after the kids.' I shoo him away. 'I'll be with you in a minute.' I take a big gulp of the water.

He goes off, and I take a few more deep breaths. In, hold, out. In, hold, out.

Get a grip, Lizzie. You're causing a scene. Alison hasn't recognised you, stop panicking.

'Are you feeling any better?' Alison is back. She sits down next to me.

'Yes, thank you.' I sip the remaining water in the glass.

'Do you often have panic attacks?'

Her question takes me by surprise. 'It wasn't a panic attack. It was a combination of the heat and not having breakfast.'

She raises an eyebrow slightly, and I remember that she's a nurse. She knows a panic attack when she sees one.

'Ah, good, you two have already connected.' George joins, a big cheery smile on his face as his eyes swivel from Alison to me. 'We're off to the park for the photos, it's only a few minutes' walk, then the meal. Are you ready?'

'Are you okay to take a short walk, little sis?' Alison squeezes my arm reassuringly then stands up.

The 'little sis' grates a bit, after all we've only just met, but her friendliness calms my nerves. She hasn't recognised me. Or maybe it isn't her. I could be wrong. Ally could have been short for Alice, Alex, Alana – or a dozen other names. But how many people have two different shades of blue eyes and a distinguishing mole like that?

It's no good trying to kid myself. It's definitely her.

'I'm fine now.' I get to my feet and look around for Nick and see that he's talking to Kenny. Isaac and Grace are huddled over Isaac's iPad so I go over to them. 'Come on, guys, it's time for the photos then lunch,' I tell them.

'We haven't finished the game yet,' Isaac protests, and Grace pouts.

'Remember what I told you about this being Nanny and George's wedding day, and how you have to be on your very best behaviour,' I say firmly. 'Please switch the iPad off, you can finish the game later.'

Isaac reluctantly does as I say. He adores his nan. I hold out my hand for Grace. 'Come on, Gracie, once we've had the photos taken we can get some fries.'

Gracie loves fries, she'd eat them for every meal of the day if we let her.

Nick is heading over to us now and Kenny has joined Mum and George. I study him, trying to see some resemblance to the little Kenny but I'd barely noticed him back then. It was Ally I'd been friendly with. And Kenny had been too young to remember me.

'I'm starving, I want to eat now,' Isaac grumbles to Nick.

'And me,' Grace chimes.

'Me too, sweetie.' Nick kisses her on the forehead. Grace is a proper Daddy's girl. 'The photos won't take long.'

We all walk to the nearby park together, with Sam, the photographer, a friend of Kenny's. He leads the way over to the pretty pergola among the picturesque flower beds with a backdrop of trees already in blossom – it's the perfect setting for wedding photographs. Sam clicks away, taking several photos of

Mum and George, then a couple of family groups. We all stand together, with Mum and George in the middle, us on the left and George's family on the right.

When Sam is finished taking photos, Alison turns to talk to Mum and George. I watch them for a moment, thinking how at ease with each other they all look, then something makes me turn and I see Nick looking over too, but his eyes are fixed on Alison.

She looks so striking in her red outfit, but the intensity of Nick's gaze alarms me. What's going on here?

5

I knew who she was right away but I wasn't going to let her know. Especially before the wedding. I need this marriage to take place.

I kept my face straight all through the ceremony, never letting any sign of recognition spark in my eyes. Revenge is best served cold they say, and that's what I intend to do. I've waited too long for this, and I can wait a little longer.

It might be twenty-five years, but I've never forgotten what she did. She destroyed our family.

I'll never forgive her. And I'm going to make sure she pays.

Look at her, walking off with Nick's arm around her shoulder, both of them clutching a hand of one of their kids. They look such a happy family unit.

Like we were until she destroyed it.

She probably thinks that her secret is safe, that no one knows what she did. That we all believe it was a tragic accident.

Maybe it was. But whether she meant it or not, she was the one who caused all that devastation.

And we've had to live with the results of what she did, had to pick up the shattered remains of our lives and try to carry on.

It was years before I realised whose fault it was and it was too late to do anything about it then. I didn't even know Lizzie's name. But I know now, and I know what she did.

Now it's time to get my revenge.

6

JUDITH

'Oh, George, this is beautiful,' I exclaim as my eyes rest on the table reserved for us in a quiet area of the pub restaurant. A round ivory lace tablecloth is covering the wooden table, and three sky-blue vases of ivory roses are placed along the centre. There are ivory napkins tied with sky-blue ribbon by every place setting. 'I didn't expect this.'

George beams and hugs me. 'Sheila's the one to thank, she slipped in before the ceremony and laid it out for us.'

I turn to my new sister-in-law. 'Thank you so much, Sheila. That's very thoughtful of you.'

'My pleasure,' she replies with a big smile.

It really has been a wonderful day, I think as we all sit down at the table. Kenny sits by George then Sheila then Alison. Nick is sitting the other side of Alison, then the children in the middle of him and Lizzie, who is next to me.

The waitress, a young woman in her early twenties, brings a bottle of champagne in a bucket of ice. George must have ordered it. She pops the cork and pours champagne in each glass, then takes a small bottle of apple juice out of the bucket and half fills two tumblers with it for Isaac and Grace.

Kenny stands up, holding out his glass. 'I'd like to give a toast to my dad and Judith, Mr and Mrs Davies. I hope you both have many happy years together.'

Together, we all clink our glasses, Isaac and Grace joining in too, their tumblers chinking loudly. George stands up and holds out his glass. 'To my beautiful wife, Judith.' He smiles at me. 'Thank you for making me the happiest man alive.' I can feel my cheeks flush. Then Grace says loudly, 'I'm hungry, can we eat now?' And we all laugh.

It's a delicious meal, prawn cocktail or breaded camembert starter followed by chicken in the basket, chips and salad. We decided not to go to a posh restaurant because of the children, and looking at Isaac and Grace tucking happily into their chicken and fries I'm pleased we chose a pub lunch.

George and Kenny are chatting away to Sheila. George told me that Sheila never married or had children of her own. She was a substitute mother for Alison and Kenny when his wife Carol died, which explains why they are so close.

'I'm so happy for you, Mum,' Lizzie says.

I switch my gaze to her. 'Thank you, darling.' Thankfully, she's recovered from the dizzy episode she had in the church. The heat and no breakfast, she said. It is warm today but not that hot and I worried that she might be having one of her episodes again, but she looks perfectly fine now.

'Sorry, Mummy!' Grace apologises quickly, looking aghast at the drink she's just knocked over.

Lizzie goes to reach for a serviette, but Alison has already grabbed one and is mopping it up.

'Accidents happen, darling,' she reassures Grace.

Lizzie thanks her, as does Nick, and they start chatting. Well, actually Nick and Alison do most of the chatting, it always takes Lizzie time to relax with people. Nick, on the other hand, is calm and at ease with everyone. He's been an asset to the company, ever since Arthur took him on fresh out of college.

23

Arthur always spoke so highly of him, and I think he would be delighted to know that he and Lizzie are married.

Arthur died so suddenly that we were shaken to the core. Lizzie was still living at home then, and we were a big support to each other in the dreadful months ahead. We were so devastated we could barely function. Nick checked in on us, always ready to help out. Gradually, he and Lizzie became close and I was thrilled when he proposed, a couple of years after Arthur's death. Lizzie didn't want to leave me on my own so she suggested that Nick move in with us, but I wouldn't hear of it. They needed to make their own home, their own life.

To be honest, it was a relief to not have the daily worry of coping with Lizzie. I know that she can't help suffering from anxiety, but it was so draining having to try and jolly her along all the while, it meant that I couldn't really deal with my own grief because I had to try and be upbeat around her. It was good to have a bit of time and space to myself, and I knew Lizzie was in safe hands with Nick. That no matter how dark her moods got he could handle them.

I glance over as I hear Nick laugh at something Alison said. He's so good with people, always interested in whatever they have to say. He rarely talks about himself, not like a lot of men who think they're the most important people in the room.

George is the same. 'Never mind me, let's talk about you,' George said at our first meeting. And he's been like that ever since. Honestly, if it wasn't for the odd remark that Sheila makes, I would know hardly anything about him.

7

LIZZIE

Alison is smiling, leaning across the table towards Nick as she chats away to him about her life in Spain, and he's hanging on to her every word.

'It sounds fantastic, so different from England. Is it a typical Spanish town you live in or are there a lot of expats there?' he asks.

'Mainly Spanish. Wherever I live I like to immerse myself in the local culture. Have you and Lizzie ever considered living abroad?'

Nick shakes his head. 'It's a lot with kids, you have to think about their education.'

She glances over at me. 'What about you, Lizzie, do you fancy a warmer climate and change of scenery?'

'Er... I've never really thought about it...'

Isaac and Grace start bickering and I turn my attention to them. They're both bored and a bit demanding. Normally Nick would help me deal with them, but he's too engrossed talking to Alison, who is now relating an anecdote about a holiday she had in Thailand when a woman collapsed in front of her and she had to do CPR. I can't help feeling a bit of a wallflower compared to her. She's so pretty, and outgoing and it sounds like she's done so much with her life. Not like me. I'm always withdrawn, anxious and have lived in this area forever.

I wonder if Nick is comparing us? He seems to be quite taken with Alison, they've really hit it off, and I can't help feeling a little jealous. And annoyed that he's making no effort to include me in the conversation.

Don't be silly, he's simply being friendly, I tell myself. *We're a family now. And there's nothing stopping you from joining in if you want to.*

'Your kids are great, really well behaved,' Kenny says.

I glance over at Kenny. 'Thanks.'

It's hard to believe that he and Alison are siblings, they look so different. He's like his mother, I realise, wondering why I didn't notice it before. He has the same dark hair and oval smiley face, whereas Alison has blonde hair and sharp features.

Maybe she follows George although he is almost bald now, I can see a slight similarity in their features. She must be four or five years older than Kenny. I remember that when I met Ally – Alison – on that fatal school trip she said her little brother hadn't started school yet. She was in the year above me and Jodie. I never thought I'd see her again, after that day.

'Time for another toast.' Alison's voice pulls me back to the present. 'I'll keep it short but want to say how great it is to see Dad looking so happy. And to have a mum again.' She raises her glass. 'Welcome to the family, Mum.' She fixes her gaze on me. 'You don't mind if I call your mum Mum, do you? It's just that we've grown so close during our vid-calls over the last couple of months and, well, my mum died years ago.' She looks a little uncertain. 'Judith said she was fine with it.'

Guilt bubbles up in me that she had to grow up without a mum and that she missed her so much she wants to grab my mum like this. I can't help feeling a bit resentful though that Mum has agreed to this and not told me. I'm not jealous, of course I'm not, but surely Mum could have mentioned it. I had no idea she and Alison were so chummy.

Mum squeezes Alison's hand. 'Of course she doesn't, we're all family now.'

'It's great to have a little sis as well as a new mum.' She grins at Nick. 'And a big brother' – then sweeps her gaze to Isaac and Grace – 'and a gorgeous nephew and niece. I can't wait for us to get to know each other better,' she gushes.

'Me too,' I reply with a smile, although it really bugs me being referred to as 'little sis'. She's much too familiar for my liking but no one else seems to mind.

I inwardly cringe every time Alison addresses my mum as 'Mum' but try not to show it. Thankfully, Kenny calls Mum 'Judith' and catches my eye and winks every time Alison says 'Mum', as if he's guessed how awkward I feel about it.

Grace wants to go to the loo, so I take her. Nick is so busy talking to Alison he doesn't even notice when I get up. I have to tap his arm and tell him.

On the way back I meet Kenny walking to the bar. 'Don't mind Alison, she's always a bit over the top,' he says. 'She's glad to see Dad happy and wants to make your mum welcome. And I'm sure she doesn't mean to monopolise Nick.'

So he's noticed it too. 'It's fine, Nick is such a good listener, everyone finds it easy to talk to him. And I don't mind about Alison, it's just a little strange to hear someone else calling my mum "Mum". I'm an only child.' I return his smile, glad that someone has taken my feelings into account.

'Lucky you, no troublesome siblings to cope with,' he jests. 'Do you want another drink? I've got everyone else's orders, but Nick wasn't sure what you'd want.' He bends down to talk to Grace. 'How about you, Gracie? Want some more juice?'

I love how he takes the time to interact with the children. Alison did at first too, but now all her attention seems to be on Nick and his on her. It's making me feel a bit uncomfortable. It isn't like Nick either to ignore me like this. I resolve to take him to task about it when we get home.

'I'll have a pineapple juice and lemonade, please,' I reply. We've already had a couple of glasses of fizz and I don't want to drink any more alcohol, not when we have the kids to look after.

When I return to the table Alison glances over at me. 'Would you believe that Nick and I worked together years ago? I worked in the office during the summer holidays while I was at college.'

Nick grins. 'Yeah, I hadn't been there long either.'

That stuns me. Alison worked at Dad's company? Why are they only mentioning this now when we've been together for the last few hours? 'Didn't you recognise each other right away?' I ask as I help Grace into her seat then sit down beside her.

Nick shakes his head. 'No, it was years ago, and Alison had long black hair then. She was going through her goth stage.'

Alison laughs. 'And Nick had a buzzcut.' She touches Nick's dark curls, and I flinch, it seems too intimate. 'I much prefer your hair now.'

'And you look better without the white face makeup and black lipstick,' he teases.

I feel uncomfortable at their easy-going banter and the knowledge that they have some sort of shared past. I want to keep my distance from Alison, not for her and Nick to be all matey. Thank goodness she lives in Spain.

'What a coincidence,' I say lightly. 'It's a small world, isn't it? And now you're a nurse and live in Spain. Do you like it there?'

'I do, but maybe I'm ready for a change. What about you, Nick, where are you working now?'

'He's still working for my dad's company. He's the Construction Manager,' I tell her proudly.

'Wow! That's a big achievement.' Then Alison frowns. 'Wait, AT Construction was your dad's company?'

I nod. 'Unfortunately, Dad had a heart attack at work.' My voice breaks a little at the memory of how quickly and cruelly my beloved father was taken away from us. 'But Nick was wonderful. He was such a support to us, he came to tell us personally about Dad's accident, took us to the hospital, looked after us and organised the funeral. I really don't know what we would have done without him.'

Alison looks really taken aback. 'I didn't realise... I'm so sorry about your dad. How awful for you both.'

'It was. It was so sudden and such a shock,' Mum says. 'And I had no idea what to do with the business, but Nick took control, he literally saved the company and worked hard building it up.'

Alison looks from Mum to me, her eyes wide. Then she turns her gaze to Nick. 'That was very good of you.' Was I imagining the edge to her voice?

Nick shrugs and stares awkwardly down at his plate. 'I had a lot of support, all the staff are fantastic.'

'Nick is always so modest,' I say.

'So that's how you two met? How fascinating.' Again there seems to be an edge to her voice.

'Yes, they quickly became inseparable, and I was delighted when Nick asked Lizzie to marry him. I couldn't think of a better son-in-law.' Mum smiles at Nick, and he flushes.

Nick is looking rather embarrassed at all this praise, so I change the subject. 'It's been great to meet you, Alison. When do you go back to Spain?'

'I fly back tomorrow,' she says. 'I'm staying over at Aunty Sheila's tonight so that I don't cramp the honeymooners' style. It's only about fifteen mins' drive from here to Gloucester.'

Mum looks a bit embarrassed but George laughs. 'What's she like?'

'Well, hopefully it won't be long before you're over again and we can all have another catchup,' Mum says.

Kenny groans. 'Don't encourage her or she'll be here every weekend!'

Alison grins. 'Wouldn't you love that.'

I listen to the banter, my mind working overtime at the freaky coincidence that not only has Mum married the man whose wife's death I was responsible for, but that man's daughter worked for my dad's company with my husband. And apparently they were very friendly back then. A friendship that seems to have rekindled today.

Alison was only there for the summer. Dad owned the biggest construction firm in the area and often gave summer jobs to the local students, I remind myself. And it was years ago.

Even so, it gives Alison even more of a connection to my family. And the last thing I want is for her to attach herself to us. I want her to go back to Spain and stay there. That way, hopefully, no one will ever find out what I did.

8

JUDITH

'Well, we'd better be going before they kick us out,' George says much later. 'It's gone six now.'

I can't believe it's that late. It's been such a wonderful day, the weather has been perfect and everyone has got on so well, which means a lot to me and George. We're both family people, liking our grown-up kids to pop in whenever they can. It would have been awkward if they hadn't got on, so we were delighted to see them chatting away happily.

We all get out of our seats and start to gather our things together.

Lizzie turns to me. 'Enjoy your honeymoon in Prague, Mum. Take lots of photos. And let us know that you've arrived safely.' She hugs me goodbye.

'I will,' I promise. I bend down and give Isaac and Grace a cuddle. They're tired so Lizzie and Nick are going straight home, but Kenny, Alison and Sheila are coming back to have a cup of tea with us.

Everyone says their goodbyes amid hugs, handshakes and cries of 'See you soon', 'Safe journey.' Then Lizzie and Nick set off home. I'm so pleased how well the day has gone, and am really looking forward to our honeymoon tomorrow. I've got a week off from the bakery where I work part-time, and George has arranged cover for his shop. It will be wonderful to spend a few days together, walking around Prague. Neither of us has ever been before but we've researched online and it looks a beautiful city with lots to see and do.

Back home, Alison goes straight into the kitchen, as if she's lived here all her life, and makes us all a cup of tea.

'Are you both all packed?' she asks, bringing mugs in on a tray. She passes me my special mug, the one that Isaac and Grace bought me for my birthday. It says 'World's Best Gran' so it's obviously mine, it's very thoughtful of her. Then she hands steaming mugs around to the others. 'What time is your flight tomorrow?'

'We have to be at the airport for eleven,' George tells her.

'Me too, I might see you there.'

It seems daft to me that she's going over to Sheila's in Gloucester when we all have to leave for the airport at the same time. 'Why don't you stay here and you can travel with us? We can share a taxi. Unless you wanted to have a catch-up with Sheila and Kenny?' I suggest.

Kenny yawns. 'I'm whacked, I was on a late shift last night, so I'll be hitting the sack as soon as I get home.' He works as a Call Centre Manager and often does a late or weekend shift. 'Besides, we all chat a lot on WhatsApp so we're pretty up to date with what each other is doing,' he adds.

'It does make sense for you to kip here, Alison,' Sheila agrees. 'It won't be such a rush in the morning for you.'

Alison turns to me. 'If you're sure, I'd love to. It would be great to spend a bit more time with you and Dad.'

'That's all settled then,' I say. It will give us a chance to get to know each other a bit better.

When they've finished their tea, Kenny and Sheila leave and me, Alison and George chat for a while. Alison has some amusing anecdotes about her life in Spain, then she and George share chats about their family holidays in Brean. Alison doesn't really talk about her mum, but George has already told me that she was only eight when Carol, his wife, died, and Kenny was four. It was so tragic. None of them has said exactly how it happened and I don't like to ask. I guess it's too painful for them. Alison and Kenny are both charming, polite and well-balanced so George, and Sheila, have both done a marvellous job helping them to deal with the trauma.

Then Alison says, 'I think we'd better turn in soon, so we'll all be fresh for our travelling tomorrow.'

George yawns. 'Good idea. I'm whacked.'

'I'll go and make you a bed up. You can sleep in Lizzie's old room,' I tell Alison.

She rests her arm on mine. 'You stay right where you are, it's been a big day for you and Dad. I'll do us all a nice cup of hot chocolate then I'll go and make the bed up,' she insists.

'Nonsense, you made the last drink,' I tell her, but she insists we both sit and rest, saying that we'll need all our strength for travelling tomorrow.

As soon as she's disappeared into the kitchen, George gets up. 'I'll go and get the clean bedding out of the airing cupboard and leave it on the bed for her,' he says. 'I won't be a tick.'

Honestly, none of them can do enough for me. I feel quite spoilt. When George comes down he's holding my tablet container.

'I think you forgot to take your tablets this morning, love. You must have been in too much of a rush.'

He hands the container to me. It's a seven-day one, with the days of the week marked on it, and I can see that Saturday's tablets haven't been touched. It's not like me to forget to take them, but then I've had a lot on my mind what with it being our wedding day.

'Thanks, George, I'd better take them now.' I open the

compartment and take out the two tablets, one to keep my blood pressure down and an aspirin to thin my blood.

George fetches me a small glass of water to swill them down. Then Alison returns with the hot chocolate and a plate of assorted biscuits for our supper.

'I'll clear these things away, you two get off to bed,' she says when we've finished.

'You use the bathroom first, love, while I lock up,' George tells me.

'Thanks. I won't be long.' I bend down to kiss him on the forehead. When I stand up again I feel a little dizzy.

'Are you all right?' George asks, reaching out to clasp my hand.

I nod. 'Just a bit tired. It's been an emotional day.'

'No regrets I hope?' His eyes are resting on mine.

'Absolutely not,' I reassure him. I'm so glad that George has come into my life. And I can't wait to go on our honeymoon tomorrow. I always wanted to go to Prague, but Arthur preferred a relaxing on the beach or around the pool holiday.

I'm halfway up the stairs when the dizziness comes over me again, and my body feels weak. It's as if all the energy has suddenly drained out of me. I hang tightly onto the banister, my head swimming.

My legs feel like they're going to give way underneath me, so I daren't move another step. I'd better sit down before I fall down, I think, trying to lower myself onto the step.

Then I lose my balance and suddenly I'm falling.

'George!' I scream as I hurtle towards the floor. 'George!!!'

9

NICK

'What a coincidence that you and Alison worked together. No wonder you were both chatting so much,' Lizzie says as soon as we arrive back home.

There's a miffed edge to her voice, and I glance quickly at her, but she's turned away to see to the kids. Grace is rubbing her eyes, it's been a long day for them. 'It is, isn't it? I couldn't believe it. Sorry, if you felt a bit excluded, I didn't mean to cut you out, it was just such a surprise to see Ally again.' I touch her arm. 'Shall I make us both a coffee and some hot chocolate for the kids?'

'Yes, please. I'll put the TV on so they can unwind for half an hour then get them in the bath and to bed.'

I put my arm around her waist and kiss her on the cheek then go into the kitchen to make the drinks. I'm glad that she's recovered from the episode earlier. I was worried that today would be difficult for her, it's been Lizzie and her mum ever since her dad died. If Lizzie had had her way, we would never have got our own place when we got married, but credit to Judith she insisted that she was ready to live by herself.

I put a pod in the coffee machine, spoon brown sugar into a

mug and put it in place then flick the switch to start it. Then I warm up the milk for the kids' hot chocolate. Lizzie's coffee is now done so I make one for myself, black and strong. The business with Alison has shaken me up a bit, and I can tell Lizzie is annoyed that I spent so much time talking to her. What was I supposed to do when her mum had just married Alison's dad? I can hardly believe it, what a small world!

I take the tray of drinks into the lounge where the kids are sitting on the sofa. Lizzie is now in jeans and a thin jumper.

'I had to get out of that dress.' She glances at the drinks. 'Thanks.'

'I'll take my drink up with me and get changed. Then I'll sort the kids out and get them to bed, you relax. It's been a big day,' I tell her.

She smiles at me. 'Thanks, love.'

I'm relieved to see her looking more relaxed, I think as I go up the stairs and head to our bedroom, taking off my suit and hanging it up. I know that she was anxious about today. It was hard for Lizzie when Judith met George. She struggled with how quickly her mum and George's relationship developed and was beside herself with worry when Judith had the mini stroke, thinking she was going to lose her mum as well as her dad.

It was a stressful time for us all, and I had to admit I was relieved when George proposed even though Lizzie fretted that it was too soon. 'Look on the positive side, George is a nice bloke, and it will be good for Judith to have someone there to look after her,' I pointed out.

Judith told me that Lizzie was traumatised years ago, when she saw a woman die from an allergic reaction while on a school trip to an amusement park. It was that which started off her anxiety and panic attacks.

'The poor woman choked to death right in front of a group of the kids. You can imagine the effect it had on them,' Judith said. 'It took Lizzie ages to get over it.'

36

I can imagine, what a terrible tragedy. Lizzie struggled with the trauma of her dad's death too. I desperately wanted to take the strain from her, so have always been caring and patient, and gradually Lizzie started to relax and blossom. It was all good for a couple of years then Lizzie started teaching, and a young lad in her class had an anaphylactic shock. Lizzie reacted quickly, got his EpiPen and saved him, but it brought the other incident back and she was such a mess she had to quit teaching.

Finally, after therapy she managed to deal with it and started teaching online. It was all fine for a while then, but her anxiety was always there, a dark shadow waiting to pounce and extinguish her happiness.

Lizzie and the kids, they're my whole life. My mum lives in France and to be honest we rarely see each other, but she's happy and I know she would call me if she needed me.

I love Lizzie, she's gorgeous, warm and kind but she's such a worrier. She always thinks that the worst is going to happen. She worries constantly about the kids, about me, about everyone.

My mind turns to Ally. It was a surprise to see her again. Fancy her being George's daughter! And a nurse too. I guess we've both moved on. We only knew each other for a few weeks years ago but we got on well, being the youngest ones in the company, I guess it was only natural that we should hang out together. It was before I met Lizzie and I've never mentioned it to her. Not that it was a hot romance between us, we were just friends, having a laugh together, and the occasional drink.

Except for that one night.

It was Ally's last day at the company. She left the UK the next day for a gap year abroad with a couple of friends. Now she's Alison and she's a fully qualified nurse.

Lizzie and I didn't do the whole 'listing our exes' thing. The past was the past, we both agreed. Although we did say we'd let each other know if an ex popped up again, just to keep each other in the picture.

Alison isn't an ex though. It was one night, years ago. There's no need to mention it to Lizzie. She seems agitated enough about Alison being all friendly with her mum. I don't want to add any more reasons for her to feel insecure.

All I've ever wanted to do is to make Lizzie feel safe and loved. I try really hard to be supportive and let her know what she means to me. I've tried hard to support Judith too.

But deep down inside I know that I can never make up for what I did. All I can do is hope that no one ever finds out. The only other person who knows is Alison. Thank goodness she's going back to Spain tomorrow.

SUNDAY

10

LIZZIE

I can't sleep. I toss and turn while Nick snores softly beside me. Eventually, as dusk begins to break, I give up, get out of bed without disturbing Nick, grab my dressing gown and tiptoe past the kids' rooms and creep downstairs to make myself a coffee.

The house is quiet, still, and daylight is just starting to creep through the curtains. I make my coffee, strong and black, I'll need a few cups of that to keep me alert today. I think about taking it into my Zen garden, as I sometimes do when I can't sleep, then decide against it and instead go into the living room and sit down, opposite the Buddha painting on the wall, nursing my hot mug as I mull over the thoughts that have been whirring in my head all night. Looking at this picture always calms my mind.

When the reality of what I'd done hit me, I'd almost had a nervous breakdown with the guilt. Mum and Dad had no idea what was wrong with me, and I couldn't tell them. How could I confess that I was responsible for someone's death? I'd been a mess, couldn't get out of bed, couldn't go to school, then one day Mum persuaded me to go shopping and in one of the stores I saw a canvas of a Buddha sitting cross-legged on the ground, hands in his lap. The background was shades of orange and the figure in brown. Written beside the Buddha were the words, 'Peace comes from understanding and accepting that which is'.

It was as if the painting spoke to me, that the words were just for me. I stared at it, taking in the message, letting it sink into my soul. I had been a child, only seven, I hadn't realised the consequences of my actions. I hadn't meant any harm. I don't know how long I stared at the painting, letting the words heal me, but Mum must have noticed because she said, 'It's beautiful, isn't it? Would you like it for your room?' I'd nodded, wordlessly. So she bought the painting, I carried it all the way home and that evening Dad hung it on my bedroom wall. That was when I started to forgive myself and heal. I brought it with me when me and Nick moved into this house, and he put it on the wall so that I could look at it whenever I wanted to.

As I sip my drink I mull over the events of yesterday. What, in the law of averages, was the chance that the husband of the woman whose death I caused would marry my mum? It was so far-fetched it seemed like something you would read in a book. Twenty-five years have passed and we've never bumped into them, probably never would have if Mum hadn't joined the Agatha Christie Facebook group. And to think it was me and Nick who had encouraged her.

I knew that she had become friendly with one of the members of the group, but I didn't realise how friendly. I'd popped in to have a cup of tea and chat with her and had been surprised to see her all dressed up, and wearing makeup.

'Are you going out?' I asked, and she confessed that she was meeting someone for lunch, George from the online Agatha Christie group.

'Are you sure that's a good idea, Mum?' I asked. 'You don't really know this man.'

'I do.' Her cheeks reddened and she fidgeted with her necklace. 'We've been talking on FaceTime a lot. He's really nice and we get on well. He's a widower, his wife died years ago.'

I was amazed to hear that she'd actually been video-calling him. And by the flush in her cheeks and the sparkle in her eyes she was quite taken with him.

Part of me was pleased for her. It had been years since Dad had died and I hated to see Mum alone and sad, but another part of me couldn't help worrying. You hear such tales about meeting people on the Internet. What if this George had picked up on how lonely and vulnerable Mum was and planned to exploit her?

'I think I should come with you,' I said to my shame. I was acting like an overprotective parent!

'You will not!' she retorted emphatically. 'I'm not a child, And I'm not stupid either. I'm meeting George in a public place and we're having lunch together. Then we're both going back to our respective homes.' Her voice had softened. 'Look, I under-stand your concern and it's great that you care so much about me, but I promise I will be fine.'

I swallowed down my fears and nodded. 'Of course you will. Take no notice of me. I hope it goes really well for you.'

'Thank you, dear.' She buttoned up her coat. 'I'll pop around when I'm back and let you know, shall I?'

'Yes, please.'

I hugged her and left. But all afternoon I'd worried and was so relieved when I got a text from her to say that she was on the train home and that George was just as lovely in person as he was online. She promised to call around later, after dinner, and tell us all about it.

She arrived in time to say goodnight to the children, tuck them up in bed and read them a bedtime story. Then she sat down with me and Nick and, with sparkling eyes, told us that she and George had hit it off right away and were planning on seeing each other again.

'He lives in Gloucester, and he has a butcher's shop there. He's driving over on Sunday and we're going out for the day,' she told us.

I wanted to ask her if he was driving home afterwards or staying the night, but I managed to stop myself. Talk about role-reversal. Instead I told her I hoped she had a super day and we'd be delighted to meet George when she was ready.

When Mum left, Nick remarked that he hadn't seen her so happy for a long time. I was still worried.

'I hope this George doesn't break her heart,' I said, and Nick pulled me in for a hug, kissed me, and told me that Mum could look after herself and to stop fretting.

A dog barks in the distance, pulling me temporarily out of my thoughts. I stand up and walk into the kitchen, putting my cup in the dishwasher. I'd expected to dislike George, but as soon as I met him I could see that he adored Mum. And they both deserved a second chance at love. George's wife had died years before, and he had moved over to Gloucester to live by his sister Sheila, who had helped him take care of the children.

'That's so tragic. How did she die?' I asked when Mum told me, but she said that she didn't know. 'He doesn't like to talk about it. He says that there's no point in dwelling on the past.'

I thought that was good advice. That's what I should do. Going over and over the past had made me ill. I had to leave it behind and move forward.

Then, a couple of months ago, Mum had a mini stroke. It was a worrying time for us all but luckily she was treated quickly, given medication and told to get on with her life. I was shaken to think that I'd almost lost my mum. So was George, and he instantly proposed. Mum accepted and I was so pleased for her.

I didn't expect them to marry so quickly, but as they both

said, there isn't time to waste at their age. I had almost lost Mum and wanted her to be safe and happy. I was relieved to think that she'd now have George to look after her.

How could I know that by bringing George into our lives, Mum was dragging up a past I desperately wanted to forget?

I don't think I can cope with this, being in such close contact with the family whose lives I tore apart. I want to unburden myself, apologise. Explain. I'm terrified of the reaction if I do, though, and worried about how I'm going to cope with the guilt if I don't. It almost destroyed me once and I don't want that to happen again.

11

LIZZIE

I'm tired but it's almost seven, too late to go back to bed, so I doze on the sofa until Grace comes bouncing in. 'I went into your room, Mummy, and you weren't there.'

She jumps on the sofa beside me. I pull her into a hug. 'I know, darling, I got up early today.' I kiss her forehead. 'Was Daddy still asleep?'

She nods and giggles. 'He was snoring.'

Typical Nick. He never has any trouble sleeping, but then he doesn't have a guilty conscience like me, does he?

'I'm hungry, Mummy,' Grace says.

'Let's have some breakfast then, shall we? Is Isaac awake?'

'Yes, he's playing on his iPad.'

I worry about the time Isaac spends playing on his iPad. Though we have safe settings, and he mainly plays educational games, I don't like him or Grace having too much screen time. We don't normally allow them to take it out with them, but relaxed the rule yesterday as we thought the wedding would be a long day, and the last thing we wanted was for them to be bored and restless.

'Can you go and ask him to come down for breakfast, and I'll get the cereal out?'

Grace nods and races up the stairs, yelling at the top of her voice. 'Isaac! You've got to come down for breakfast!'

Well, I doubt if Nick will be still asleep now, I think as I go into the kitchen and get the cereal bowls out of the cupboard.

Isaac and Grace come charging down the stairs at the same time as a message pings in from Nick.

Just having a shower and I'll be with you.

It seems crazy to message each other when we're in the same house, but we both often do if we're in different rooms. The kids yell enough without us doing it.

I put the kettle on for a coffee, we both like instant first thing, and sit down at the table as the kids tuck into their breakfast. I try to remember what time Mum and George are catching the plane, I want to phone her and wish her a safe journey before they go, but I don't want to wake them up, yesterday was a full day for them. Then, just as Nick comes in, hair wet from the shower and wrapped in his dressing gown, George phones.

'Hi, George, I was about to—' I start to say but he cuts me short.

'Lizzie, love, I'm so sorry but your mum's had an accident.'

I can hear the quiver in his voice and my hand flies to my mouth. *Oh God, Mum!* I grip my mobile tight as I stammer. 'What sort of accident? Is she...?' I can't utter the words that are swimming in my mind. *Please God, don't let her die.* I throw a panicky look at Nick and motion to let him know I'm going out of the room.

'It's not serious, fortunately, but she's fractured her ankle. She went a bit dizzy last night and fell over. Thank goodness Alison was here, we persuaded her to stay over so we could travel to the airport together. She knew exactly what to do. She drove us to A&E and stayed with us. She's cancelled her flight too so that she can stop and look after Judith. I've told her that I can manage but she insists.'

Last night? 'Why didn't you let me know last night? I would have come straight over.'

'We didn't want to trouble you, love. We knew it wasn't serious and Alison was here to help. She is a nurse after all.'

But she's my mother. I should have been told straight away. The words are screaming in my head but I force them back. I'm overreacting. They didn't want to worry me late at night, that's understandable.

'Are you sure she's okay? Have the doctors checked her out thoroughly?'

'Yes, Alison insisted. Judith's ankle is a bit swollen but the fracture doesn't require surgery, so they have given her a surgical boot and she'll have to walk with the aid of a front-wheeled walker for a while, as the hospital didn't think she'd be safe using crutches. Obviously we've had to cancel the honeymoon. We'll go later when your mum's ankle is better.'

That makes sense. I feel sorry for them both though, they'd been looking forward to their short trip to Prague. 'I'll be right over,' I tell him.

'There's no need, dear, Judith is having a rest right now. It was a long night. And Alison is here so Judith is being well looked after. Come along this afternoon when we've all had a bit of shut eye. I promise you that your mum is okay.'

I swallow back my protest that I want to see my mum, make sure for myself that she is all right. I'm being selfish, of course they all need to rest. They were probably in A&E for hours. They must be exhausted.

'I'll come over later then. Please give Mum my love.'

Nick comes in as I end the call and puts his arm around my waist. 'What's up?'

I tell him what's happened. 'Luckily Mum was only halfway up the stairs when she went dizzy, what if she was almost at the top? Or had hit her head on something?' I tremble as I realise how this could have all been a lot worse. I could have lost my mum forever. No one knows more than me how fragile life is.

Nick holds me in his arms and caresses the back of my head as I nestle against his shoulders. 'I understand that you're worried, but George has assured you that Judith is okay so please don't get yourself in a state. Leave the kids with me when you go and see her later. I wouldn't think your mum is up to them bouncing around just yet.'

'Thank you,' I tell him. I don't know what I'd do without Nick, he's so calm which is a good thing as I'm anxious enough for both of us.

Sometimes his laidback attitude drives me nuts and I know he gets irritated when I'm overanxious. But everyone's different, aren't they? And we both adore each other and have each other's back which is the most important thing. We trust each other completely.

I do a quick Internet search on fractured ankles, it can take six to twelve weeks to heal, might need a cast and Mum will need lots of rest. She won't be able to go to work at the bakery, so she will be home alone when George goes to work. He has an assistant at the butcher's shop but he'll fret if he isn't there himself, overseeing things. I'll have to visit her every day and do any chores she needs.

I'm worried all morning, but the kids keep me busy. Finally it's three o'clock and I grab my bag. 'I'll go and check on Mum now then. I won't be long,' I tell Nick.

'Be as long as you need, the kids are happy playing in the garden and I've got some weeding to do,' he tells me.

I decide to walk to Mum's, she only lives a couple of streets away and it's a warm day, the fresh air will help me get myself together. I don't want to turn up all anxious because then Mum will worry about me.

I'm so deep in thought that I hardly notice the short journey, I know it so well that I'm sure I could walk it in my sleep, and realise with a jolt that I'm there. I stand in front of my family home for a few minutes, my mind going back to the day we moved in.

Dad was so proud and Mum so happy. Our former house was a decent sized semi in a nice enough area but Dad had always wanted to live in this part of Worcester and had been over the moon when his company did so well he could afford to buy this four-bedroomed detached house, in the corner of a leafy cul-de-sac, with its big rooms, conservatory and large garden. We all felt at home there immediately.

Truth be told, I didn't want to leave. The house held so many memories, and by leaving it I felt like I was leaving Dad behind. Nick really wanted us to have our own house though, and Mum thought it was for the best too, so I agreed as long as I was in walking distance of Mum. We visited each other every day until she met George and still see each other several times a week. I wonder if that would change now they are married.

I have a key but since George moved in I don't let myself in unless I know Mum is home alone. It's only polite. Mum does the same when she comes to mine if Nick is home.

Alison opens the door a couple of minutes after I ring the bell. 'Hello, Lizzie. Mum's expecting you,' she says with a smile. 'Best not to stay too long though, we don't want to tire her out.'

I feel a bit put out at her use of the word 'Mum' again. And that she's only been here five minutes and she's telling me how long I can stay in my own mother's home. She's only looking out for Mum. And she is a nurse, I remind myself as I step inside.

'How is she?' I ask as Alison closes the door.

'A bit shaken up, and her ankle is painful but we're all thankful that it wasn't a lot worse.'

So am I. I've been trying not to dwell on the fact all day that if Mum had been near the top of the stairs and fallen she could have broken her neck.

'I've been so worried about her. Is she in the lounge?'

'Yes. Excuse me, I was in the middle of loading the dishwasher.' Alison strides off towards the kitchen, and I head into the lounge.

Mum is sitting in an armchair, her foot is in a black surgical boot and propped up on a pouffe. A front-wheeled walker is placed against the back of the chair. She looks pale and drawn but her face lights up when she sees me.

'Hello, Lizzie. It's nice of you to pop in and check on me, love. Where are the kiddies?'

'I thought it best to leave them with Nick today. They can be a bit boisterous.' I sit down on the opposite arm of her chair and give her a hug. 'Are you sure you're okay? Do they know what made you go dizzy?'

'They said that my blood pressure was very low. Which is unusual, it's normally a bit high.' She looks puzzled. 'I take tablets to keep it down, as you know.' Mum has been on tablets to lower her blood pressure since the mini stroke. 'Alison thinks it must be the stress of planning the wedding. Apparently emotional stress can cause low blood pressure and as I'm taking blood pressure tablets to lower it as well it must have plunged too low.'

I hadn't realised it had all been stressful for Mum, she seemed so happy. There had been the mini stroke though too, I remind myself.

'When the swelling goes down I'll be able to get about a bit easier,' Mum adds.

I look at her pinched face and dark eyes. 'Is it really painful?'

'A bit but that's only to be expected. I've got some strong painkillers and Alison said the swelling will go down after a few days.' She grimaces. 'I'm going to be out of action for a bit though. And obviously we've had to postpone our honeymoon.'

I take her hand in mine. 'Well don't worry, I'm going to look after you. I'll visit every day to make sure that you're all right and do the chores for you, so you just concentrate on getting better again. Or George can drop you off at our house every morning and pick you up when he finishes work, if you want. Then I can be with you all day.'

'Thank you, darling, but you've got the kiddies to look after, and your job to do.' Mum squeezes my hand tight. 'Alison has taken leave from work and is going to stay for a while to look after me.'

I'm taken aback at this. 'You mean she's not going back to Spain?'

'No, she said she's due some leave so is happy to stay here for a bit. She can spend some time with her dad and look after me. Isn't that kind of her?'

Alison appears in the doorway then. 'Can I get you a drink before you go, Lizzie?'

She says it pleasantly enough and her face is wreathed in a friendly smile, but I feel really put out. This is my mother's house, my family home, I'm the one who should be offering her a drink. And the way she said it is almost as if she's limiting my time with Mum, one drink then I have to go.

I know that it's a good job that Alison was here when Mum had the fall but I really wish that she wasn't staying to look after her. I don't want her here, living in Mum's house.

Any day she could remember who I am, what I did. I can't bear her knowing. And then everyone else will know.

I've never told Mum exactly what happened on that day. I was too ashamed. I'm terrified that if it comes out Nick and Mum will be disgusted with me. And what about George and his family? How will they feel when they find that I'm responsible for Carol's death? It might destroy Mum and George's marriage before it's had time to really begin.

'I've not long had a drink, thanks, but I'm not rushing off yet. The kids are fine with Nick and I want to spend some time with Mum,' I say politely.

'That's only natural. She is rather weak though so we don't want her to tire herself out. Shall we say half an hour? I think that will be enough for Mum today.'

I can feel myself bristling at her attitude. Anyone would think Alison is the daughter, not me. 'Of course I won't tire her out, she's my mother.' I force my lips into a smile. 'Mum said you're staying for a bit longer to help look after her. That's kind of you but there's no need. I only live a few minutes away and I can look after her.' I was about to say that Mum could move in with us but she probably won't want to do that as she and George have just got married.

'You have the children to look after, and your work, Lizzie.' Alison's gaze meets mine. 'It's absolutely no problem. My contract with a doctor's surgery has just finished so I've told the agency that I'm taking a few weeks' holiday.'

'A few weeks?' I repeat. I don't want her here that long! I won't be able to cope. 'There's really no need. we don't want you losing wages. Honestly, we can manage.'

'I don't like to pull rank but I am a trained nurse. And it's not been long since Mum had the mini stroke. Dad suffers from high blood pressure and I don't want him to have any more stress either. So I'm going to stay with them until Mum is mobile again.' Her voice is firm, brooking no argument.

I feel panic rising up in me, like a hot liquid pouring into my veins. It sounds as if she's intending to stay for weeks. I don't want her here, around Mum. If she and Mum start chatting about how her mum died, they might realise that I was there that day. And it wouldn't take Alison long to realise what part I played in her death. She might have put two and two together years ago but then I was just a girl she met on a trip. Now I'm her stepsister.

'I can take time off work and come over when the kids are at school. There's no need for you to put your life on hold.' I sound desperate even to my own ears.

'You've got enough on your plate, Lizzie. I don't want you stressing and wearing yourself out, I know you suffer from anxiety. It's better all around for me to stay here with them so I can help. It will be good to spend time with Dad. Now let me go and make that coffee. White with two brown sugars, isn't it?'

Alison is determined to stand her ground, and I can't help wondering why she wants to stay on here instead of returning to her job and life in Spain. It's not as if she knows Mum that well. Or that Mum is in serious danger, she's fractured her ankle but is otherwise fine. I live nearby. I can help. And how does Alison know I suffer from anxiety? Have they all been talking about me? Although I did have that panic attack at the wedding.

'Please don't worry, Alison will take good care of me,' Mum says when Alison goes off to make the drinks. 'Now tell me, did you enjoy yourself yesterday? I must say that everyone seemed to get on so well and we will have some wonderful photographs.' She sighs. 'I wish we were going on honeymoon to Prague today as we planned.'

Poor Mum, she must be so disappointed. 'You can go as soon as your ankle's better, Mum.' Then I realise that I haven't seen George yet. 'Where's George?'

'He's popped to the supermarket for a few bits. We didn't get much in as we were meant to be away.' She sighs. 'George is going back to work tomorrow. He said he knows I'm safe with Alison here, and he doesn't want to pay someone to work there if he can do it. Especially as he'll need time off when we can actually go to Prague.'

I can see that makes sense but it seems a shame for him not

be here when they only got married yesterday. This is supposed to be their honeymoon.

Alison returns with the drinks and puts them down on the coffee table.

'Dad said that you have a spare key, Lizzie. Would you mind giving it to me until I get one cut? Then I can let myself in if I have to pop out without Mum having to get up and drag herself to the door.' She holds out her hand expectantly.

I do mind. That means she will have a key to my mother's house and I won't. But I tell myself not to be childish and hand it to her. 'If you could give it me back as soon as you've got one cut.'

'I will. Thanks.' She slips the key into her jeans pocket then walks over to Mum and plumps up the cushion behind her head. 'I'll leave you two to chat while I start preparing dinner. It's best if you sleep down here for a while, Mum, we don't want you struggling with the stairs. Luckily there's a shower in the downstairs toilet so you'll be able to freshen up.' My dad had an extra shower fitted when I was a teenager because I kept hogging the bathroom and making him late for work. It's come in very handy over the years. 'I'll continue sleeping in Lizzie's old room.'

I'm staggered at this. She's only been in the family for one day but now she is sleeping in my bedroom, looking after my mother and deciding when I can visit her. And worst of all, she is calling my mum Mum. It's almost as if she's trying to push me out. But why?

Have all these years without her mother made her desperate to replace her? Is that why she's taking over mine?

12

LIZZIE

Nick is peeling potatoes when I get home. 'The kids are playing upstairs so I thought I'd make a start on the dinner. Sausages and mash okay?' he asks, glancing over his shoulder at me. Then he frowns, puts the potato peeler down and walks over to me, obviously noticing that I'm upset. 'What's up? Is it your mum?' he asks, placing his arm around my shoulders.

I'm so agitated the words come pouring out. He listens intently, stroking his chin.

'Lizzie, hun. I get you feeling a bit pushed out, but I'm sure that isn't Alison's intention. She's a nurse, and as she has finished her current contract it's perfectly reasonable that she'd stay to look after your mum – and George. This must all be a strain for him and he's getting on a bit too.'

Which is exactly what Alison said. But it doesn't make me feel any better.

'I guess so. But she's my mum. I should be looking after her. Alison has completely taken over, she's even sleeping in my room.'

Surprise flickers across his face. 'Your *old* room. You haven't lived at home for years, Liz. You can't expect Alison to sleep on the sofa when there's an empty room she can use.'

I feel my cheeks flush. I know I'm being unreasonable but I can't help it.

'It just feels wrong. And she's calling mum "Mum". As if she's *her* mother.'

'It's probably out of respect, she doesn't want to call her Judith, the older generation don't like that, so she's gone for "Mum".'

Nick is always calm and reasonable but right now he's annoying me.

'I don't call George "Dad".'

Nick pulls me into him, wrapping his arms around my waist. 'I can completely understand how you're feeling, Liz. Since your dad died it's been only you and your mum. Even though she's with George now, ever since the mini stroke you've run yourself ragged trying to look after her, and work and look after the kids. But this is your chance to take a break. Now Alison is here you can step back a bit. I know it's hard for you, you're an only child so you're not used to sharing your mum. But look on it as help rather than...' He pauses.

'Rather than what?' I snap. He'd better not be trying to suggest that I'm jealous of Alison, that this is some kind of competition. That is not what this is about. I pull myself angrily away from him and go over to the fridge to get some milkshake for the kids. I take out the bottle and turn back to Nick, who is leaning against the worktop now, hands in his pockets, head to one side.

'Rather than feeling guilty that you're not the one doing the caring,' he says cautiously. 'Give yourself a break.'

I consider his words as I take two plastic beakers out of the cupboard and pour the chocolate milkshake into them.

He's right that as an only child I've always felt responsible for Mum, especially after Dad died. Maybe I should embrace the fact that Alison is here to help instead of assuming that she's deliberately pushing me out. As Nick said, she's a nurse, and she's just being professional and looking after 'a patient'. And yes, she's obviously concerned about the effect it will all have on George, her father.

'I'm sure that Alison doesn't mean to be so bossy but nurses have this efficient, assertive attitude, don't they? They're used to dealing with anxious families,' he adds.

'I guess...' I say slowly. Am I blowing this all up because it's my fault that Alison's mum died? Maybe the guilt is making me think that Alison's trying to push me out and take my mum away from me, as payback. But she doesn't know what I did, does she? She wasn't watching. And she doesn't even recognise me. If she did, she would have said something as soon as she saw me.

'Mum looks so tired and fragile though. And she has this big black boot on her ankle.' I swallow. 'She wants to see the kids. She asked me to take them over, but Alison said not to bring them yet.'

'Only because your mum needs to rest up for a few days, and the kids, well they can be a bit lively, Liz. Also, do you want them to see their nan looking so weak? It might upset them.'

Right again. Nick's calm, rational personality is one of the things I love about him. I can lean on him, turn to him for support when my anxiety spirals out of control.

It's also one of the things that drives me nuts about him.

We both turn as we hear a yell from upstairs. Isaac and Grace are arguing. Again.

'I'll go,' I'm already hurrying towards the door.

'I'll finish the dinner then,' he says.

I head up the stairs into Isaac's bedroom where the loud voices are coming from. I walk in to find Lego all over the floor, Isaac red in the face and Grace sitting on the floor, tears streaming down her face.

'She's ruined it. I spent ages building Superman and she's knocked it all down,' Isaac shouts. 'She spoils everything!'

'Isaac pushed me,' Grace sobs.

I pick her up. 'You have to remember that she's only little, Isaac. She didn't realise that it would all topple over.' Having Isaac helps me forgive myself for what I did. I was only seven then, as he is now. You don't realise what you're doing at that age. You don't understand the danger.

'I'm only little too!' Isaac shouts and he runs out of the room.

I cuddle Grace and look around at the Lego bricks scattered on the floor. Poor Isaac, he'd been so happy to get the Superman Lego for his birthday and had worked hard to build it up. I realise how annoying it must be for Grace to come in and ruin it, but she didn't mean it. He's right though, he's only seven. He's only little too. He was only two when Grace came along and had to grow up quick. Did he resent that, I wonder?

Sometimes when I was younger I longed for a sibling to play with, but there were bonuses too. I got all my parents' attention, I never had to share, I could build a jigsaw or a Lego model knowing that no one would come in and destroy it.

Nick is right. The kids need me, I should be glad that Alison is going to look after Mum. I've got my hands full here. I should embrace the fact that I now have a stepsister to share the burden with.

If only that stepsister wasn't Alison.

I have to stop letting this eat me up. I should be more tolerant with Alison, I was the one who did wrong, not her. I'm lucky that she clearly doesn't realise who I am or what I did. I should support her and show my appreciation that she's looking after my mum.

'I'm happy now,' Grace says so I put her down and she runs off to play.

I go back down to help Nick with the dinner but everything

is cooking nicely so I lay the table. 'You're right, maybe I am overreacting a bit. I'll go around to Mum's tomorrow when I've taken the kids to school and take a bunch of flowers for Alison, to show her that I'm grateful for her help. Then we can have a cup of tea and a chat. I'll let her know that I'm willing to share the load.'

'That sounds a good idea. I'm sure Alison will appreciate that,' Nick says approvingly.

Tension now eased we all chat away as we eat dinner, then I take Isaac and Grace up for their showers while Nick clears away and loads the dishwasher.

A little later Nick calls up the stairs. 'Alison's asked me to pop around and help her move the spare bed downstairs for your mum. I won't be long.'

I hear the front door close behind him before I can ask him how Alison contacted him. She hasn't got his number. Has she?

Mum probably gave it to her so she could phone. But why didn't she phone me and ask if Nick could pop around, that would be the normal thing to do. My mind is working overtime. Alison turning up has really rattled me. She hasn't messaged me at all. Not even to give me an update on my mum. Yet she has my husband's number and seems very friendly with him.

I remember the sparkle in Nick's eyes when he was talking to her at the wedding yesterday, how they both got on so well, and a snake of unease slithers through me.

Exactly how friendly were they all those years ago?

13

JUDITH

Alison and George are being really kind but I feel useless. My foot is so painful I can't put any weight on it, I'm having to use a walker to get around, like an eighty-year-old. I really wanted to go up to bed last night, our wedding night, but after the fall I couldn't manage it. The pain was so excruciating. I slept downstairs on the sofa, and George slept in the armchair because he refused to leave me downstairs on my own, but it was so late by the time we got home from the hospital that we overslept this morning. And now here they are, both running around after me while I sit on the sofa with my foot up on a pouffe. I want to be the one to look after them. I feel so stupid for falling down the stairs like that and putting myself in this position.

'I'm so sorry, I've ruined everything.' A sob catches in my throat. We should be on our honeymoon in Prague, but now, thanks to my fall, we can't even cuddle up in bed together. I feel so helpless and miserable.

George sits down beside me and hugs me tight. 'It isn't your fault you fell. And I'm just grateful that you weren't seriously injured. Or killed.'

I know he's right, it could have been a lot worse, but I don't want to be hobbling about like this. I want to be able to move around. I want us to go to Prague as we planned.

Oh stop having a pity party and be grateful that you didn't break your neck, I tell myself. *Your ankle will be a lot better in a few days.*

'Are you sure you'll be all right if I go into the shop tomorrow?' George asks when we all sit around the table eating the roast beef dinner Alison cooked – with George's help I managed to manoeuvre my walker into the kitchen. 'It does seem daft to pay someone else to come in, and there's not much I can do here. I know Alison will look after you.' He squeezes my hand. 'It won't be long before you're back on your feet again.'

'Of course. And you must go up to bed tonight, you can't get a decent night's sleep in that chair. I'll be fine down here on the sofa. I can get myself to the loo and into the kitchen for a drink.'

'Are you sure?' he asks. 'I hate to leave you down here alone.'

'Nonsense. I'm a big girl, I'll be perfectly okay. And I can phone you in the unlikely event I need anything.'

'I think she's right, Dad, you need your rest and that chair is no good for your back,' Alison pipes up.

George finally agrees. 'But I'm not having you sleeping on the sofa until your ankle is better enough for you to climb the stairs. We can bring the spare bed down from the office room and put it into the back room for you. At least then you'll have some privacy and can sleep in a decent bed.'

'That's a lot of bother for everyone. I'm sure I'll be able to make the stairs in a couple of days, even if I have to crawl up!' I don't want me and George separated like this. And I certainly don't want him and Alison dragging that bed down, it's heavy.

'Dad's right. It could be a week or so before you're ready for the stairs, Mum. It's not just going up, it's coming down too. We don't want you falling again. You might not be so lucky next time. I'll ask Nick to come over and help us.'

I protest that I don't want to trouble him, but Alison waves my concerns away. 'I'm sure he won't mind.'

I know he won't. Nick will always do anything to help, but I feel such a nuisance putting everyone out like this.

Nick comes around straight away, and he and Alison bring the bed down between them, laughing as they quibble who is going to take which end, but Nick insists on going down first. Then they push the sofa over a little in the back room to make space for it. I have to admit that it's much comfier to sleep in the bed than on the sofa. Alison sees Nick out and they stand chatting on the doorstep for a while, they seem to have quite a connection considering as they only worked together for a short time years ago. But then Nick is always friendly.

George brings me a cup of hot chocolate and we sit together in my make-shift bedroom, chatting. A little later I hear the front door close then Alison pops her head around the door.

'I think I'll turn in, I'm tired. Is there anything you want before I go up, Mum?'

'No thanks, love, I'm fine. George has made sure of that.'

'Great. Goodnight, both. See you in the morning.' Alison blows us a kiss and closes the door behind her, then I hear her going up the stairs.

'Are you positive you'll be okay down here?' George asks as he helps me into bed. 'You can manage going to the loo by yourself?'

'Definitely,' I tell him. 'Now off you go.'

He gives me a big hug and a kiss, reminding me to phone him if I need him, and goes off to bed. I lie for a while going over the events of last night.

I've never felt dizzy like that before. Alison said it must be the stress of the wedding but I hadn't felt stressed. The wedding went really well and everyone got on great. Lizzie was a bit strange though, she seemed awkward around Alison. Whereas

Nick was the opposite and chatted away. Especially to Alison. Like tonight.

I think back to last night. George had to remind me to take my blood pressure tablet. I was sure I'd taken it in the morning, but then I was busy getting ready for the wedding. Is that what caused me to go dizzy, because I didn't take it at the right time? Although the doctor at the hospital had said my blood pressure was low – which was unusual. It doesn't make sense.

I close my eyes as weariness comes over me.

14

Well, that was easier than I thought it would be, I think to myself as I sit in my room this evening, my mind going over the events of last night. It's so satisfying when a plan starts to come into place. You plot and scheme, try to think of all the things that could go wrong, wonder if you can pull it off. Then bingo! It's working.

There's a long way to go, of course. This is only the first stage but I can't believe how easy it's been. How gullible she is. They all are.

I get my list up on the notes app on my phone and scan it, although the next stage is imprinted in my mind. I almost started to put it in action today, but I know that I have to take my time and not rush things.

It all has to appear believable, logical. I don't want any probing or asking questions. As much as I'm longing to rush in and get it all over, now I have to be patient and continue building up trust. I'm going to make her pay for what she did, rip apart her family like she did to mine. I know she was a child. That's no excuse.

I bet she's forgotten all about it, got on with her life, never giving a thought to what she took away from me. Well, see how she feels when I take away everything she loves.

MONDAY

15

LIZZIE

'Is Nanny's foot better?' Isaac asks the next morning as we set off for school.

'Not yet, it will take a little while but Aunty Alison is looking after her and I'm going to see her when I've dropped you off at school.'

'I want to see Nanny too,' Grace protests.

'You can in a couple of days, darling. I tell you what, when you come home tonight why don't you both make her a Get Well card and I'll take it around to her tomorrow. She will love that.'

'I'm going to put hearts on mine,' Grace says.

Isaac rolls his eyes. 'Girls!'

'You can do whatever you want. Nanny will love it.' She will too, Mum adores Isaac and Grace. 'Now let's get into the car or we'll be late.'

After dropping the kids off I stop at the supermarket to get a bunch of flowers and a box of chocolates then go to see Mum. I'm a bit disappointed to see Alison's hire car parked in the drive, I was hoping to get some time to chat to Mum alone.

Never mind, it's a good thing someone is with her, she must still be a bit unsteady on her feet, I remind myself.

I search in my bag for the door key then remember that I gave it to Alison, so I ring the bell. It doesn't work. Frustrated, I knock on the door. No one comes. I knock again. It takes a while before Alison opens the door, and she looks surprised to see me. 'Oh hello again, Lizzie. You're an early bird.'

'I came straight from dropping the kids off at school,' I reply.

She looks at the flowers. 'They're beautiful. Are they for Mum? I'll make sure she gets them.'

She's blocking the door. I'm not sure if it's on purpose, but I hand her the flowers. 'No, they're for you, to thank you for looking after Mum.'

Her eyes widen in surprise and as she takes a step back, I squeeze past her into the hall. 'I've got a box of chocolates for Mum, to cheer her up,' I say as she closes the door behind me. 'By the way, the bell doesn't work.'

'I know, I took the battery out so that Mum wouldn't be disturbed when she was sleeping. I was about to help her have a shower, actually.'

Alison follows me as I walk through into the kitchen. Everywhere is spotless. Alison definitely has it all under control.

Help Mum shower? 'I can do that. I'm sure she'd prefer me to...' I hesitate to add 'than a stranger' because Alison is family now.

Her expression is sympathetic. 'Actually, Lizzie, I think Mum would prefer me to help her, seeing as I'm a trained nurse – and patients usually feel awkward when their immediate family do intimate tasks for them.' She pauses. 'I know that you and Mum are close and it must be hard for you to allow someone else to care for her, but it really is important that Mum's handled carefully, we don't want the fracture to get worse.'

I feel like I'm being immature and selfish. 'I see. Well, there must be something I can do to help. Washing or ironing perhaps? I don't want to leave it all to you.' I look around. 'Where is Mum?'

'She's in the back room getting undressed. If you really want to help' – Alison takes a piece of paper out of her pocket – 'there are a few things we need from the shops, perhaps you could get them? Mum will be showered and dressed when you come back, and we can all sit and have a cup of tea together.'

So now I have to go to the supermarket again. I should have phoned to ask if they needed anything but I reckon that Alison would have found some excuse to put me off coming. 'Yes, of course. Anything to help.' I take the shopping list off her and scan it, there's not a lot there. 'I'll only be about an hour or so,' I say. I need to start work by eleven or else I'll never get through the assignments I have to mark before I collect the kids from school, which means I'll only have about half an hour with Mum. Thank goodness I don't have an online class today.

The supermarket is crowded so it takes longer than I thought. I whizz back round to Mum's, surprised to see Kenny's car in the drive. I park behind it.

Kenny opens the back gate before I can press the bell. 'Hi Liz, I was listening out for your car. Sheila's here too. We're sitting out in the garden. Come and join us.' He looks at the shopping bags I'm holding. 'Let me take those.'

'Thanks.'

As I walk through the back gate, I hear a tinkle of laughter and look over to the patio on the right where Alison and Mum are sitting beside each other on the cushioned garden chairs, facing the lawn. Their heads are bent towards each other, laughing, and neither of them have noticed me yet. Mum's foot, clad in the protective black boot, is perched up on a pouffe. It's great to see her up and about.

'It's good to hear you laughing, Mum,' I say as I walk down the path to join them. The garden is mainly lawn and patio with a few well-tended flower beds, easy to manage Dad always said, and Mum has kept it the same.

Mum turns her head and smiles at me. 'Oh hello, Lizzie. Alison said you were getting some shopping for us. That's very kind of you, dear. Come and join us. Alison is telling me about some of her adventures in Spain.'

I sit down in one of the chairs opposite, taking in Mum's sparkling eyes. She's still a bit pale but she looks happy, I'm pleased to see. I've been so worried about her.

'Did you manage to sleep okay?' I ask her. 'Nick said that you're sleeping in the back room on the bed from the spare room.' The back room is right at the rear of the house and is hardly used now. I feel like Mum's being shut away, but she probably wants the privacy if she has to sleep down here. It's right by the downstairs shower room, too, I remind myself, and it's a big, spacious room, with a deep beige pile carpet, a soft duck egg sofa – the same blue as the curtains – matching armchairs and pouffe.

'You're comfy there, aren't you, Mum?' Alison answers for her. 'I messaged Nick to ask him to help bring the bed down. He was round straight away. Very kind of him.' She looks a bit smug.

'I guess Mum gave you his number?' I'm determined not to let her know that I'm bothered that she has Nick's number and messaged him not me. The fact that they worked together for a short time years ago shouldn't concern me at all.

'Yes, I didn't want to disturb you and it was quicker to message Nick direct. I knew he wouldn't mind. Judith said he will do anything for anyone.'

'He will, and we don't mind at all. We want to help. Is there anything else I can do while I'm here?'

'I've got it all under control, Lizzie, but thank you. I know you're busy with your work and the children.' She gets to her feet. 'Now can I get you a drink?'

'Oh let me...' Alison has been looking after Mum all morning, I don't want her waiting on me too.

'No, I insist.'

For a moment I'm tempted to stand my ground, but then I nod. 'A tea would be great, thank you.'

Alison looks at Mum inquiringly. 'Not for me, thanks dear. If I drink any more I'll have to go to the loo again.'

'Are you managing okay, Mum?' I ask as I sit down in Alison's place.

She pats my hand. 'I'm being very well looked after. I'll be back on my feet in no time.'

'Of course you will,' Sheila says.

As we all sit and chat the conversation turns to anecdotes about George's family. I feel left out, but Mum looks as if she's enjoying it. I'm pleased that she is happy, she's been on her own so long, and that they're all getting on so well. But I can't help feeling like an outsider in my childhood home.

It's as if George has moved in his whole family.

16

LIZZIE

I notice that Mum has gone quiet and is letting the conversation flow around her. She's a bit pale and there are bags under her eyes. 'How are you *really* feeling?' I ask her quietly as the others chat around us. It's one of our little habits, to add the 'really'. We used to say it to each other in the dark days after Dad died. It meant, 'Don't tell me you're fine like everyone else, tell me the truth.'

Her eyes meet mine and I can see the exhaustion in them. 'My ankle throbs a bit but the painkillers help, and I'm tired, which Alison said is only natural. It's only been just over a day since the fall.'

It should be me looking after her, not Alison who she hardly knows, I think with a pang of guilt.

'I don't know what I'd do without Alison,' Mum continues. 'It's so lucky that she's a nurse and can take the time off.'

'I don't mind at all,' Alison pipes up, she obviously over-heard. 'I'm happy to look after you. I lost my mum when I was young and I feel the loss even to this day.'

A shiver courses through me as her eyes hold mine and a

sad smile plays on her lips. 'I know that Lizzie would be devastated if anything happened to you.'

My hand shakes so much tea spills from my cup. I break the gaze, turning my attention back to Mum, trying not to show how unnerved I am.

That sounded a really pointed remark, and the way she looked at me. Was she having a dig? Does she realise that it was my fault her mum died? But then why hasn't she said something?

The answer hits me so hard I almost drop the cup from my hand.

She's after revenge. That's why she's all over my mum, making herself indispensable, replacing me. It's her way of getting payback.

By the time I get home I've calmed down and talked myself out of thinking Alison is out to get me. She can't possibly know about my part in her mother's death. How could she? She didn't see what I did, no one saw. It's my own guilt that's tormenting me. The knowledge that I robbed her and Kenny of their mother. Fortunately, Kenny wouldn't even remember me, he'd only been four years old, and he was with his mother all the time.

The mother I killed.

'You have to forgive yourself for this, Lizzie, it was an accident and you were a child,' Bridget, my therapist, told me many times. And I managed to, eventually. Until Alison came into our lives.

I think of Isaac. Would I blame him if the same thing happened when he was on a school trip? Of course I wouldn't. No one would.

I have to put it out of my mind and get on with my work. I've got a new student to deal with. He hasn't joined an online session yet but has sent over his first assignment already. I need to stop thinking about Alison and keep calm and focused.

I make myself a cup of calamine and honey tea then carry it over to the kitchen table where my laptop is placed, ready for me to start work. I start it up, taking a long sip of the tea, and open the first assignment.

I enjoy my job teaching English as a second language. Most – but not all – of my students are overseas and really eager to learn. I'm a conscientious tutor and Nick is always telling me that I put too much pressure on myself, but I get a lot of pleasure out of seeing them progress, it's a good feeling to know that I'm helping someone. It's an atonement of sorts for causing someone's death, a little voice in my head says.

I take my time marking the assignments, making sure that I give constructive feedback, then grab a sandwich and a cold drink. I've just finished my sandwich when my phone rings. It's Jodie. We've been friends since school and honestly Jodie has saved my sanity at times. We don't get to see each other much now we both have a family, but we make time for a catchup chat every week or so.

'Hi, do you have time to chat?'

The sound of her bright, friendly voice lifts my spirits. 'Good timing,' I tell her. 'I've finished my work for the day and have half an hour before I pick the kids up from school.' I take my phone into the living room, sit down in the comfy chair, tucking my legs underneath me. 'How are things with you?'

'Same old. Freddie is adorable but refuses to sleep, me and Rob are going around all bleary-eyed and shattered. Millie was a much easier baby,' she says. Jodie and Millie's dad, Kyle, are divorced, and she's been with Rob a couple of years now, he's Freddie's father.

My mind goes back to those baby years when I was so drained I could barely function. Nick did his best but he was working very hard to keep the company afloat. Mum came to the rescue, though. She was such a support then, cooking meals for us, doing the washing and ironing, even though she was working part-time herself. I don't know what I'd have done without her. She offered to take Isaac for a few hours so I could catch up on sleep, but I wouldn't let her. I couldn't bear him to be out of my sight, thinking I was the only one who could keep him safe. I woke up in the night to check on him constantly, sometimes sitting on the chair by his cot watching him sleep, making sure he was breathing. I was ill with anxiety and lack of sleep, barely eating.

'Do you remember what a mess I was when Isaac was born? I don't know how I'd have got through without Mum and Nick's help,' I remind her.

They had both been worried about me, exchanging anxious looks, whispering to each other in concerned voices, speaking to me softly, slowly, as if I was a child. They couldn't understand why I was so tired and anxious when Isaac was such an easy, happy baby, a good sleeper, content to kick and gurgle in his playpen while I got a few jobs done, but I was scared to take my eyes off him, terrified that something would happen to him. That Karma would take him away from me. Like it had taken my dad. It was a really dark time for me.

'Lucky you. I wish my mum was here,' Jodie says with a sigh.

Jodie's parents live in Portugal. They've been over for a few visits but it's not the same as having a mum on hand to help. I'm lucky. I know that.

'Anyway, how did the wedding go?' she asks.

'The wedding was lovely but Mum had a fall...' I explain what happened and how Alison has stopped over to look after Mum.

'That's a bit of luck that she's a nurse,' Jodie says. 'What's she like?'

I take a deep breath. Jodie is the only one – apart from my

therapist – who knows what happened that day on the school trip. She was sitting beside me. She didn't realise until years afterwards, like me, that I was to blame. Haltingly, I explain.

'Shit! I bet that creeped you out!'

'It did, but she doesn't seem to recognise me...'

'I'm not surprised. We were all so young and look totally different now. And if she did, all she would remember was a young girl she spoke to. I keep telling you, Lizzie, you've built all this up too much in your mind.'

She's right. I know she is. But the guilt is so suffocating. 'She knows Nick too, they both worked at Dad's company just before he died.'

I hear Jodie gasp. 'Wow, that's really weird, Liz. A double coincidence. You couldn't make that up.' Suddenly Freddie starts wailing in the background. 'Sorry, got to go. I'll call you later,' Jodie says, and she's gone.

Leaving her words going round and round in my mind. She's right, it is weird that not only is Mum married to the husband of the wife whose death I caused, but also that Nick worked with his daughter. And now that daughter is all over Nick and Mum, but very cool with me.

Is it really all a coincidence or is there something going on here?

17

NICK

It's been a tough day at work and I can't wait to get home, but as I'm about to get into my car a text pings in. I look at my phone expecting it to be from Lizzie and am surprised to see that it's Ally again. I open it.

Hi Nick, would you mind popping in after work and helping me move a few things around in the back room to make Mum more comfortable? I'm afraid she's going to be downstairs for a while. A x

Funny how quickly we've slipped back into the easy friendship we had years ago. We're older, different people, but our connection is still there. I should go straight home but how can I refuse? Ally can't move the furniture by herself and I don't want her to wait for George to come home, all that lifting wouldn't be good for his high blood pressure.

Besides, Ally was a good friend once. And I need her loyalty, she could blow my life apart.

It will be easier to go there first, so I reply that I'll pop in from work. Then I message Lizzie to let her know that I'll be a bit late home, so she doesn't worry that I've been in an accident or something. Lizzie always imagines the worst-case scenario, which I understand after what happened to her dad.

'Thanks so much,' Ally says as she lets me in half an hour later. 'I'm really grateful.'

'No problem, we all appreciate you looking after Judith.' I follow her into the lounge where my mother-in-law is sitting in the armchair, her bad ankle resting on a pouffe. 'How are you feeling?' I ask her, giving her a peck on the cheek. She looks pale and tired, I notice.

'I'm fine. I'll be right as rain in a couple of days,' she says weakly. 'Sorry Alison had to bother you. You're busy enough.'

'I'm never too busy to help you,' I tell her. It's true. I'll do anything for Judith and Lizzie. It began with guilt, but now it's love that drives me. Although the guilt never goes.

'Nick is going to help me bring a wardrobe or chest of drawers down so that you can access your clothes and a few personal things. Which do you prefer, Mum?'

Judith looks worried. 'Oh please don't go to all the trouble. I'll be back upstairs in no time.'

Ally squeezes her hand. 'It's going to be a while before you can get up and down those stairs, Mum, so let us make it a bit easier for you.'

'Well, it would be good to have the small chest of drawers,' Judith agrees. 'And there's a freestanding clothes rail folded up in the office room, we can put some of my clothes on that.' She must feel such a burden. One of the things I've always admired about Judith is that she's so fiercely independent. 'Thank you both.'

'It's no problem at all,' I reassure her.

I look around, we'd pushed the sofa to one side yesterday to make room for Judith's bed but it's still very cramped. 'How about we move the sofa out into the conservatory? There will be plenty of room for it if we move the wicker sofa and chairs from there outside. The weather's nice enough.' The conservatory leads off from the back room so it will be a fairly easy procedure.

'That's a great idea.' Alison's smile lights up her face. It's really nice how much she cares for Judith and everything she's trying to do for her. I remember how friendly and helpful she was all those years ago when we both worked together. 'Probably best if we move the stuff out of the conservatory first.'

She opens the patio doors leading to the conservatory and steps inside. I follow her. The wicker sofa and chairs aren't very heavy, and we each take a chair outside then carry the sofa between us. We place them on the patio.

'They look good here, don't they?' Alison says. 'I'll see if I can get a cover for them in case it rains because they'll probably be out here for a couple of weeks.'

'There's one in the shed,' I tell her. 'Right, let's get the big sofa out first. Are you sure you are okay carrying it? It's heavy.'

She raises an eyebrow in amusement. 'Nick. I'm a nurse. I'm used to heavy lifting.'

I guess she is. 'Okay then. But I'll lead and go backwards.' I don't add that it's the most difficult position, but she raises her eyebrow again to let me know she's guessed why I've made that choice. I admire how calm and confident she is. Not like Lizzie who is always convinced that the worst is going to happen at any time.

We go back in and together we lift the sofa and carry it into the conservatory, me walking backwards very slowly, as the last thing I need is to trip up and injure myself. We set the sofa down, it fills the space of both the wicker sofa and chairs but there's still room to move around it. I wipe the back of my arm across my forehead. Then we put the chest of drawers and clothes rail in place for Judith.

'Oh this looks wonderful.' Judith has come out of the lounge now and is leaning on her walker in the doorway. 'I'll be very comfortable in here. Thank you.'

'That's the idea,' Ally tells her. 'Do you want any clothes brought down?'

'George will see to that when he comes home. And Lizzie will pop in tomorrow and help too,' Judith replies. 'You both take a rest now, you've done enough.'

'If you're sure.' I glance at my watch. It's almost six thirty. 'Actually I'd better get back home now, Lizzie will have the dinner ready.'

'At least have a drink before you go. It's thirsty work carting furniture around.' Alison goes into the kitchen and comes back with two opened bottles of beer. 'They're chilled,' she says. She looks at Judith. 'Do you want a drink, Mum?'

'No thanks, love. I'm going to sit in the lounge and wait for George.' Judith leans on her walker as she goes out. I hate to see her this way, but hopefully it won't be for long, and she's in good hands with Alison.

I take a long swig out of the bottle, Alison does the same.

'This takes me back,' she says with a grin.

I nod, recalling how we always used to have a bottle of beer after we finished work. Our little ritual as we moaned about the day.

'It does. You've got a good memory to remember that from all those years ago.'

'It comes with the job,' she says. 'I remember everything.'

The words seem loaded. I glance at her guiltily, but she is smiling.

'I still can't believe that you're a nurse,' I say, shaking my head. 'Who would have thought it back then when you were a goth.'

'And I still can't believe that you're the Construction Manager of the company now. Who would have thought it back then when you were just a junior assistant.' She takes another swig of beer. 'You've done well for yourself, Nick.'

'What can I say? I felt I owed it to Arthur to keep the company going.'

'I'm sure you did.' Our eyes meet and she holds my gaze for a moment. Panic worms its way into my stomach.

I hope I can trust Ally to keep my secret. She has the power to shatter so many lives.

18

LIZZIE

Jodie's words have started a spiral of worry in my mind. I take some deep breaths to calm myself down. *It's all a coincidence*, I repeat, *a coincidence*. Finally I feel a little calmer. I've learnt coping tactics to see me through over the years and this is one of them. Now I need to get back to work then it will be time for the school run. I log onto the site to check the ratings for the session, as I do every day.

It's important that I deal with any complaints straight away. I'm self-employed and the ratings are visible for students to see and decide whether to book me. So far I've got a solid line of five stars and I'm proud of that. The knowledge that so many people are happy with my work helps me cope. I glance at my overall performance ratings then freeze as my eyes rest on a single star. And it's been added today.

I have never had a one-star rating. Never. Who has left it and why? I'm a good tutor, I know I am, and can't think of any instance recently when I've upset a student enough for them to mark me down like this.

It's one bad rating, I remind myself, *you have lots of good ones*. But it niggles at me. I can't wait for Nick to come home so that I can discuss it with him.

I pick the kids up from school and take them to the park for a while. They love playing on the swings and slide, and it burns off some of their energy and I enjoy watching them play, so happy and carefree. Like I was once.

'Push me, Mummy!' Grace calls. She's sitting on a swing trying to push herself up with her feet. Isaac is on the slide, going down backwards as usual. I walk over to Grace. 'How high do you want to go?' I jest as I gently push her. 'Do you want to touch the trees?'

'Right up to the fluffy clouds!' she giggles.

'Mum, watch me!' Isaac calls. He's on the climbing frame now, swinging along the bars. I wave to him then continue pushing Grace. I love this time I spend with my children and am proud that I pulled myself up out of my despair to be a good mother to them.

I'm never going to get that low again, I vow. I owe it to my family.

When we get home I give the kids a snack then they sit at the kitchen table and make a Get Well card for Mum while I prepare the dinner. I'm doing cottage pie with extra carrots and peas to go with it, they're the only vegetables that the kids will eat. Nick messaged earlier to say he would be late so I'm guessing a problem has come up at work.

Nick finally arrives home when I'm draining the vegetables, he looks a bit flustered.

'Everything okay? Trouble at work?' I ask.

He gives me a big hug and kisses me slowly, and I feel my own tension fade away. Nick's love keeps me safe, and sane. I don't know what I'd do without him.

'Ally texted and asked me to drop in on the way home to help her move some furniture around for Judith, to make the back room more comfortable for her. It's going to be a while before she can manage the stairs.'

'That's a good idea. Though, she should have mentioned it when I was there this morning, I could have helped.' I frown at him. 'Why didn't you say you were going to Mum's?'

'I was on a call to a client so I texted you in a hurry.' He sniffs appreciatively. 'That smells good. Anything I can do to help?'

I push away the niggle that Alison messaged him again when she could have told me. It feels like she's deliberately excluding me. *It was for Mum, to make her more comfortable*, I remind myself. 'It's cottage pie. You can lay the table and call the kids down, please. They're playing upstairs.'

'I'm on it.' Nick takes the plates out of the cupboard and places them on the table, then fetches the cutlery. 'How's your day been?' he asks as he lays out knives, forks and spoons.

I want to tell him about the one-star rating but I know he'll shrug it off and tell me to focus on all the four and five stars I get. Which I guess I should but it's niggling me. 'Okay, I took Alison some flowers this morning to thank her for looking after Mum. And a box of chocolates for Mum to cheer her up. Did they tell you?'

'No, there wasn't time for chit chat, I wanted to get home as quickly as I could.' He looks over at me. 'That was nice of you. I'm glad you're cutting Ally a bit of slack. She's only trying to look after your mum.'

I nod. 'I know.'

'I'll go and call the kids.'

I chew my lip as he walks out the kitchen, and I hear him shout up the stairs to Isaac and Grace. Nick's probably right and Alison is only trying to help, but I'm concerned with how quickly she's integrated herself with my family. And how chummy she is with Nick. And how he still calls her Ally, as if they were really close. I can't help wondering if there's more to their history than he's told me.

TUESDAY

19

JUDITH

'Good morning, darling, how are you feeling?'

George's cheery voice wakes me up out of deep sleep. I blink open my eyes as he kisses me. 'I've brought you a cup of tea. I thought we could spend a few minutes together before I go to work.'

He sits on the end of my bed. 'Or would you prefer to sleep a little longer?'

'No, I want to sit up and talk to you.' I try to get myself up and George immediately helps me, propping the pillow behind me. 'Bad night?' he asks sympathetically.

'I've been disturbed in the night with a terribly upset stomach but it's passed now,' I tell him. 'I feel so tired but I'm sure I'll soon liven up.' I grimace. 'What a way to spend a honeymoon.'

He reaches out for my hand and gently strokes it. 'Don't even think about that. The main thing is that you get well again. We can go on honeymoon later.'

'You're right. I'll soon be on my feet again.' I've got to stop being such a grouch. It could have been a lot worse.

We chat for a while as we drink our tea, then George has to leave for work. 'Take it easy today, don't push yourself too much,' he tells me as he kisses me goodbye.

'I won't,' I promise. I'm determined to get up, have a shower and put a bit of makeup on, it will make me feel and look a lot better. Lizzie will pop in again today and I don't want her worrying about me.

But when I try to get out of bed I feel dizzy and nauseous. I'm sitting on the side of the bed, holding the headboard for support, when Alison comes in.

'Mum, you should have called me!' She rushes to my side.

'I went giddy, I'll be okay in a few minutes,' I say weakly. 'I had a bit of an upset stomach last night and it's left me feeling a bit shaky.'

'Falls can really knock you about at your age, Mum. Your body takes longer to heal, you need to take it easy.'

It still feels a little strange that she calls me 'Mum' and I can tell that Lizzie doesn't like it, but Alison did ask my permission and it seemed petty to object. We've got quite friendly over the past couple of months, when she's phoned George for a chat, and I think she's just trying to make me feel part of the family.

'I've got a fractured ankle, that's all,' I say, feeling fragile. 'It shouldn't affect me like this. It's been three days now. I want to be able to get out and about.' Tears well up in my eyes. I'm frustrated with how helpless I feel. It's all I can do to hobble to the loo. I blink the tears away. I'm stronger than this. 'Me and your dad, we should be in Prague now. And instead I'm sleeping downstairs by myself and can barely get out of bed.' Yesterday I'd thought I was making progress but now I feel frail again.

'Don't stress yourself, Mum. Tummy bugs only usually last twenty-four hours so I'm sure you'll feel much better tomorrow. Now why don't you get back in bed and I'll bring you a bit of breakfast? How does a lightly boiled egg and some toast sound?'

I feel so weak that I reluctantly let her help me back into bed. My stomach is churning too much to eat, but I know that I need to build my strength up. 'Maybe just some dry toast,' I suggest. It's so frustrating. I was hobbling about yesterday and thought that I was on the mend but now I'm exhausted again.

While Alison goes off to make breakfast, I check my phone and see a message from Lizzie, asking how I am and saying she's tied up with work most of the day but will pop in before she picks the kids up from school. I reply back that I've got a tummy bug so it's probably best if she keeps away, as I don't want to pass it on to her and the kids. She answers that she hopes I feel better soon and will phone me later and attaches photos of Get Well cards the kids have made me. I smile as I look at them. Grace's card is literally covered in hearts whereas Isaac has drawn a picture of an old lady in bed – which I presume is me. Then Alison returns with my breakfast.

'Has someone called?'

'Lizzie messaged. I've told her not to pop in today, I don't want her to catch this bug,' I explain.

'Good idea. I think you need to rest today.' She puts the tray down on the chest of drawers by my bed that Nick brought down yesterday. She really has gone out of her way to make me comfortable. 'I've made you some peppermint tea, it will help settle your stomach.'

'Thank you. It's good of you to look after me like this,' I tell her. I'm grateful to Alison, she never rolls her eyes and makes me look like a nuisance but I feel one. I'd be more comfortable if Lizzie was looking after me, but I know she has enough on her plate. And she doesn't seem to be herself since the wedding.

'I was looking forward to seeing the kids though.' I show her the photos on my phone. 'Look at the cards they made me.'

Alison uses her fingers to enlarge the images. 'They're great. They're smashing kids, aren't they?' She puts my phone down on the bedside cabinet and takes the plate of dry toast off the tray. 'Try and eat, Mum, even if it's only a couple of bites,' she urges me.

I take a nibble of the toast and chew it slowly. Suddenly nausea swills in the bottom of my stomach again. 'Could I have a glass of water, please? I feel queasy.'

Alison jumps up and dashes out, returning a couple of minutes later with a bowl and a glass of water. She hands me the glass and puts the bowl down on the floor beside my bed. 'In case you feel sick and can't get to the loo quick enough,' she explains.

'Thanks.' I take a big gulp of the water. 'I don't understand why I have such an upset stomach,' I say when the nausea subsides a little. 'If I've somehow caught a bug then surely one of you would have it too.'

'I was wondering if it might be your medication. Let's keep an eye on it and if the nausea persists I'll check with the doctor.' Alison takes my temperature and blood pressure. 'You're a bit high but nothing to worry about.'

'I'm exhausted,' I tell her, feeling my eyes closing.

'Have a little nap. I'll tidy around and then go and get some shopping.' Alison points to a bell on the table. She must have brought it in earlier. 'Ring this if you need me. I don't want you exhausting yourself trying to get around on your walker. Have a rest today and build your strength up first.'

'Thank you.' I'm so grateful for what she's doing for me. Kenny and Sheila too, he popped in last night and brought me some flowers and a couple of magazines from Sheila. They've all welcomed me into the family with open arms.

George is so kind and considerate, nothing is too much trouble, and I really enjoy his company, we have such a lot in common. I was surprised but thrilled when he proposed, telling me that he was so worried that he'd almost lost me when I had the mini stroke that he wanted us to get married as soon as we could. Truth be told I was lonely since Lizzie married Nick. We are all still close, of course, but I missed having someone in the house. And the mini stroke frightened me too. Luckily George had been stopping over that weekend. What if it had happened in the middle of the night when I was alone?

20

JUDITH

I start to feel better as the day progresses, and Alison helps me negotiate the back steps again so that I can go outside to get a bit of fresh air. I sit on the wicker sofa that Alison and Nick moved from the conservatory and my mind drifts back to when Lizzie was young and we used to have a picnic on the lawn. Such precious times.

My phone buzzes. Lizzie is FaceTiming. 'How are you, Mum?' she asks when I accept the call.

'I'm a lot better. Alison is really looking after me, so there's no need to worry about me,' I tell her. 'How are you?' She looks a little tired, I think, although it's hard to tell on my small phone screen. 'Thank you for the photos of the kids' cards. I love them.'

'They're cute, aren't they? They spent ages making them. I'll bring them with me tomorrow. I'll drop by after the morning school run and we can have a cuppa and a catchup.'

'I look forward to that.'

We chat for a bit longer, then Alison comes out with a glass of water and my tablets. She waves to Lizzie. 'Hi there.'

'Hi, Alison. Just checking in on Mum.'

'She's doing fine.' Alison turns to me. 'Sorry to cut you short, Mum, but it's time for your tablets and I think you should have another rest. I don't want you to exert yourself.'

'I am a little tired,' I admit. So I say goodbye to Lizzie then I take my tablets, and Alison helps me into the back room and onto the bed. My eyes close as soon as my head touches the pillow.

I wake to enticing smells coming from the kitchen. Alison must be preparing dinner. I ease myself up and reach for my phone. I'm disappointed when I notice a missed call from George. It would have cheered me up to speak to him, but I must have been out for the count. I immediately call him back but his phone rings out. Then I notice the time, gone six – goodness, I've slept for hours! George is probably on the way home, he never answers his phone when he's driving. I slip my phone into my pocket and reach for my walker. Leaning on it I propel myself forward. I hate using it, it makes me feel like an old lady and is a bit awkward to manoeuvre, but at least I'm mobile.

'Can I help?' I ask as I shuffle into the kitchen.

'It's all under control, thanks,' Alison says cheerfully. She looks over her shoulder at me. 'How are you feeling now?'

'The nausea has gone. I think I'm through the worst.'

'That's good. Why don't you sit yourself down and I'll make us both a drink. Dad will be home soon.' She shakes the kettle to check how much water is in it then flicks it on. 'Tea okay?'

'Please. I noticed I missed a call from George. I can't believe I slept through my phone ringing.'

Alison pulls out a chair and helps me into it. 'That's because I turned your volume down. I hope you don't mind but you looked so tired, I wanted you to have some undisturbed rest.'

I'm a bit taken aback that she's meddled with my phone.

She's a nurse, she's used to making decisions to look after people, I remind myself. 'Not a problem. I'll turn it back up now.'

Alison makes the tea as I take out my phone and turn the volume back up, then she sits down beside me.

'That smells delicious.' I sniff at the aroma that is filling the kitchen. There's no sign of any saucepans on the stove, so whatever she's making is in the oven. 'What are you cooking?'

'Something very simple, a sausage casserole with roasted vegetables. It's Dad's favourite.'

I hadn't realised that. But then, there's a lot about George that I still don't know. It was such a whirlwind romance.

'I hope you like it too?' she asks, suddenly looking worried.

'I'm sure I will. And thank you, I appreciate you cooking dinner for us.'

We sit and chat as we drink our tea then George comes in. 'Oh good, you're up and about.' He strides over, gives me a big hug and a wrapped gift. 'I couldn't resist getting you this. I hope it cheers you up a bit.'

I open it eagerly, it's a black velvet jewellery box. I gasp when I open it up and see the gold locket inside. 'It's beautiful,' I say.

'Open the locket,' he tells me with a smile.

So I do and tears well in my eyes when I see that it holds a photo of me and George on our wedding day. My hand flies to my mouth. 'Oh George. What a wonderful present.'

He leans over and kisses me. 'A wonderful present for a wonderful lady.'

I put my hand on his cheek and stroke it tenderly. 'And you're a wonderful husband.'

'Has Sam sent the wedding photos over then?' Alison asks, admiring the locket.

'Only this one, because I asked him for one. He said the others will be ready in a couple of days.'

We all sit around the table eating our meal and chatting away. It feels so natural, as if the three of us have known each other for ages instead of only fairly recently. Then Alison goes upstairs to chat to a friend on FaceTime and me and George go into the lounge and watch TV.

George wraps his arm around my shoulder and I lean against him, loving the closeness of it. It's so good to feel stronger now. Tomorrow I'll see if I can make the stairs, I decide. I want to be able to snuggle up to George in bed, not sleep down here alone.

'Shall we have some warm milk and honey then we'll hit the sack,' George says, yawning.

'That sounds perfect.'

George returns a few minutes later with a couple of mugs on a tray and two slices of jam sponge. 'Alison made this earlier and insists we have a slice for supper.'

'That's kind of her.' I take the plate off him and dip my fork into the cake. It's soft, and melts into my mouth. 'This is luscious.'

'She's always been a good cook.'

Alison pops her head around the door just as we've finished our supper. 'I'm off to bed now, do you want me to help you settle down, Mum?'

'No thanks, love. George will help me. And thank you for the cake. We really enjoyed it.'

'Good, I'll see you in the morning then. But if you need me, give me a ring. Night.'

'Night, love. I think it's time we turned in too.' George stands up and holds his arm out to help me up. I cling on to it, but as soon as I pull myself up I feel dizzy. The next thing I know I'm in bed with George sitting beside me, his face etched with worry,

'What happened?' I ask.

He shakes his head. 'One minute you were fine the next you

keeled over. Luckily I caught you or you might have fractured your arm as well as your ankle.'

'I don't understand why I keep feeling dizzy,' I say. 'It was just like when I fell down the stairs and fractured my ankle.'

'Alison is worried too. She's keeping an eye on your blood pressure and it is a little high but nothing to worry about.'

But I am worried. I've only fractured my ankle, which yes is painful, but I shouldn't be feeling so weak and dizzy. Something isn't right.

21

I look down at her sleeping. She looks peaceful and, hopefully, will stay that way for a while, long enough for me to do what I have to do. As I watch her, her chest rising as she breathes in and out, I think how easy it is to end someone's life. One minute they're alive and breathing and the next minute they're gone. Forever. There's no going back with death.

It would be so easy to kill her. I could do it quickly now with a pillow over her face. Or I could take my time, do it slowly. A little too much medication, a little something added to her food, a fall. It's not the ending her life that's the problem, it's making sure that I don't get caught out for it. That it doesn't look suspicious.

I thought hard about this, I've been planning it for a long time, waiting for my chance to come. Which has the most effect, to kill the person who wronged you, or to kill someone they love and make them live with that loss, like we had to? I keep changing my mind, swapping from one to the other. I can't afford to make a mistake, I need to get this right.

WEDNESDAY

22

JUDITH

I've had a bad night, tossing and turning restlessly. It felt like I had some kind of fever. Images flash in my mind. Alison holding a glass of water for me, George wiping my forehead with a cool flannel. And something else, it's at the back of my mind, lurking, but I can't grab it. I'm sure it's important but it's no use, it's eluding me. Maybe it was just a dream.

I lie still to get a sense of how I'm feeling before I try to get out of bed. My stomach seems to have settled, but I feel weak, and my mouth is dry.

I can hear movement and then the door opens and, to my surprise, Sheila walks in, holding a mug in her hand.

'Morning, dear, how are you feeling today?'

What on earth is she doing here?

My surprise must be evident because she smiles. 'Alison had to go out for a bit, so she asked me to stay with you. She was worried about leaving you alone. She said that you picked up some sort of tummy bug and went dizzy again last night.'

'Has Lizzie been? She said she was popping in when she dropped the kids off to school.' I'd been looking forward to seeing her. George's family are being kind but I miss the familiar company of my daughter and grandchildren.

'She phoned and as you were still asleep I took the liberty of answering, I hope that's all right. She said that she had to work this morning so would drop by later.'

'Yes, thank you. And for the tea. I'm feeling a lot better but my head aches,' I tell her.

Sheila crosses the room and puts the mug down on the bedside table. 'I'm not surprised. Alison said that you've had a bad night. Tossing, turning and calling out.' She props a pillow behind my back. 'She came down to check on you because she was worried you might get out of bed to go to the loo and go dizzy again.'

'I had a couple of bad dreams. I feel so guilty at how much I'm putting on Alison, when I barely know her. She must be wishing George had never met me!'

'Nonsense! We are all delighted that you and George have got together. Mind, George is very worried about you, the poor lamb. He didn't want to go into work today but I said I'd take the train over and sit with you. Kenny's going to pick me up later.' Sheila points to the mug she's just brought in. 'I could see that you were stirring so I've made you a cup of tea. Alison said you like one when you wake.'

'Thank you.' I try to sit myself up but I can't. It's like my bones have turned to jelly and I have no control over my movements.

'Here, let me help you.' Sheila helps me sit up and props the pillows behind me for support. 'You really have been in the wars lately, haven't you?'

I wonder where Alison has gone but I don't like to ask, she's entitled to her privacy.

Sheila hands me the cup of tea. 'Drink this up. You're probably a bit dehydrated now. I've put some sugar in it to give you energy.'

'Thank you. You're all so kind.' Tears fill my eyes at the care George, Alison and now Sheila have shown to me. I've barely been in the family five minutes but they've all taken me under their wings. It really is kind of them. Lizzie and Nick are doing their best to help too. And it's all my fault, being so clumsy as to fall down the stairs. I could have broken my neck. And I've ruined everything. We should have been in Prague, but instead everyone is running around looking after me.

You went dizzy and fell. There was nothing you could do, I remind myself. *Now stop feeling sorry for yourself!*

I'm not used to feeling like this. I've always been a strong woman. I've had to be, what with Lizzie being how she is, and then Arthur dying suddenly, and in such a dreadful way too.

'Do you think you can manage a bit of food?' Sheila asks. 'A lightly boiled egg and toast maybe?'

Actually, I do feel hungry, I could manage an egg today. 'Thank you. I'd appreciate that,' I reply.

She goes out to the kitchen, leaving me to sip my tea. It's cooled enough to drink now and soothes my dry throat. I wrap my hands around the mug and drink it slowly. As soon as I've finished it I'm going to have a shower, get dressed and put on some makeup. I'm determined not to be an invalid. I'm stronger than this. I'm a fighter. I always have been.

I put my empty cup back on the bedside table then my eyes rest on a black pen lying there. I stare at it, my mind swimming as a memory springs into it. Someone holding the pen out to me, wanting me to write something but I can hardly hold the pen. *What was it? Who was it?* I remember the feeling that I had when I woke up, that something important was lurking at the back of my mind. If only I could remember it.

Sheila returns a few minutes later with a tray holding two plates of toast and two partly shelled eggs in egg cups. 'Tuck in,' she says, placing one on my lap, and I realise how hungry I am. I need to build myself up then I'll get stronger.

'This is so kind of you, thank you,' I say.

'No problem, you're family now and we all look after each other.' She sits down on the chair and tucks into her egg.

'You're all very close, aren't you?' I remark.

'We are. When poor Carol died George moved to Gloucester so I could help him with the children. We're a unit, us four.' She takes a bite out of her toast.

George never talks about Carol's death, all I know is that it was because of some kind of allergic reaction. 'Past is past, no point going over it,' he said, so I never pushed him for information. Now though, I'm curious.

'Yes, it was a real tragedy, wasn't it? So devastating for you all.'

Sheila pauses, spoon in hand about to scoop into her egg again. 'The thing is, Carol wasn't supposed to be going on the school trip that day. Another mum had to drop out so she stepped in at the last minute. If she hadn't, she'd still be with us.'

A school trip? Surely it couldn't be... 'Goodness, that is awful. George said she had a bad allergic reaction to something?'

'Peanuts. She always avoided them but one of the kids on that trip must have had them in their lunchbox. I guess Carol thought she'd be safe as they were eating outside. She collapsed in front of Kenny and Alison. Poor Alison ran for her EpiPen but didn't get it in time.'

I force my voice to stay calm as I ask, 'Where were they?'

When Sheila tells me the name of the park and the year, my fears are confirmed.

George's wife is the woman who died on Lizzie's school trip when she was seven.

If Lizzie learns about this, it could bring her trauma back. I can't let her find out and be plunged back into that darkness again.

23

LIZZIE

'Morning, Lizzie, Judith's still asleep, dear. I'll get her to call you later,' Sheila says when I phone to see how Mum is this morning. 'How are you and the children?'

'We're all good, thanks.' I'm a bit put out that she's answering Mum's phone, but then tell myself if Mum was asleep and Sheila heard it ringing, it's quite natural for her to answer it.

'Glad to hear that. I must get on now. Bye, dear.'

Then she's gone.

I drum my fingers on my desk. Surely Mum shouldn't be this tired. I know she has fractured her ankle, and she caught a tummy bug, but something doesn't feel right to me. Maybe she should see the doctor. I'll mention it to Alison when I visit her later. I try to put my worries to one side as I start marking my assignments.

The morning flies by and before I know it it's lunchtime. Mum hasn't called me back. I check my phone in case she's sent me a text and I missed it. Nothing.

She must be awake by now. Maybe Sheila has forgotten to tell her that I called? I make myself a cup of green tea and call

Mum. It rings and rings, and I chew my lip anxiously. *Is she still asleep?*

Relief floods through me as Mum finally answers, but she sounds breathless. 'Sorry, darling, I went to the loo.'

'Are you feeling any better, Mum? Sheila said you had a bad night.'

'I did. I went all dizzy again and I think I was a bit delirious in the night. Alison said she thinks it's the co-codamol, it can make you feel sick and dizzy apparently. She popped out to get me some other painkillers, and a bit of shopping.'

'That's good. I've been worried about you. I'm sorry I couldn't come over this morning but I've had so much work. I'll drop in before I pick the kids up from school.'

'Don't worry about me, darling, I'm in good hands. The whole family are rallying around me. Kenny came over to collect Sheila and brought me a custard slice and a magazine. I'm being taken care off. You look after yourself. You've enough on your plate. You can leave it until the morning if you want.'

'No, I want to see you. I'll drop by about two thirty.'

'I'll see you later then, darling. I'm looking forward to having a chat.'

'Okay, Mum.'

She sounds chirpy enough, I think in relief when we've ended the call. And I have to admit that George's family are being really helpful. I should be grateful for that and stop feeling like they're pushing me out.

I make myself some lunch and take it out into the garden to eat it. It's mild today and I always feel better when I'm outdoors. It calms me down to sit in the little Zen corner Nick made for me. Our garden isn't very big, there's a lawn for the kids to play on, a couple of swings, a few flower beds and a shed for Nick. In the top corner, the one that gets the most sun, is my Zen garden.

I guess an outsider would say it's nothing special, a little rockery with cacti plants, a big Buddha statue, a peace lily, a tree of life plaque on the shed wall and a mosaic table with two chairs. I put my cup on the table and sit down, taking in deep breaths of fresh air. This corner always makes me feel calmer. Nick had noticed how much my Buddha painting meant to me, so made this precious garden for me when I was struggling so much to cope after Isaac was born.

I'd only recently returned from maternity leave after having Isaac when that terrible incident with a boy at at school having a bad allergic reaction made me realise what I'd done. That I'd killed someone. The burden of carrying that secret dragged me into despair, but I was too afraid to share my guilt with anyone so tried to carry on. Until I had a total breakdown.

The doctor gave me some antidepressants which made me feel calmer, and Mum persuaded me to stay with her one weekend, so she could help look after Isaac while I rested. When I came back home Nick took my hand, led me out into the back garden and showed me the beautiful garden he'd spent all weekend making for me. 'Somewhere for you to sit and relax,' he said, and I'd cried at his thoughtfulness and love.

That was the turning point for me. Gradually, as I sat out here breathing in the peace, I healed again. When Grace was born I managed to calm my anxiety. I had two children to look after now. I had to keep strong for them. Mostly I managed it, but the guilt and remorse never left me, it was always there, like a coiled poisonous snake, waiting to pounce.

Now I can feel it building again. That suffocating feeling that one day I would pay for my actions.

I can't let it in. I have to hold it all together. But as I sit here the memories resurface and explode into my mind, and I am plunged back to that fateful day when I was only seven years old.

24

LIZZIE

Then

I was so excited. I was going on a school outing today to an amusement park with a zoo, and we were having a picnic lunch there. All the class was going, and the class above us. Mum got me some treats to take, crisps, chocolate, an apple. 'What do you want for sandwiches, Lizzie? We have cheese, ham or peanut butter,' she asked.

'Peanut butter,' I instantly replied. It was my favourite, I had a peanut butter sandwich every night before I went to bed.

'Cheese is better for you,' Mum said persuasively. She was always trying to get me to vary my diet, but I was insistent. I wanted peanut butter. I had no idea how much I would regret that decision, how I would wish I'd agreed to have cheese.

Both classes were excited as we got onto the coach and set off. I sat by my best friend Jodie and we chatted away about what we would do at the park, the animals we would see, the rides we would go on. A couple of children's parents were accompanying the teachers, and I'd wanted my mum to come but she couldn't because she had to work. If only she had come things would have been different.

There were a few groups from other schools at the park too, it was really busy. We all had to queue to go on the rides and to go into the reptile house to see the big snakes and lizards. I was scared of the snakes but Jodie said she wasn't. We were licking our ice cream cones, talking about the snakes, when a girl from another school accidentally bumped into me and knocked my ice cream out of my hand.

'Sorry!' she said, and I fought back the tears as I saw my delicious ice cream splattered on the ground. I had been enjoying that ice cream and I didn't have enough money to buy another one.

Then a lady came over. 'What's happened, Ally?' she asked.

'It was an accident, Mum. I didn't mean to knock her,' the girl protested.

'It's okay, Ally. Accidents happen.' The lady looked kindly at me. 'What's your name, love?'

'Lizzie,' I replied, determined not to cry.

'I'll go and get you another ice cream, Lizzie. I'll be back in a minute,' she promised.

True to her word, she returned a few minutes later with an even bigger ice cream cone, with two flakes in it. I was delighted and thanked her profusely. Jodie eyed the cone enviously, so I gave her one of the flakes, dipped in ice cream.

I saw Ally, her mother and little brother a few times throughout the morning and we all waved at each other.

Then lunchtime, we sat down on the wooden benches in the picnic area to eat our packed lunches. Ally, her mother and little brother were sitting at another table, but me and Jodie waved to Ally and called her over, so she squeezed onto the bench next to me and we all chatted away.

Jodie had a cheese roll and Ally had egg and cress sandwiches made with thin brown bread, they looked so dainty and tasty. My mum usually gave me thin brown bread too but we were out of it that morning, so Mum had to use the thick bread Dad liked. It was twice as thick as Ally's bread and the crusts were hard. I bit into the middle of the bread, nibbling around the crusts as I chatted to Jodie and Ally.

'Right everyone, put your rubbish in your lunchboxes and let's get going,' our teacher said.

I didn't want to put my crusts in my lunchbox. Mum would scold me if she saw I had left them, she was always telling me to eat my crusts, but I couldn't eat these, they were thick and hard. I needed a bin. Only there wasn't time to find one, everyone was getting up to follow the teacher. I'd be left behind.

Ally's lunchbox was open. Her empty crisp bag was in there, and her chocolate bar wrapper. I glanced at her, she was busy talking to her friend and not watching me, so I quickly scooped up my crusts and thrust them into the empty crisp packet. Then I shut my lunchbox, got up, shouted goodbye and went off with the rest of my class.

We were going to see the chimps when suddenly there was a commotion in front of us. I could see Ally's mum standing by the bin, holding her throat, she was crying and wheezing. She couldn't seem to breathe.

Ally screamed something about getting a pen and raced over to the table where her mum had left her bag. There was a crowd around her mum now, teachers and other mothers all trying to help. Her little brother was standing all alone, crying, then one of the mums held his hand and talked to him, trying to comfort him.

Ally returned a couple of minutes later shouting, 'I've got it!'

I couldn't see what she was holding, but a teacher grabbed it off her and bent down by her mum. I couldn't see properly because there were so many people around. Soon the sirens sounded and an ambulance pulled up.

'Stand back! Stand back!' the paramedics shouted as they ran over and the crowd parted.

But it was too late. Ally and her little brother's mum was dead.

25

JUDITH

Sheila's words keep going over and over in my mind. The woman who died from anaphylactic shock on Lizzie's school trip all those years ago must have been George's wife.

It is too much of a coincidence for it not to be.

Then another thought occurs to me. What if Lizzie's peanut butter sandwiches had been the cause of the poor woman's fatal allergic reaction? I know that they didn't go to the same school but they might have sat at the same table.

It's a big if. Surely there would have been other children with peanut butter sandwiches, or a peanut snack bar.

Poor Lizzie had been so traumatised, she'd actually witnessed the poor woman die. If she even suspected that it was her sandwiches that caused it, it would destroy her. As it was she refused to eat peanut butter ever again. I think she had it in her head that she might have a bad reaction like that too, although I tried to reassure her that eating peanuts could only kill you if you were allergic to them, but she still refused. Wouldn't even let me have peanut butter in the house. And still won't have it in her house. That was the start of her anxiety problems.

They got worse when she became a teacher and a child in her class suffered an anaphylactic shock too. She saved him, but it seemed to push her over the edge. She had a total nervous breakdown and never returned to teaching in a classroom. Even now, her anxiety is always hovering in the background, ready to rear its head when there's any setback or problem. Poor Lizzie lives on her nerves.

My phone rings. It's George, checking up on me again. The sound of his voice always cheers me up.

'Hello, darling, how are you feeling today?'

'Much better,' I tell him. 'I think I'm over the bug now and Alison has got me some different painkillers. We think the co-codamol doesn't agree with me.'

'Perfect. I've messaged Alison to let her know I'm bringing some lamb chops home for tea. We'll soon have you on your feet again.'

He knows that I love lamb. 'Thank you, darling.'

We chat for a while and then George has to go as a customer has come in.

'Do you want a cuppa, Mum? And shall we sit out in the garden for a bit?' Alison asks.

'That sounds a good idea,' I reply. I reach for the wheeled walker which is placed by the bed and she rushes over to help me.

I shake my head. 'Please let me do it. I'm sure I can manage. And if I can't, I'll ask you for help, I promise. I have to try to be independent.'

She nods and steps back. 'Of course.'

I carefully make my way out into the garden – Alison rushing to open the back door for me, as I'd have struggled to open it by myself. I manage to get over to the table by myself, though, and sit down on one of the chairs. It's a warm day, clear blue sky and it feels good to be outside. I'm getting better, getting stronger. I'm not going to let this ankle defeat me.

'Here you are, Mum. Two sugars and milky, just as you like it.' Alison puts my mug down in front of me and sits opposite me, still holding her mug. 'Isn't it a gorgeous day?'

'It certainly is.' I pick up my tea and sip it, my mind still going over what Sheila had told me. It must have been so awful for Alison and Kenny to see their mother die like that, goodness Lizzie was traumatised enough! George – and Sheila – had obviously handled the situation really well and given them a lot of support.

I wonder whether to mention it to Alison, to let her know that Lizzie had been on the same school trip, and how badly it had affected her to witness her poor mother's death. But I don't want to bring it all up again, it must be such a painful memory for them all. It was twenty-five years ago, and everyone has changed so much, no wonder they didn't recognise each other. Lizzie has black hair now, she always hated being auburn, and Alison looks totally different from the photos George has shown me of them all when they were younger.

Then an image of Lizzie having the panic attack at our wedding flashes across my mind. Had Lizzie somehow recognised Alison? Was that what had triggered her anxiety?

My hand shakes a bit, slopping tea out. I put the mug down on the table.

'Are you all right, Mum?'

'Oh yes, just a bit clumsy,' I reply. How can I tell her that I'm worried that Lizzie might have recognised her, and about the consequences if she has? There is no telling what Lizzie will do when she crashes.

26

LIZZIE

After lunch I text Mum to say that I'm on the way, and she replies that they're sitting in the back garden. I'm so relieved, Mum must be feeling better then. I decide to drive there, so I can go straight to the school to pick up the kids afterwards. I grab the cards they made Mum on Monday and slip them in my bag.

Kenny's car is parked outside the house so it looks like I won't get time alone with Mum. Again. I was already worrying about seeing Alison. Every time I see her, or Kenny – although I know he was too young to remember me, and I hardly had any contact with him – the guilt overwhelms me and I live in fear that Alison's going to remember me, guess what I did and tell everyone, but I can't let that stop me from seeing Mum. She needs me to look out for her.

I shout over the gate, annoyed that Alison hasn't returned my key yet. She has had plenty of time to have one cut. I'm starting to wonder if she's doing it on purpose, to make me feel the outsider while she cosies up to my mum.

'Coming,' Kenny calls. I hear him unlock the bolt and the

gate opens. 'Hiya, Liz. Judith said you were on your way. How are you all?'

His big smile and friendly chatter puts me at ease right away. 'We're all good, thanks.' I glance around and see Mum sitting in the comfy wicker chair from the conservatory, her feet up and a cushion behind her back. There's a glass of water and a half-eaten sandwich on the table in front of her. Sheila is sitting beside her, chatting. Mum waves to me and I walk over to join them. There's no sign of Alison.

'How are you, Mum?' I kiss her on the cheek and sit down on the empty chair beside her, my eyes anxiously scrutinising her face, noting the dark shadows under her eyes and her pallor.

'I'm so tired, Lizzie. I can't believe how much this fall has knocked me about. That and the tummy bug.'

I hold her hand in mine. It's cold and clammy despite the warmth of the day. She has a blanket over her knees. I glance at the half-eaten sandwich. 'Are you eating, Mum? You need to keep your strength up.'

'I'm trying but I've lost my appetite.' Her voice is very quiet, as if she hasn't got the strength to talk. 'Alison's made me soup and plenty of hot drinks so don't worry, I won't waste away.'

'Are you in a lot of pain?' I ask her.

'A bit, but that's only to be expected.'

Sheila pats her hand. 'Things take longer to heal when you get to our age, dear.'

Then I remember the kids' cards in my bag. I open it and take them out, handing them to Mum. 'Here's the Get Well cards Isaac and Grace made for you.'

Mum's face lights up as she looks at them. 'Bless them, they're so cute. I'll put them on my bedside cabinet when I go back inside.'

Sheila looks over at the cards too. 'Ah, they must have spent ages making those.'

'They did. They love their nanny. They can't wait to see you,' I tell Mum.

Then the back door opens and Alison comes out. 'Oh hello, Lizzie,' she says brightly. 'I thought you were too busy to pop in today. I know that your work is important, you have to keep on top of things, don't you, in this online world. People are too quick to leave a bad review.'

That seems an odd comment when I've just had my first low review ever. *Don't be silly, why would Alison leave you a bad review?* Anyway, ratings and reviews can only be left by people who've used the site.

'I phoned Mum this morning and told her I'd pop in and see her before I picked the kids up from school,' I reply.

'Good idea not to bring the kids with you, Mum's ankle is still swollen and if they knock it, it will be really painful for her. Now, can I get anyone a drink? I've got some homemade lemonade.'

'Yes, please, dear,' Sheila says. Mum agrees and I add, 'That's good for me too.' But Kenny says he has to be off.

I watch Alison go back into the house, hoping Sheila will leave with Kenny so I can talk to Mum in private, I've only got an hour before I pick up the kids, but to my disappointment Kenny leaves alone, telling Sheila he'll pick her up in a couple of hours.

'He's got a meeting, he only popped in to check if we needed anything,' Sheila says.

Well, it looks like I'm not going to get a chance to speak to Mum alone. I never seem to get the chance to do that nowadays. Maybe it's for the best. Maybe I shouldn't tell her what I did. Mum might feel that she has to tell George and then everyone will know, and I've no idea how they will take it. They might all blame me, hate me. It could make things difficult for Mum too.

'How are you doing with your walker? Are you managing to get around?' I ask her.

'I can a bit, but it's rather tiring. When I feel a bit stronger Alison is going to take me to the shops in a wheelchair. She said she can borrow one from the hospital. It would be nice to get out a bit.'

'That would be great. I can fit a wheelchair in my car, you can come over for an hour and see the kids.'

'I look forward to that. Will you bring them to see me from school tomorrow?' she asks. 'I do miss them.'

'I think it's a bit soon...' Alison has returned with our cold drinks on a tray.

I'm determined not to let her keep overruling me. 'Nonsense, it will be good for Mum to see them. They've always been very close.' I take the glasses from the tray and hand one to Mum.

'You'll have to excuse me if I seem to be overprotective, Lizzie.' Alison swallows, her eyes holding mine. 'But when you lose your mum young, like Kenny and I did, I guess it makes you that way. I'd hate anything to happen to your mum.'

27

LIZZIE

'I know you've only got my best interests at heart, Alison, but I really want to see the children, so please bring them after school tomorrow, Lizzie. Just for a little time,' Mum says.

'I will,' I promise. I don't look at Alison. I can't. My mind is in turmoil. It sounded an innocent enough remark, but the way Alison said it, her eyes piercing into mine... it sounded like a threat. And it's not the first time she's mentioned 'something happening to Mum', I recall.

When I do look up, Sheila and Alison are walking back to the house together, deep in conversation.

Mum is sipping her drink slowly and the colour starts to return to her face. 'Ah, this is just what I needed. And to see you,' she says happily.

'I'm glad to see you too.' I put my arm around her shoulder. 'Are you sure you're all right, Mum? You look a bit troubled. You know you can tell me anything.'

She sighs and rests her head against me. 'Oh Lizzie, I'm in a bit of a tizz because everything's gone wrong since the wedding. We should have gone to Prague for a honeymoon, and instead

I'm stuck in here, feeling helpless. I can't even go upstairs to bed.'

A sob catches in her throat, and my heart goes out to her. Is it all a coincidence that everything has gone wrong since Alison arrived? And it all started with Mum having that dizzy spell.

'Can you remember much about your fall, Mum? How long did you feel dizzy?' I ask as I move out of the hug to give Mum space to finish her drink.

'It was so sudden. I'd been feeling a bit tired all evening, probably the excitement of the wedding. Alison made me a hot drink, and I went to bed. I shouldn't have gone up the stairs really, my head was swimming. I tried to hang on to the rail to stop myself falling but it was too late, I hit the floor. I must have passed out. I don't know anything else until I woke up in hospital. George said Alison called an ambulance, dealt with everything. I don't know what we'd have done if Alison wasn't here. Thank goodness she didn't go back to stay with Kenny as she planned.'

Lucky or planned? Alison makes Mum a warm drink. A few hours later Mum is dizzy, falls and fractures her ankle. Is that simply a coincidence?

Stop it, Lizzie, you're being paranoid.

The door opens and Alison comes out again. 'Oh, you're looking a lot perkier, Mum. I think a chat with Lizzie has done you good.'

'It certainly has.' Mum pats my hand. 'It's lovely to have so many people drop by to see how I am.'

I'm so pleased that she's perked up. It worries me to see Mum weak and upset. She's always been so positive and strong. I wish I could stay longer but I have to go and pick Isaac and Grace up now. 'I'll message you later, Mum,' I promise.

'I look forward to it. And seeing you tomorrow.' Mum's eyes meet mine. I feel like she's holding something back. That she wants to talk to me but can't because of Alison and Sheila.

Is she suspicious of Alison like I am? After all, everything was fine until she turned up. And it feels like Alison was warning – or threatening – me when she said 'we don't want anything to happen to your mum.'

Was my earlier thought that she might be out for revenge correct or am I being paranoid? I'm sure Nick would say I am. Maybe I am. But I'm going to keep a close eye on my mum, and I'm going to get my key back so that I can go and see her whenever I want, not when Alison allows me to. If she does remember me and is planning a twisted revenge, then I need to be on alert.

I wonder if it would be best if I told Mum, and Nick? That would stop Alison if she is planning anything. I don't want anyone to know what part I played in that awful tragedy, though. It was an accident, and I was so young. I would do anything to go back in time and prevent it. But if I have to tell everyone to keep my mum safe, then I will.

I hope I don't have to, though. I can't bear to see Mum's face when she learns what I did. And what about Nick, will he be angry and upset that I've kept it a secret all these years? Especially as he knows Alison and they are old friends.

Or maybe more than friends.

28

LIZZIE

I've just got back with the kids, given them a snack and let them play out in the garden, when a message pings in from my boss. She wants to speak to me urgently.

My stomach plunges. Yvonne has only ever sent me a message like that twice before. And both times it was when a student was upset over their assignment marks. I hope that hasn't happened again. I try to be fair, and most of my students are great, but you get the odd one who thinks their work is better than it is. Yvonne has always been so supportive, but any type of complaint makes me nervous. And there was that one-star rating too.

I check the kids are okay and phone Yvonne, my mind going over the last few assignments I've marked. None of them had low marks, nothing to complain about.

'Hello, Lizzie. Thank you for getting back to me.' Yvonne's manner is crisp, businesslike.

This doesn't sound good, she's usually warm and friendly.

'That's okay. Is anything wrong?'

There's a pause. 'We've had a complaint about you on the company website, Lizzie. A potential customer said they contacted you for information about a course and your manner was very unprofessional.'

I'm stunned. I've never been unprofessional, and boy have I had some awkward customers, but I've always been polite to them.

'Did they leave their name?' I ask, casting my mind over all the queries I've had the past few days. With email queries I always have the emails as proof, but we tutors don't record phone calls, and there have been a few phone enquiries regarding the course. The calls had been brief and pleasant – although there was that man the other day who seemed to be deliberately awkward, I recall.

'No, it's on the website posted as anonymous, but we still have to take it seriously, Lizzie. Have you a record of the queries you've dealt with over the past couple of weeks? I could ignore it if it was a general anonymous complaint, but your name was specifically mentioned.'

I've been set up, I can see that and am now sure it was that man the other day. I tell Yvonne about him. 'He was a bit shirty and wanted me to assure him that he would pass the course, which obviously I couldn't, but I was very polite and professional, I promise.'

'It's the first complaint we've had about you, Lizzie, and I'd be willing to put it down to an awkward customer, but you have three one-star ratings online too.'

Three! Another two must have gone up since I last checked.

'Do you know who left them?' I ask.

'No, they were all anonymous.'

Someone is out to discredit me. Why?

'Look, you've worked for us for a few years now and there's never been any complaints before, so I'm prepared to overlook this providing we don't have any more.' She hesitates. 'Are you struggling a bit, Lizzie. Do you need to take time off?'

I probably do, I acknowledge, I haven't been myself since

Mum's fall but I need to pull myself together. I can't afford to lose this job.

'No, I'm fine,' I tell her. 'There won't be any more complaints, I promise.' Although I'm not sure how I can promise that when I didn't do anything to deserve these and have no idea who is out to get me.

What's happening to my life? Everything seems to be going wrong.

I've just finished the call when Nick phones. 'Hey, how are you doing?' he asks, his voice warm and comforting.

'Okay, how are you? You're not phoning to say you'll be late, are you?'

'Yes, sorry, we've got a bit of a problem so I need to stay late and sort it out. Look, don't bother with cooking, just fix something for the kids and I'll bring a takeaway for us.'

I wish he wasn't working late, I was hoping to pop over and see Mum again tonight and ask Alison if I could have my key back, tell her I'd have one cut for her tomorrow.

I'm sure Nick doesn't want to work late either, I remind myself as he ends the call. It's good that he's so dedicated to the company. It could have gone under when Dad died if it wasn't for Nick.

'I'm hungry,' Isaac says, running in with Grace right behind him.

I glance at the clock, it's gone five. 'How about spaghetti hoops on toast?' I suggest.

'Yes, please. Can I have two pieces of toast?' he asks.

'And me!' Grace pipes up.

'Of course. Now go and wash your hands and I'll start making it.'

Later, when the kids are tucked up in bed, I give Mum a call to check how she is. It rings out and out. Then George answers.

'Hello, Lizzie, your mum is asleep. She was shattered so went to bed early. Can I take a message, love?'

Asleep again?

'I'm worried about Mum, George. She's always been so lively and outgoing, but since the fall she seems exhausted all the time.'

'I know, I'm concerned too. Alison said that you and Judith were sitting out in the garden this afternoon and it tired her out. I guess it will take her a bit of time to build up her strength again.'

Is Alison blaming me for visiting my mum? She fractured her ankle. It shouldn't affect her like this, I want to shout. 'Maybe Mum should get checked out by the doctor, just to make sure everything is all right.'

'I suggested that but Judith doesn't want to. She feels that she's wasting the doctor's time when other more seriously ill people need his help.'

Which is exactly the sort of thing Mum would say.

'We'll give her a couple more days then I'll call the doctor myself if she hasn't improved,' George continues. 'I'll let her know you called, love. Give the kiddies a hug from us both. Love the cards they made, by the way.'

'Thanks. Will do. Bye George.'

George ends the call. I tap my chin with my phone, deep in thought. Mum has always been a bundle of energy, I can't help but worry how this fall has knocked her about.

Mum is everything to me. It was devastating when we lost Dad and I can't bear to think of losing my mum too.

Alison and Kenny lost their mum at a very young age because of me, I think guiltily. It must have been so terrible to have to grow up without a mother, and for poor George to lose his wife. An image of Carol, smiling as she hands me the double flake ice cream, flashes across my mind and I screw my eyes tight. It haunts me that I was responsible for her death. And ever since I realised it was my fault I've been consumed by an enormous feeling of foreboding that one day I would pay.

29

LIZZIE

Before

Watching Carol die, choking and gasping for breath, seeing Alison and Kenny's distress and everyone running around in panic had been the start of my crippling anxiety. One minute their mother had been alive and the next she was dead. It terrified me that someone could die so quickly, but I hadn't known then that it was my fault.

Night after night, I had horrible dreams about it and every day I was scared that my parents, my friends, or even I would suddenly die. It seemed to me that there was nothing you could do to prevent it, one moment everything was okay and the next moment you could be gone. I woke several times in the night and went in to check on my parents. I was so riddled with anxiety that Mum took me to counselling. The school also arranged for someone to come in and talk to us because several children, including Jodie, had witnessed the terrible event too, and were distressed. Gradually I got over the trauma and realised that it was something that didn't happen often and it was because of an allergy.

I'd just returned from maternity leave after having Isaac and was standing in for a teacher who was away when one of the boys in my classroom went into an anaphylactic shock. I'd checked the board in the staffroom so that I was aware of medical conditions and allergies but hadn't expected it to be a problem in a classroom situation. All was fine until halfway into the lesson. The boy, Jamie, started going red in the face and choking. My mind went back to the dreadful day Ally's mother had died, and I sprang into action, grabbing the EpiPen he kept in the green bag. I saved him, thank goodness, but I was puzzled how it had happened. He hadn't been eating peanuts. We asked if anyone had anything with peanuts with them and everyone said no. Then we discovered that the little girl next to him had a snack bar in her pocket. Reading the label, we saw that it contained nuts. Just being close to it had caused Jamie to go into shock. An image of Ally and Kenny's mum emptying Ally's lunchbox into the litter bin flashed into my mind. The lunchbox that contained my peanut butter coated crusts. It was then when I realised what had happened. It was all my fault. I'd killed her.

The guilt and mental anguish drove me to the point that I could barely function. I couldn't stop thinking about how the woman who had been so kind to me, bought me an ice cream, was dead. That Ally, the girl I'd sat by, chatted to, and her little brother no longer had a mother. And it was all down to me. My actions had caused it.

I longed to go back in time and change things. I rewrote the scene over and over again in my head, only this time I put my crusts in the bin, not in Ally's lunchbox, and Ally, her little brother and her mum all waved to me as they went home together, holding hands. How could that one little mistake cause so much tragedy? I felt that I didn't deserve to live when I'd robbed two children of their mother. My mind was in torment. I really think that only the fact that I didn't want to leave Isaac motherless gave me the strength to carry on.

Nick and my parents were supportive but didn't understand my devastation. 'You saved his life, Lizzie,' they kept pointing out. I couldn't bring myself to tell them about my part in Ally's mum's death and the weight of the guilt was drowning me, I didn't know how to cope. I had to give up teaching because I was too anxious that it might happen again and this time I wouldn't be able to save the child.

More years of therapy helped me to deal with it and move on. I still couldn't face teaching in school though, so Nick suggested I taught online, which I've been doing ever since.

Now, it has all come flooding back. And I'm scared that Mum is in danger. She's married George, a widower, whose wife, Carol, died of an allergic reaction after I put my crusts in their daughter's lunchbox. And his daughter, Alison, is looking after Mum, who has suddenly had an accident and is always feeling ill.

It all seems too much of a coincidence.

THURSDAY

30

LIZZIE

'You look tired, can you take an hour off today to rest?' Nick asks as we all sit at the table eating breakfast the next morning.

'I didn't sleep too good but I've got the morning off, so I'm going to do some shopping then see Mum,' I reply. I don't tell him that I was awake half the night worrying about her and have decided on a plan of action. Instead of asking Alison for my key back, I'm going to get another key cut for myself, then I can come and go as I please. I'll drive over to Gloucester and see George, as there's a place that heels shoes and cuts keys just around the corner from his butcher's shop. I'll take George a cup of coffee and have a chat with him and ask him if I can borrow his keys so I can get one cut, explain that I don't want to be dragging Alison to the door every time I visit Mum.

'Good idea. And let me treat you to something nice, I'll transfer some money to your bank.' We have a joint bank account for bills, etc, and a personal account so that we have our own money to spend.

'Thanks, Nick.' I smile at him.

'You deserve it.' He reaches over and clasps my hand. 'I'll drop the kids off to school too. You have a long soak in the bath before you go. That always relaxes you. I'll go and run it for you.'

'Really? That would be heaven.'

Nick pushes his chair back. 'Lavender or jasmine?'

'Jasmine, please.' As he walks past me he bends to kiss me and we hug for a moment before he goes upstairs.

The bath relaxes me, and I feel quite calm and determined as I drive to the shopping precinct where George has his butcher's shop, park in the multi-storey car park then stop off at the coffee shop for two takeaway coffees – black for George and white decaf for me, I'm wired up enough without having caffeine – and a custard slice, George loves them. Another thing he and Mum have in common. He's busy serving a customer but looks up and smiles when he sees me.

'Morning, love, is one of those for me?' he asks with a smile.

'Yes, I thought you might need one.' I walk over to the counter and slip behind it, as I always do when I take him a coffee.

'You're spoilt today, George,' the lady he's serving says with a smile. 'Is this your daughter?'

'Stepdaughter,' he says. 'And yes, she does spoil me.'

He wraps up some chops and hands them to the lady, telling her the price. She rummages in her purse and hands him a ten pound note. As I watch George put her money in the till and take out the change, I think how strange it is that I'm here bringing him a coffee and his daughter is at home looking after my mum. She's just come over from Spain, you'd think she'd want to spend time with her dad.

She's looking after your mum because she's a nurse.

She doesn't have to shut me out though. She's doing that on purpose.

George picks up his coffee as the lady leaves the shop.

'Thanks for this, love.' He takes a gulp, despite it being hot. Mum is always telling him not to gulp down a hot drink because it's bad for him but he never listens. 'What brings you over this way?' he asks. 'Everything okay?'

'I need to get some new trainers for Isaac and thought I'd get a few things for Mum while I'm at it. I'll drop them off on my way home.'

'I'm sure she'll appreciate that. And it will cheer her up no end to see you.'

'How's she doing?'

He purses his lips. 'Still struggling, I'm afraid. I hate to see her like this. And to think of her downstairs at night on her own.' He takes a bite out of the custard slice. 'I wish she could stay upstairs with me, but as Alison said, she'd be trapped up there. At least if she's downstairs she can get out into the garden.'

'It must be hard for you both. I'm going to get Mum a book to read and some treats to cheer her up.' I pause as I wonder how to phrase my request. 'I was wondering if I could borrow your door key, so I can get a copy made for myself. I gave mine to Alison and obviously she's been too busy to get one cut yet. I don't want to have to ring the bell and disturb her, she's doing so much for Mum.'

'Of course, love.' He digs his hand in his pocket and fishes out his keys, slipping off the door key. 'There you are.'

'Thanks. I'll bring it back right away.'

'No rush, love. I'm here all day.'

I pop to the key cutters first and bump into George's customer again, getting some shoes heeled. 'Hello, love, how's your mum? George said she's had a bit of a fall. What a shame they couldn't go on honeymoon. He'd been so looking forward to it.'

'Mum was too. But hopefully her ankle will heal soon and then they can go away again.'

She nods. 'I must say I'm delighted they both met. Poor George has been under so much financial strain, he was even thinking he would have to sell his shop and he's had it for years. Now he's living with your mum so he doesn't have to. It's wonderful how it all worked out.' She smiles at me, pays for her paper and goes.

I hadn't realised that George was thinking of selling the shop. Mum never said. Perhaps that's why she asked him to move in after her mini stroke, it helped both of them out. I guess he's going to sell his house now instead.

I get myself a key cut, then take George's keys back to him. It's such a relief to have a key to Mum's house again. Now Alison won't be able to shut me out.

And, more importantly, I can let myself in and find out exactly what she's up to.

31

LIZZIE

I get the trainers for Isaac and go to the newsagents to buy a book for Mum. There's a couple of detective books by a popular author so I get those. I think she'll enjoy them, and it will help pass the time for her. Then I set off to see Mum.

I park my car around the corner and walk to her house, not wanting to alert Alison to my arrival. Alison's hire car is in the drive, but I don't call out as I put my newly cut key in the lock. This is my mother's house. I'm entitled to be here. I have more right to be here than Alison does, in fact.

The quietness hits me as I step inside. No talking, no kettle boiling, no radio or TV on. Alison must be out, maybe she's gone for a walk. Good. Now I can have a chat to Mum alone.

I close the door quietly behind me and take the first turning to the left into the lounge. Empty. Everything is clean and tidy and there's no sign of anyone. I walk through into the back room. Mum is lying in bed sleeping. Again.

I walk over to her. She looks so peaceful.

'Mum,' I call softly. 'Mum, it's Lizzie. How are you? I've bought you a couple of things.'

No answer.

A flutter of fear rises in me. It's not like Mum to sleep so deeply. Surely... I hold my breath as I look down at her then let it out again as I see her chest rise and fall. She's breathing. She's fast asleep though. There's not a murmur from her. I take hold of her hand and am relieved that it feels warm.

I'm not sure what to do. I open the kitchen door and step inside. All spick and span. I go over to the window and look out into the garden. There's washing blowing on the line but no sign of Alison.

She must have gone to the local shops, it's a warm day and they're only a short walk away. I put the bags down and go back into Mum. Still sleeping. So I take the opportunity to scout around, see what I can find. I go upstairs and open the door to Mum and George's room. The bed has been made, there's no clothes hanging around and the window is open to let in some fresh air. Then I notice that the bottom drawer of the dressing table is half open, that's where Mum keeps her personal papers. She was probably looking for her passport, what a shame that she can't go on honeymoon after all.

Hang on, Mum hasn't been in this room since the morning of the wedding. Surely that drawer hasn't been open all this time?

Has someone been mooching?

I walk over to the drawer and pull it out a bit more. The passport is there. I move it out of the way and something urges me to look a bit further. I take out the zipped document case where Mum keeps her will and life insurance.

I unzip it and look inside.

Both are gone.

Mum told me before she got married that she and George have agreed to keep their finances separate, and she is still leaving everything to me in her will. Maybe she's asked George to take her papers to the solicitors for safe keeping. I go to shut the drawer then stop myself. I don't want to alert anyone to the fact that I've been looking around. After all this is George's room too now.

I go to what was my room next. Alison has established her presence already. There are some photos on the chest of drawers of her, George, Kenny and Sheila, and some personal nick knacks about. My eyes rest on the photo by her bed, a woman with dark curly hair, wrapping her arms around a young Alison and Kenny. Her mother. They look exactly as I remember them that fateful day. My head swims and I reach for the headboard for support, sinking down onto the bed. They all look so happy together, and I destroyed that.

Suddenly I hear the front door open and voices. Alison isn't alone.

I walk over to the doorway and try to listen. If I step out any further they'll be able to see me, as the stairs run up opposite the front door.

'Where's Judith?' It's Kenny. *What's he doing here?*

I edge out a bit further.

'In bed in the dining room. She'll be asleep for ages,' Alison replies.

She's said that with such certainty. How does she know how long my mum will sleep?

Did Alison drug her so she could mooch through Mum's personal things? Has she taken her will? Jumbled thoughts are racing through my head.

I've been so consumed with guilt that I've overlooked the fact that none of us know much about George and his family. The wedding happened so quickly, then came Mum's fall and suddenly George's family are practically living here. Is Alison – or one of the others – drugging Mum to make her confused so that they can get money out of her?

32

LIZZIE

I creep down the stairs softly, wanting to hear what Alison and Kenny are saying.

As I reach the bottom step I hear the kitchen door open and then Alison gasp. 'What's that shopping doing here? Someone's been here.'

She walks out of the kitchen as I reach the dining room. 'Lizzie! What are you doing here?'

'I came to see Mum. I bought some things for her.' I can't get over how shocked she looks. Anyone would think that I'd walked into her house unannounced instead of my own mother's home.

'How did you get in? Did I leave the door unlocked?' She looks confused.

I take the key out of my pocket and jangle it. 'I have a key.' I wasn't going to tell her how, I don't have to explain everything to her.

Kenny steps out now to join her. 'Hello Liz,' he says with a grin.

'Hi Kenny, is everything okay?'

He shrugs. 'Day off. I thought I'd drive over and catch up with this one before she goes back to Spain.'

Hope springs up in me. 'You're going back?'

'Not yet. Not until your mum is better.'

'It seems to be taking her a long time to recover. She had the fall almost a week ago.' I fold my arms. 'I'm going to book her an appointment with the doctor, get her checked over.'

'Recovery in older patients can take longer, Lizzie,' Alison explains patiently. 'I think Mum is a bit depressed too, which is only natural. People often are when they have an injury that restricts their mobility. If she doesn't improve over the weekend, I will call the doctor on Monday. After all, I'm her medical carer.'

'She's practically knocked out, Alison,' I point out. 'It's almost as if she's been drugged.'

I leave the words hanging there and walk out. I want to check if Mum is awake.

'Lizzie, is that you?' Her voice is weak, barely more than a whisper, and my heart constricts.

I go over to her and kneel down, holding her hand in mine. 'Yes, it's me, I popped in to see how you are. I've bought you a couple of books to read. And a few of your favourite treats. How about I help you sit up and make you a nice cup of tea?'

'That would be welcome, dear,' Mum says and tries to edge herself up.

Alison has followed me in and immediately hurries over to Mum. 'Let me!' She steps in front of me, lifts Mum and puts an extra pillow behind her back. 'There you are.'

'Thank you, dear,' Mum says.

I feel a bit put out, I'm quite capable of helping Mum sit up.

'Sorry, it's just there's a special way of helping a patient into a sitting position,' Alison says, looking a bit contrite. 'Look, why don't Kenny and I go and have a catch-up in the kitchen and leave you to talk to your mum for a bit? I'm sure you'd like some alone time with her.'

Yes, I would and I'm grateful that Alison has recognised this. Maybe I'm being over suspicious of her, after all. 'That'd be great. Let me just make the drinks first.'

'Already done.' Kenny comes out of the kitchen with a tray loaded with four mugs. 'Tea for Judith, decaf for you, Liz, and coffee for us two. Have I got that right?'

'Perfect,' I tell him. 'Thank you.'

Kenny puts our two mugs down on the table then he and Alison go through into the other room.

I'm so pleased that they've left us alone, and reassured too. 'Are you feeling any better, Mum?'

'I'm just so tired, Lizzie. I don't know why. And I'm feeling so confused. My head feels all fuzzy.'

She really doesn't look her normal self. 'Mum, any time you want to see me, call me or message me. I'll come straight over. It's no problem.'

'I haven't got my phone, darling. Alison's taking care of it for me. She said I need to rest and she doesn't want me disturbed by constant texts and phone calls.'

I'm furious at this. How dare she! That phone is Mum's life-line, her only way of contacting people and calling for help.

Is that why Alison has taken it? Does she want to make sure that Mum can't call for help if she needs it?

33

LIZZIE

Well, she's gone too far this time.

'She's got a cheek. You drink your tea, Mum, and I'll go and get your phone back. You need it.'

'I don't want to cause a fuss, darling,' Mum says weakly, but I'm already marching out into the kitchen.

'How dare you take my mum's phone off her, Alison. She needs that. Give it back to her immediately!' I demand.

Kenny throws me a look of surprise then turns to Alison. 'Did you?'

She looks flustered. 'Well, yes, but only because she needs to rest and honestly, her phone is pinging all day with notifications. You wouldn't believe it.'

I would actually, I know how many FB groups Mum belongs to. She's quite active on Instagram too. 'That doesn't give you the right to take her phone from her. You're depriving her of the means to contact anyone and call for help for one thing.'

Alison looks confused. 'I'm here if Mum needs help. And it's only today that I've taken her phone away. It's in her best interests. You can see how tired she is.'

'To be fair, Al, you shouldn't have done that,' Kennys says, and I'm so glad for his support.

'Give me her phone, please.' I'm still holding out my hand.

Alison opens a drawer and takes out Mum's phone – she actually hid it in a drawer, now I'm even more furious – and hands it to me. 'Thank you.' I look her straight in the eye. 'And I have to say that I'm very concerned that it's been almost a week since Mum had her fall and she isn't getting any better. I know a fractured ankle takes a while to heal but she should be all right within herself, not tired and listless as she is.' I pause, my eyes still on Alison's face. 'I'm concerned that she isn't getting the care she needs.'

Fury sparks in Alison's eyes. 'Your mother isn't in any danger from me, if that's what you're insinuating. And I resent your manner. I cancelled my flight back to Spain to look after your mum.'

'Exactly. *My mum*. Not yours.' I pause to let that sink in and push away the thought that it's my fault Alison hasn't got a mother. I have to put Mum's health first. 'I will be coming to check on her every single day in future and calling the doctor on Monday if there is no improvement.'

I pick up the bag of shopping I'd left in the kitchen and return to the back room. Mum's sitting up now.

'Thank you, darling. I hope you and Alison haven't fallen out over this,' Mum says worriedly when I hand her the phone. 'She's been very good to me and I'm sure she didn't mean any harm.'

'Maybe not, but she shouldn't take your phone away.' I sit down beside Mum. 'She said it was because you had a lot of notifications coming in and she didn't want you to be disturbed. Shall I turn the notification off for FB and Insta until you feel better?'

Mum nods. 'Good idea. I don't have the energy to answer them all at the moment.'

I turn the notifications off and we sit and chat for a while. 'I've bought you a couple of books to read, and some treats,' I say, handing the bag to Mum.

She looks at the books in delight. 'I haven't read these. Thank you, love. That will keep me occupied a bit.' She delves into the bag again. 'Oh, strawberry creams and a bottle of mango juice. That's so kind of you.' She smiles at me. 'I'm sure I'll be right as rain soon. I'm determined to overcome this. It's ridiculous that I'm so weak. It's really getting me down.'

I'm relieved that Mum has got her fighting spirit back. 'I've got to go now, Mum.' I need to do a few hours' work before I pick up the kids from school. 'I'll phone you later. And I'll pop around tonight when Nick's home.'

When I collect the kids from school they're both bursting with energy. Grace shows me a painting she's done. 'It's us,' she says. I take it out of her hands and look at it. *My Family* is written at the top by her teacher and underneath Grace has copied it in lopsided letters. Then there are six matchstick figures, which I identify as me and Nick, Grace and Isaac. The white-haired lady and bald man holding hands are obviously Mum and George. Grace has drawn hearts all over the picture. I smile as I see it and think what a lovely family we are.

'That's a fantastic picture, Grace,' I tell her, and she grins with pride.

Isaac has a gold star for his story and is very pleased with himself.

'Well done,' I tell him. 'Well done both of you.'

I take them to the park as a reward. As they go up and down the slide I sit on the bench and think about my mum. I can't have this hanging over me all the time about my part in George's wife's death. I need to deal with it. As soon as Mum is stronger I have to confess everything to her. And to Nick. Then Alison will have nothing on me.

And hopefully it won't tear my family apart.

I let the kids play for a good half an hour to tire them out then we pop into the supermarket before we set off home.

As soon as I open the door I feel like something is off but I can't put my finger on what. I go into the living room. Everything looks fine.

'Can we watch the TV?' Isaac asks.

'Okay, for half an hour or so while I cook dinner,' I tell him, turning it on and selecting their favourite programme. The kids settle down, one on each end of the sofa, and I go into the kitchen and unpack the shopping. Everything is exactly as I left it. I can't shake off my uneasy feeling though and I go upstairs, checking every room. Nothing is out of place.

I must be imagining it. My anxiety is getting the better of me. I go back down into the kitchen and put the oven on. I'm going to do something simple tonight, fishfingers, chips and beans. The kids love that. Me and Nick can order a takeaway later and open a bottle of wine. It would be good to have a relaxing evening together after such a fraught week.

I open the freezer and take out the fishfingers, shake them onto a tray. Shake the chips onto another tray.

Then I open the cupboard to get a tin of beans – and I freeze. I haven't eaten any since the day I learnt that Alison's mum had died because she was allergic to peanuts, and I've never, ever bought any, but there, on the shelf in front of the beans, is a jar of peanut butter.

34

NICK

'We're going to need you to go up to Leeds and sort things out, Nick. We can't afford to lose this contract,' Graham, the project manager, says, coming into the office.

Just what I need! I know there have been a few problems on the Leeds development site but didn't realise they were that bad. I look up from the calculations I'm working on. 'I need to get this finished. Can you send Phil?' Phil is my right-hand man and very reliable.

'No can do, he's off work with the flu. He phoned in first thing this morning, he's croaking like a frog. He'll be off for at least a week.'

That only leaves me then. I really could do without this, it means I'll be away a couple of days, at the earliest, and it's almost the weekend. I don't want to leave Lizzie, she's been edgy again since the wedding, and especially after Judith's fall, but I can't refuse. I'm the Construction Manager, it's my job to deal with onsite problems.

'Nick.'

I snap my attention back to Graham. 'When do you want me to go?'

'We need you onsite first thing in the morning, so you need to travel up this afternoon. You can leave work now to avoid the rush-hour traffic. I'll get you booked into a hotel for a couple of days. I'll deal with these costings.'

I know when I'm beat. Besides, this contract is important to us, we don't want any delay in the building work. 'Sure. No problem.'

Hopefully, it will only take a day or two, but you never know with these things. Thank goodness Alison is staying with Judith and can keep an eye on her, at least Lizzie won't have to worry about her mum. I'm glad too that I had that conversation with Alison the other night when she asked me to help bring the bed down. She's assured me she won't breathe a word of what happened all those years ago to Lizzie. I think I can trust her. I have to.

I'm about to leave when I get a message from Alison. She wants to talk to me urgently.

What the hell is going on now? I don't want to go around and talk to Alison. I need to get home, explain to Lizzie that I have to work away and get on the road as soon as possible. But I can't refuse, can I? Something has obviously happened for Alison to want to talk to me. My mind starts working overtime.

What if it's Judith? Has she got worse? Lizzie is worried that her mum is taking too long to recover, has she had a relapse? Or maybe it's something to do with Lizzie herself, she and Alison aren't exactly hitting it off.

Whatever it is, I need to sort it before I go away otherwise all this could blow up in my face.

My family, my future and maybe even my freedom depend on keeping Alison onside.

35

NICK

When I arrive at Judith's, Alison calls me into the kitchen and holds out a mug of coffee. She must have had the kettle on the boil.

'Judith's asleep in the living room so I thought I'd let her rest for a while, then she can sit up and chat with Dad when he comes home. He will like that.'

'How's she doing?' I take the mug from her. 'I was worried that something had happened and you wanted me to break it to Lizzie.'

Her eyes meet mine and I can see the concern there, see her hesitate as she wonders how to phrase whatever it is that she's going to say, and I brace myself. This isn't looking good.

'It's not Judith I'm concerned about.' She pauses. 'It's Lizzie.'

'Lizzie!' I almost spurt out my mouthful of coffee. 'Why? Is she okay?' Now I think about it, Lizzie had sounded strange on the phone when she spoke to me earlier today.

Alison stares down into her cup then raises her eyes to mine. 'I can see that Lizzie suffers a lot from anxiety. That was a panic attack she had at the wedding, you know that, don't you?

She said it was because she hadn't eaten but it was definitely a panic attack.'

I frown. Yes, I know it was a panic attack but I wasn't about to tell Alison too much of our business. I owe my loyalty to Lizzie. 'Why would she have a panic attack?'

'I think maybe because she felt like she was losing her mum?' Alison tilts her head to one side. 'They're very close, aren't they? And Lizzie seems a little possessive. I mean, she seems to really resent me being here but I'm only trying to help.'

I wonder where this is leading. Lizzie is close to her mum, yes. And yes, she does suffer from anxiety but she's had it under control the last few years. At least I thought she had. What is Alison trying to say? I wish she'd just spit it out, I need to get on my way to Leeds. I haven't even told Lizzie I have to go away yet, I want to tell her face to face, check that she can cope without me there.

'Look, can I be honest? I don't want to cause trouble between the two of you but I am very concerned.'

My mouth is suddenly feeling dry and I take a few mouthfuls of my coffee before I reply. My brain is racing. I hope Lizzie's paranoia isn't returning. 'Go ahead.'

'Lizzie is acting a little strange. I went shopping with Kenny today and when I came back I found her upstairs. Apparently she'd gone over to Dad's shop to borrow his key so that she could have one cut. I had meant to do that but it slipped my mind.'

I'm considering this from Lizzie's point of view. Judith has a key to our house too. They've both always popped in to see each other whenever they felt like it, sometimes leaving a bunch of flowers or a cake for the other one to find when they came home. Lizzie had given her key to Alison so it probably did bother her that she couldn't come and go as she used to.

'I don't think that's really strange. Lizzie has the kids, and her work, so she probably wants a key so she can pop in when she had a spare moment, and you might be out. She wouldn't want to keep pestering you for her key back so went to get another one cut.'

Alison nods slowly. 'I can understand that. But when I left Judith she was quite perky and said she was going to sit and watch a bit of TV. When I returned she was asleep, almost comatose in fact. And Lizzie was upstairs. She came down looking very guilty and practically accused me of drugging her mother.'

'Lizzie had probably gone up to get something for her mum. And I'm sure she didn't mean to accuse you, Alison, she's so worried about Judith. She hates it that she can't look after Judith herself. She's an only child and they're both very close.' *Especially since Arthur died*, I think, but I don't say that to Alison. I don't want to bring it up.

'I think she hates me,' Alison replies flatly.

'Of course she doesn't,' I reassure her.

'Then why is she accusing me of hurting Mum?' Alison puts her arm on mine. 'Has she said anything about it to you?'

I shake my head. 'Nothing at all. I'm sure she doesn't think anything of the kind.'

Alison bites her lip. 'You haven't told her about us, have you? That could be why she dislikes me.'

'No, I haven't mentioned it. I mean, it was years ago. We were only friends.'

Something flashes in Alison's eyes. Was it hurt? 'I thought we were more than that.' She strokes my arm.

'It was one night,' I reminded her gently, moving away a little. 'And we both agreed that it was a mistake.'

A mask comes over her face. 'Even so, it might bother Lizzie so I'm glad you haven't mentioned it. Don't worry, I won't either. It will be our secret.' She flicks her eyes to my face. 'I won't tell her about that other thing either. All your secrets are safe with me.'

36

LIZZIE

I stare at the jar of peanut butter, my heart racing, my breath coming out in shallow gasps. Someone has been in my house. Someone has put this jar in my cupboard. Two questions are burning my mind. *Who and why?* I take a few deep breaths, force myself to calm down. I don't want the kids to come in and see me in this state.

Finally, a little calmer, I rush to get my anxiety band from the drawer by my bed. I've tried hard not to wear it for the past few months, even though my stress levels have been building. I know that Nick worries about me when I put it on, he sees it as a sign that I'm not coping, rather than that it helps me cope. I slip it on and ping it against my wrist. Twice.

It has to be Alison. Mum has a spare key to our house, as we do to hers, Alison must have taken it and sneaked in when I went to get the kids from school. She must have recognised me after all. She's remembered that I was eating peanut butter sandwiches and realised that it was me that caused her mum to have that anaphylactic attack, so now she wants to remind me what I did.

Is it a threat too? Is she warning me that she knows I killed her mum and now my mum is at her mercy?

By the time Nick gets home I'm a wreck.

'What's up?' he asks, his eyes growing concerned as they scan my face.

I glance at the kids who are watching the TV and beckon him into the kitchen. I point to the jar of peanut butter on the shelf. I still haven't been able to bring myself to touch it. 'I came home and found that in the cupboard.'

'Peanut butter? I thought you hated it.'

'I do. I didn't buy it. I never buy peanut butter. You know that.' I fix my eyes on his, imploring him to believe me. 'Someone sneaked into the house and put it there.'

His eyes widen and for a moment he doesn't say anything. I can see all the emotions crossing his face, surprise, disbelief and finally concern. He takes my hands in his. Then I see his eyes narrow as they rest on the band around my wrist and, looking down, I see that there's already a red mark around it. I hadn't even realised that I'd been flicking it so much. He moves his eyes back to my face. 'Lizzie, darling, who would do that? And why?'

'Alison,' I whisper. 'She must have borrowed Mum's key and sneaked in and put it there while I was picking up Isaac and Grace from school.'

I can see that he doesn't believe me. I can see something else too, panic in his eyes. Now he's noticed I'm wearing my band he thinks my anxiety and paranoia have come back. Well maybe it has but it's only because Alison is playing games with me. I look at the jar of peanut butter. It's real, I'm not imagining it.

'Lizzie, love, why on earth would Alison do that? It doesn't make sense.'

This is my chance to tell him but I can't. The words won't come. I've never told Nick what I did and I can't now, not after all these years. I know from my therapy sessions that it wasn't my fault, but I can't get away from the fact that someone died because of my actions. And I'm increasingly certain that Alison does remember me and surely as a nurse she now knows that just being near peanut butter could cause a fatal allergic reaction. What if she blames me too?

And she wants to make me pay.

'Daddy!' Grace comes in for a drink, sees Nick and squeals in delight. She runs over and hugs his legs, she's so small she can't reach any higher. He bends down and swoops her up into the air and she squeals even louder. 'How's my little princess?'

He cuddles her then puts her back down again and she runs off to play. He looks over at me. 'I've got to go to Leeds for a couple of days to sort out a major problem on the construction site there.'

'You've got to work away?' My breath catches in my throat. 'Is anything wrong?' I hope this isn't bad news. I know there have been some redundancies at the company and I don't want to be stressing about Nick's job as well as my own.

He wraps his arm around my shoulder and hugs me. 'Nothing to worry about. There's a problem at a construction site up in Leeds and I've got to sort it out. I've got to drive up there now so I can be onsite first thing in the morning.'

This often happens, one of the drawbacks of being the Construction Manager is that Nick's often called away to deal with a problem at one of the sites in another part of the country. It was the same for my dad, he often had to work away when I was younger. Dad worked hard to build up his company, and Nick works hard to keep it afloat. I'm proud of him. Dad would have been too.

I wish that I hadn't mentioned the peanut butter to him now. He's going to worry about me while he's away.

'Are you going to be all right? I can't really refuse to go.' He looks worried. 'You're not really worried about that peanut butter, are you? One of the kids must have put it in your basket when you were going around the supermarket. They're always doing that.'

I guess he must be right. I want him to be right.

'Maybe,' I say. 'But please, Nick, take it out of the cupboard and throw it away. I don't want to risk the kids touching it.'

'Okay, but you know that it's only harmful if you're allergic to peanuts. Otherwise it's perfectly safe.' He picks up the jar.

I back away as if the jar could bounce out of his hands and attack me. 'I don't want to risk it.'

Nick puts it in his bag. 'All gone.' Then he holds out his arms and I go into them, resting my head on his chest, and inhale the faint sandalwood smell of his aftershave. I wish he didn't have to work away.

We hug, then he kisses me. 'I'll be back before you know it,' he says.

He goes upstairs to say goodbye to the kids and pack his case. I follow him.

'It's probably a good job Alison is looking after Judith, you'd struggle to find time to look after your mum with me away, work and the kids,' Nick is saying as he zips up his case. He stands up and looks at me. 'Seriously, Liz, are you going to manage okay?'

I don't want him to worry about me, he needs to concentrate on his work. 'Of course. It will only be for a couple of days. I'll have to take the kids with me when I visit Mum over the weekend but she won't mind, she'd love to see them and surely she'll be stronger by then. I can take something with me to occupy them.'

He pulls me into another embrace. 'Look after yourself. I worry about you.' He kisses me soundly on the lips, and I hug him tight. I love him so much, I think as I return his kiss. I wish he wasn't going. I'm scared to be here alone, especially now that someone has sneaked into the house.

I pretend to go along with Nick's theory that one of the kids slipped the peanut butter into my shopping basket, but I know they didn't. I would have seen it when I put the shopping away. I want to ask him not to go but I bite back the words. I have to be strong.

Nick has always been my safe space. Meeting him healed me. I love him and my little family, and I live in constant fear that I will lose them. I try so hard to keep my anxiety at bay, to focus and stay strong from them. Now I can feel it building again. That suffocating feeling that one day I will pay for my actions.

37

NICK

I wish I didn't have to go away and leave Lizzie, I think as I drive up to Leeds. Alison's right, she is taut with anxiety. I've seen it building ever since the wedding, actually before the wedding. Lizzie was concerned that her mum had rushed into marriage with George too quickly, that she didn't know enough about him. But anyone can see that they're happy together. And they're both just a couple of years off retirement, it's only natural that they would seize the chance of happiness while they could.

I agree with Alison, that Lizzie probably feels she's pushed out by the marriage. She's an only child and was adored by both her parents. When Arthur died, Lizzie and Judith became even closer, and they relied on each other for everything. I understand that Lizzie would want to hang on to that connection, but she has me and the children now, we're her family. Surely she can let go of her mum a bit. And she should be grateful that Alison has stopped to look after her, I know I am. Lizzie would be run ragged if she had to do it all and that could cause her to have a breakdown again.

She's already worked herself up into such a state that she's taken to wearing that damn anxiety band around her wrist again. She hasn't worn that for ages. At one time she was never without it, her therapist encouraged her to get one. It's basically a coloured elastic band that she snaps against her wrist every time she feels anxious. The 'snap' as the band springs back onto her wrist is supposed to get her 'out of her head' and back to reality. For Lizzie it signifies comfort, a coping mechanism. But for me it's a cause for alarm.

Because when Lizzie is wound up things start to happen. Taps left on, doors left unlocked, things put in strange places, cookers and irons left on. I have to follow her around checking everything. Once she put Isaac in his pram in the garden then started working and forgot all about him. Luckily I came home for lunch and found him screaming, Lizzie came down at that moment, her face ashen, saying Isaac was missing from his cot. 'Oh, you've got him, you could have told me!' she said when she saw him in my arms. She wouldn't believe it when I told her I'd found him in the garden. Absolutely denied it until I took her out and showed her the pram. Another time she left the iron plugged on and unattended when Isaac was a toddler, Judith popped in and found Lizzie hanging out washing in the garden and Isaac crawling around unsupervised. I was so worried that harm would come to the children.

Now that worry is resurfacing. I can't believe that she's got herself in such a state over a jar of peanut butter. Of course one of the kids must have picked it up and she didn't notice. How else would it get there? She's on edge all the time at the moment. And I can't believe that she's actually accused Alison of drugging Judith.

And now she's on her own with the kids. Normally Judith would be there to keep an eye on things but there's no one. And I'm worried what's going to happen.

There's only one thing I can think of, and that's to phone

Jodie. She's got her hands full, I know, but she's the only other person who knows how much Lizzie struggles, and she's her oldest friend.

Luckily my car phone is hands free. I call Jodie.

'I need your help,' I say.

38

LIZZIE

That jar of peanut butter is on my mind all evening as I give the kids their tea and get them to bed, forcing a smile on my face, acting like nothing is wrong when my mind is whirling. And my thoughts are spinning out of control. Alison's to blame, I know she is. Everything has gone wrong since she came into our lives. Mum's fall, how weak Mum's becoming, she's always so exhausted. I'm suspect that Alison's dosing Mum with something and is trying to make me think that I'm imagining things.

She wants to push me to a breakdown, I'm sure of it, and I'm scared how far she will go. And the way she's sidling up to Nick, sending him messages, getting him to come over on his own on the pretext of helping to do things she should be able to do herself. Or could ask Kenny and Sheila to do. They're always there. I'm sure she's trying to cause trouble between us. Maybe even take Nick from me. Have my mum, my husband. My life. The ultimate revenge to take everything from me.

Now I do sound paranoid.

A text pings in. I glance at the screen and see it's from Jodie.

Want a catch up when I've got Freddie down?

That's exactly what I need. Jodie will understand. She knows what went on that day, she understands what I've gone through all these years.

Love one. The kids are in bed so call me when you're free.

I text back.

I grab a glass of wine and curl up on the sofa in the lounge already feeling myself destressing. Jodie is the one person I can talk to freely about this and who will believe me. I take a sip of my wine and let the smooth liquid flow down my throat. Jodie will help me find a way to trap Alison and show everyone what she is doing.

I jump as the phone rings. Jodie is vid-calling me. She grins at me through the screen and raises her glass of wine. 'Hiya. What's up?'

'Nick's away and I'm on my own and I think Alison is trying to kill my mum and set me up for it.' The words gush out like Prosecco from a bottle you've shaken then taken the cork out of.

Jodie's eyes widen. 'Crikey! I didn't expect you to come out with that! What the hell has she been up to?'

I love how she listens to me and never makes me think that I'm crazy. How she instantly believes me and wants to know more. Jodie is the best friend anyone could have.

'I don't know where to start...'

'Anywhere you want. I'm listening.'

So I tell her everything, it literally pours out of me. How I think Alison is responsible for my mum's fall, for how tired she is, how Alison has made threats against Mum, how she's trying to push me out, how she's always all over Nick. And finally about the jar of peanut butter I found in the cupboard.

Jodie shrieks 'No way!' at that.

'She's out to get her own back because it's my fault her mum died,' I say. 'The trouble is, how far will she go?'

Jodie listens and calms me down. 'Liz, you have to let this go. You'll make yourself ill. You were a kid and what happened was an accident. Look, why don't you and the kids come and stay with me for the weekend? I don't like you being there on your own without Nick.'

She's worried about me. I can hear it in her voice. Nick is too.

Am I having a breakdown again?

I'm worried about me too. And I don't want to stay here alone, so I agree to Jodie's suggestion of staying with her tomorrow night. It will be nice to have a chat over a glass of wine and Jodie is good for me, she has such a no-nonsense attitude. I'm coming home on Saturday night though, before Rob comes back. He doesn't need me and my kids there.

I tell Nick about my plans when he phones later that night.

'That's great. You and Jodie can have a catch-up,' he says, clearly pleased. 'I'm hoping I can sort things out up here in a couple of days, love. I should be home by Sunday evening.'

I hope he is. I miss Nick. And I've decided that when he comes home I'm going to tell him everything. I'm going to tell Mum too. I can't keep carrying this guilt around with me.

And then Alison will have nothing on me.

39

It's time to put the plan in action. I can't hang about much longer, the clock is ticking. I have to be careful though that no one suspects me. And that it looks like an accident. I've got no intention of going to prison so I need to plan it carefully. Cover all possibilities.

Judith is a lot weaker now, I've made sure of that. And as for Lizzie, the anxiety is eating her up. She's jumping at her own shadow, paranoia is taking over. I would have loved to have seen her face when she found that jar of peanut butter in the cupboard. I bet that sent her over the edge. I can imagine her, leaning against the side, her chest tightening, taking deep breaths to try and control her panic attack.

Apparently she's been eaten up with guilt for years but I have no sympathy for her. She got to have her mum while she was growing up. And look at her now, living in a comfortable house, loving husband and family. She's got it all. Well, not for much longer.

I look at the signature again. It's good, but then it should be the time I took practising it. No one would ever guess it was a forgery.

I smile and I put it in the envelope. Soon Lizzie will lose everything. And I will gain it all.

FRIDAY

40

LIZZIE

I wake up the next morning feeling brighter. I'm not going to let Alison drag me down into a pit of despair again. I owe it to my kids to keep strong. I tell Isaac and Grace over breakfast that we're going to stay at Jodie's that night and they're delighted. They both get on with Millie, and Grace adores playing with Freddie.

While the kids eat breakfast I check my tutor page and am relieved to see that there aren't any more one-star ratings. Maybe it was just a disgruntled student who didn't get the grade. There are several assignments to mark and a couple of students want a one-to-one session. I'll do that this morning, then I'll visit Mum this afternoon before I pick the kids up and go to Jodie's.

The morning whizzes by. It's gone two before I've finished everything so I grab a quick sandwich and head over to Mum's. I was hoping to pack our overnight bags and go to Jodie's straight from school, but I'll have to come back and do that. It doesn't matter, it's more important to see Mum.

I'm surprised to find Kenny's car parked in the drive. Again. Honestly, he and Sheila practically live there. I'm a bit annoyed too, it means I won't have time to talk to Mum alone. Maybe that's for the best, though. Perhaps I should tell Nick about my part in George's wife's death first, then Mum.

I'm glad now that I got a key cut, I think as I put the key in the lock and open the front door, calling out, 'It's only me, Mum,' as I step into the hall.

Sheila comes out of the kitchen, her face registering surprise when she sees me. 'Oh hello, dear. I didn't hear you knock.'

I wave the key I'm holding. 'I let myself in.' I want to say what are you doing here again, but it sounds rude so I opt for, 'Have you dropped by to visit Alison?'

'She's popped out for a bit so she asked me and Kenny to sit with your mum.'

'I would have done that. She should have phoned me.'

'Alison knows how busy you are, dear. You have the children, and your work. And Nick said you haven't been yourself just lately.' Her eyes meet mine and I wonder exactly what Nick has told her. And when?

'Do come and join us, we're in the garden.'

Determined not to be stung by being invited into my own mother's garden, I follow her outside. Mum is sitting at the table, laughing at something Kenny is saying. It looks a happy family scene and my heart lifts at hearing her happy.

'Hello, Lizzie. Are you feeling better?' Kenny rises to his feet to greet me.

Another one who thinks I've been ill.

'I haven't been unwell, just busy with work,' I reply. 'How are you all?' I sit down in the chair next to my mum, guessing it must be Sheila's chair but she can sit the other side of the table. 'How are you, Mum? It's so good to see you out and about.'

'Hello, Lizzie. I'm feeling a lot stronger today.' She turns to face me. 'It's so lovely to see you. How are the kiddies?'

'They're good.' I relate the kids' latest escapades to her and soon we're both chuckling.

Sheila and Kenny show no sign of going home. I guess they are intending to stay until Alison gets back. I really want to talk to Mum in private. Then Kenny's phone rings, he answers, beckons to Sheila and they go indoors. I take my chance.

'Mum, why does everyone think I've been ill?'

She looks at me in surprise. 'Because Nick told us so.'

'What? When?'

'He came by yesterday and was talking to Alison. They were huddled up together in the kitchen. They're quite friendly, aren't they? I guess it's because they used to work together at Arthur's firm. Anyway, when Alison came back in I asked her what Nick wanted, and she said that he'd told her you were ill.' She looks worried. 'Has your anxiety come back, love? I see that you're wearing your band.'

Embarrassed, I pull the sleeve of my top down, my mind in a whirl. Nick came to see Alison before he came home yesterday and didn't mention it to me?

And why are they so close? Has he told me the truth about their relationship all those years ago? Or was there something between them then and now they've taken up where they left off? Am I right to worry that Alison is trying to get the ultimate revenge by taking my husband from me.

41

LIZZIE

'Are you all right, Lizzie?'

Mum's words pull me out of my thoughts. 'Yes, I'm fine.' I want to confide in her but how can I when Alison, Kenny or Sheila are always here? It's like they won't give us chance to be alone. I feel that they're deliberately trying to cause a divide between us.

Mum yawns. 'Oh goodness, I wish I wasn't so tired all the time.'

I can't believe that she's so exhausted again. I look at her worriedly. Maybe I shouldn't go to stay with Jodie. Maybe I should stay home and look after my mum.

'Why don't you come home and stay with me for the weekend, Mum? I can look after you, give Alison a break.'

Mum looks at me in surprise. 'But George is home the weekend and we're hoping that Sam will send over the wedding photos. I can't wait to see them. Besides, you have enough to do with Nick away.'

I stare at her. I haven't mentioned that Nick's away yet. I guess he told them yesterday. During the visit he didn't bother to tell me about, when he also told them that I was ill.

Although to be fair he didn't get much chance, I remind myself, I was so worked up over that peanut butter and he had to get away so quickly.

He could have messaged and told me once he got there though. But then he had that problem at work to deal with. Thoughts are ping ponging in my mind and I bat them away, reciting the mantra my therapist told me. *That thought can wait.* It helps break the relentless whirl of thoughts consuming me.

'Lizzie, love, you'll make your wrist bleed.'

Mum's voice breaks through my tumble of thoughts. I blink. Then I look down at my wrist and am astonished to see the red welt that's formed there. I hadn't been aware that I'd been pinging my band.

Alison returns just then. She looks surprised to see me. 'Oh hello, Lizzie. Are you feeling better now?'

Not another one.

'I'm perfectly well, thank you,' I reply.

'I've been reading one of those detective books you bought me,' Mum tells me. 'I haven't got very far, I'm afraid. As soon as I read a couple of pages I start to feel sleepy. But it's very good. Thank you for thinking of me.'

'I'm glad, I know how you like solving the mysteries.' I smile at Mum then notice that her eyes are already closing.

'Are you tired, Mum?'

'I am. I think it's all the fresh air, and the chatting. I'd better go and lie down for a little while.'

Alison is at her side immediately. 'Let me help you.'

'Thank you, dear. See you soon, Lizzie. Love to the kiddies,' Mum says.

I watch as Alison helps her up. On one hand she really seems to care for Mum, but she's very possessive over her too.

'We'd better go too,' Sheila says. 'Leave Alison to get on.'

'It's lucky that you can share a lift. How far away from each other do you live?' I ask them.

'We live together,' Sheila says. 'George moved in with me when Carol died, so I could help look after Alison and Kenny.'

I'm surprised to hear this, but it isn't until I get back home that a memory pops into my mind. George's customer said that George had money problems and had been about to sell his shop when he met Mum. I'd thought she meant that now he was living with Mum he was selling his house to solve his money problems. But it seems it's Sheila's house.

So how has moving in with Mum solved his money problems?

And why does Mum think that George owns the house, not Sheila?

My mind is whirling. George was struggling to make ends meet when he met Mum. Within a couple of months she has a mini stroke and he moves in with her. Then the very day they get married Mum goes dizzy and has a fall.

An image of Mum's open document folder flashes into my mind. Someone's been looking at her will and personal papers. Was it George?

42

NICK

I'm in the canteen having my break at work when I hear someone say loudly, 'Nick Williams, well I'll be damned. It's been years! What's brought you here?'

I spin around to see Ian Skilmore standing behind me. He was an apprentice at Arthur's company at the same time I was. He was a skinny thing back then with a mop of fair hair. He's put on some weight since and lost most of his hair. I never really took to him, he sneaked around tattling about everyone. He left the company years ago and I haven't seen him since. He must be working for the contractors we've hired.

'Hello there, Ian. How are you doing?'

'Good. Good.' He puffs out his chest. 'I live up in Leeds now and I'm the supervisor of the building firm.' He looks me up and down. 'How about you?'

'Still at AT. I'm the Construction Manager, I've been sent to sort out the problem here.'

'I see. Construction Manager, eh? Well, you've done well for yourself.'

'It's been a lot of graft but I didn't want the company to go under when Arthur died, for Judith and Lizzie's sakes. They suffered enough.'

Too late I see the gleam in his eyes. I shouldn't have said that. I shouldn't have let on that I had any connection to Judith and Lizzie.

'Friends of theirs, are you? I didn't know you were so close to our dear departed boss. Or to his wife and daughter.'

I don't like the sneer on his lips and calculating look in his eyes. He knows nothing, he wasn't even at work on that day, I remind myself.

'I wasn't. But I was the one who found him and called for an ambulance. Gradually Lizzie and I became close, we got married a few years ago and have two children now.'

'Lucky you,' Ian retorts. 'That worked out well for you, didn't it?'

'A man died, Ian, and in horrible circumstances,' I say icily. 'I don't think that's any call for a celebration.'

I turn on my heels and walk away, determined not to show the fear that gripped me at Ian's words. He was a nasty piece of work back then. We were all pleased when he left not long after Arthur's death. I hadn't expected to bump into him again.

I hadn't expected to bump into Alison either.

I feel like my world is being turned on its axis and I'm clinging on for dear life.

43

JUDITH

The sound of talking mixed up with cups and plates clanging wake me up. I glance at my clock and see that it's gone six. Goodness, I've slept for hours again. I hear the murmur of George and Alison's voices but I can't hear Kenny and Sheila. Perhaps they've gone, I think in relief. It would be nice to have my home to myself for a while. The whole family seem to have moved in since my accident and I'm finding it a bit much, especially when I feel so vulnerable.

I sit up and swing my legs off the bed but they feel like lead. Why am I feeling so shattered? I was fine until that stupid fall.

Since then nothing has ever been the same.

It was just a fracture, painful but not debilitating. Yet now I feel like an invalid and it's a horrible start to married life, but I've got to pull myself together and fight this. I can't allow myself to wallow and get depressed. I've always been strong, always held everything together. I look at my walker. I loathe that thing. If only I could get about without it, I know I'd feel a lot better, but my foot is still painful. Too painful to even attempt getting up the stairs. I long to be back in our bedroom, with George.

The door opens and George steps in. 'How are you, darling?' he asks gently.

'I'm a bit woozy but I'll be okay in a few minutes,' I tell him weakly.

'Don't overexert yourself, love. I can bring your dinner in on a tray. Mine too. We can eat it together.'

'Thank you, darling, but I want to eat with you and Alison. Have Kenny and Sheila gone?'

'Yes, Kenny's going out tonight.' He sits down beside me and puts his arm around my waist. 'Let me help you up. Lean on me.'

I lean my head against his shoulder as he helps me to my feet, then pushes my walker towards me.

'I need to go to the loo first, and I want to tidy myself up a bit. You carry on into the kitchen and tell Alison I'll be along in a couple of minutes.'

'Okay, love. If you're sure you can manage.'

'I can.' I'm determined to. I need to get stronger, to get my life back. And to speak to Lizzie about what I've learnt about George's wife. She has to hear it from me first. The trouble is whenever she pops in someone else is always here. Maybe I should wait until Nick returns and tell him? He'll know how to break it to Lizzie. Or will she think that's a breach of confidence? I really don't know how to handle this.

George opens the door for me, and I shuffle the few steps to the downstairs bathroom. Once I've been to the loo, I freshen up, comb my hair and put a bit of lipstick on. There, I feel more like my usual self. I make my way to the kitchen where George is laying the table. He smiles as I come in.

'Ah, you're looking better already.'

'I feel it,' I reply. 'And that smells delicious.'

'It's steak and kidney pie, Dad brought it home for us,' Alison says with a smile. 'I've put some oven chips and peas with it. Is that okay?'

'Perfect. Thank you, dear. It's so kind of you to do all this.' I make my way over to the table and George rushes to pull out a chair and help me to my seat.

It's a really enjoyable meal. We sit and chat, George entertains us with stories about his customers, and Alison with anecdotes about some of the patients she's encountered. I can't believe how difficult some of them are.

'I must say you're very patient,' I tell her.

'I try to be. I understand that people get stressed and worried so I try to make allowances.' She spears her fork into her pie and cuts a slice. 'The ones I really find difficult to deal with are the ones with mental health issues. They are so convinced that what they believe is right, and sometimes there's no convincing them otherwise even though their version of events is totally unrealistic. One man was so fatigued he was certain that his wife was putting something in his food to harm him because she wanted his insurance money. The poor woman was beside herself trying to convince him otherwise. It turned out he had an iron deficiency, and once he was on iron tablets for a few days he was much better.'

I pause and stare at her. 'Maybe that's what's the trouble with me! Do you think I could be lacking in iron?'

'They did blood tests at the hospital, Mum, when you had the fall, and they would have picked it up then,' Alison reassures me.

'Then what is it? Why am I so drained all the time?' I look from Alison to George. 'I hate being like this. It's as if I've suddenly turned into an old lady.'

George reaches over and squeezes my hand. 'Oh darling, you've had a lot happen in the last couple of months, the TIA, me moving in, a wedding and then the fall.' A worried look crosses his face. 'Maybe I shouldn't have rushed the wedding. I just wanted to be with you and keep you safe, but maybe it was too soon after your mini stroke.'

'Now, Dad, don't go blaming yourself.' Alison smiles reassuringly at me. 'I'm sure that now you've got different painkillers you'll be back on your feet in no time, Mum.'

I hope she's right.

We all chat for a while, then, when the meal's finished, we go into the living room to relax. 'Did Sam send over the wedding photos?' I suddenly remember as George sits by me on the sofa. I'm anxious to see them but I know that Sam is a professional photographer and will want to edit and filter to make them look the best they can. Plus he's doing them for free, as a wedding present to us, so paid work will come first.

'No, he said he'll try and do them at the weekend. He's been mad busy at work,' George tells me.

He turns on the TV and we watch a film but after a couple of hours I start yawning and my eyes start to close.

'I think you need to go to bed,' George says gently. 'I'll be turning in myself soon. It's been a long day.'

'I guess you're right.'

George helps me up. 'You go and get yourself ready and I'll bring you your night time toddy,' he tells me.

After a quick wash, brushing my teeth and changing into my nightie I get into bed. George comes in and sits himself down on the edge of the bed, holding out a steaming mug that contains my nightly hot milk and honey. 'This will help you sleep.'

I take the mug. 'Thank you. You go up if you want to. You don't have to stay with me until I've drunk it.' George always insists on sitting with me until I've finished my drink and am tucked up ready to sleep.

'It's no problem. I'll worry that you won't settle all night,' he says, settling down on the edge of the bed and holding my hand. 'I can't wait for you to get well enough to sleep upstairs again. I miss you.'

'I miss you too,' I reply. He's gazing at me tenderly as I sip the drink. It's warm, sweet and comforting. I finish it off and hand the mug back to George, feeling my eyes closing already. He kisses me and wraps me in a big hug. 'Sleep tight, darling. See you in the morning. Love you.'

'Love you too,' I whisper as sleep claims me.

SATURDAY

44

JUDITH

George is surprised to find me sitting up in the chair, reading, when he comes in to say goodbye before he goes to work the next morning.

'Goodness, you're up early!' he exclaims.

'I woke up and my foot wasn't hurting much,' I tell him. 'And my head feels so much clearer. I think I'm on the mend, darling.'

'That is good news.' He bends over and kisses me. 'What's that you're reading?'

'A detective book Lizzie bought me the other day. It's very good.' I mark my place and put the book on my bedside table. 'I thought I'd read for a while.'

'Excellent. But make sure you don't tire yourself out.' George's eyes are full of concern. 'I have to go to the shop early today so I'm getting something to eat in town, but Alison is in the kitchen making breakfast. She'll look after you.'

'I'll go into the kitchen and help her,' I tell him. I reach for my walker and am delighted that I don't need to lean on it so much this morning. I'm finally getting better. I wonder if it's because I didn't take a couple of my painkillers yesterday, I slipped them into the drawer on the bedside cabinet so Alison wouldn't realise. I really don't think I need as many as she's giving me, they could be the reason I feel so exhausted.

'I should be able to move back upstairs to sleep, soon,' I tell George as we both make our way into the kitchen. I'm determined. We haven't even spent a whole night together since we got married.

'I'm so pleased you're feeling stronger.' He pats my hand and then pushes open the kitchen door.

Alison looks around. 'Morning. I didn't expect to see you up, Mum. I was about to wake you.'

'She's feeling very alert this morning, which is great news,' George says. 'Well, I'm off to work, I'll see you both tonight.' He pulls out a chair for me to sit down at the table, kisses me and then he's gone.

'Good to see you looking stronger, Mum.' Alison hands me a cup of tea and a couple of tablets. I take my blood pressure tablet but leave the others, swallowing it with a sip of my tea. I wrinkle my nose, the tea tastes bitter. I noticed that yesterday too and wonder if the tablets are affecting my taste buds. I've heard that can happen with some medications. Even more reason to leave them off. I can take a couple of paracetamol if the pains start to bother me. The swelling is going down now although my ankle is still tender.

'Not drinking your tea?' Alison asks, turning around, then her eyes rest on the tablets. 'And you haven't taken all your tablets either.' She looks concerned. 'It really is important that you take them, Mum.'

'I'm going to try and manage without them, I think they're making me feel woozy,' I tell her. 'And I fancy some fruit juice rather than tea.'

'Let me get it for you...'

I shake my head. 'No, thank you. You've been marvellous, you really have and I appreciate you looking after me, but I need to pull myself together and get up and about. I've got a fractured ankle but that shouldn't stop me living my life.'

'Just be careful. You've been so depleted. We don't want you to have another mini stroke.'

'I won't. I'll grab myself a drink then go and have a shower.'

I can feel her eyes on me as I go over to the fridge. Am I imagining it or is there almost an air of panic about her?

I open the fridge, take out the carton of orange juice and pour myself a glass. Then I put the empty carton in the bin. As the lid flips open I see an empty bottle of antihistamine. I frown and turn to Alison. 'You use a lot of that, don't you?'

'Yes, I have a few allergies, luckily not as lethal as Mum's were.'

A worm of suspicion wriggles into my mind.

Antihistamine can make you feel sleepy. And if you added it to a drink it would probably give it a strange taste. She looked panicky when she saw that I hadn't drunk my tea or taken my tablets. Has Alison been putting some in my food to make me ill? Or been giving me a stronger strength tablet than I need?

But why would she do that? Why would she want to harm me?

I like Alison, she's warm and caring, but I don't actually know her well, do I? We had a few FaceTime calls, and now she's living in my house, making my food, giving me my medication.

Have all my years of reading Agatha Christie books made me too suspicious or could Alison be responsible for my exhaustion and fatigue?

I have a shower and get dressed, politely but firmly refusing all Alison's attempts to help me, and go out in the garden. My progress is slow with the walker but I manage it. I need to put some distance between me and Alison. I need to think.

There are so many coincidences. George's wife died on Lizzie's school trip, Nick and Alison worked at Arthur's company. Alison is a nurse and her contract ended just in time for her to look after me when I had a fall.

Are they coincidences or is something more sinister going on?

45

LIZZIE

Jodie and I sat up quite late talking last night, she listened to all my fears and agreed with my decision to tell Mum, and Nick when he comes back home, everything. 'It's the only way you're going to get closure on this,' she told me. 'And they will all understand, no one will blame you for something that happened when you were Isaac's age.' She's used Isaac as an example on purpose, to drive it home that I was very young and didn't know the results of my perfectly normal childish actions. And she was right.

I've just drained my coffee cup the next morning when a message pings in from Mum, telling me that she feels a lot better today and could I pop in and see her at some point.

'Here's your chance to tell her everything.' Jodie reaches across the table and squeezes my hand reassuringly. 'The kids will be fine with me. You'll feel a lot better once you've got this out in the open.'

I look at her gratefully. 'I know. Thanks for the pep talk last night and for looking after the kids. Are you sure though? You've got your own kids too and Freddie's being so fretful.'

'The more people are around the better he is. Besides, Rob

will be home after lunch and he'll help. And no, he won't mind you being here,' she adds, pre-empting my next question. 'Now get a shower and off you go. You're doing the right thing.'

So half an hour later, I'm driving to Mum's house, determined to tell her everything and hoping she will understand. She's the only one who can help me with this. Thank goodness George is at work so there's no chance of him overhearing. Of course the whole bloody family might be there, but hopefully we'll find a way for us to talk alone.

Alison looks surprised when I let myself in. 'Mum said you were coming, Lizzie, but I wasn't expecting you so early. She's in the garden again getting some fresh air,' she adds.

'Thanks, I'll go out to her,' I say already heading over to the back door. Obviously Mum wants to talk in private, but I doubt if Alison will leave us alone for long.

Mum smiles up at me, and I lean over and kiss her cheek. 'How are you, Mum?'

'I'm feeling stronger.' Her eyes meet mine and I can see urgency in them. 'I need to talk to you, Lizzie.'

I'm immediately alarmed. What's so important that Mum needs to talk to me? She does look stronger though, there's a bit of colour to her cheeks.

'What is it?' I ask. She shivers as a breeze blows past. 'Do you need a blanket?'

'I've got her one. I do think you should come inside, Mum, there's a nip in the air today,' Alison says, rushing over to us with a blanket. Having a private conversation with Mum is going to be difficult as my new stepsister obviously intends to stick around.

'I'll be fine. I want some fresh air,' Mum says.

'I'll load the washing machine then I'll make you both a hot drink.' Alison heads off back to the house.

'I need to say this quickly before she comes back out.' Mum holds my hands, her eyes fixed on my face. 'Lizzie, darling, the woman who died on that school trip all those years ago was George's wife, Carol. Alison and Kenny's mother. I found out a few days ago, Sheila told me the details of how Carol died, the amusement park they were at, and the date and venue match.' She rubs my hands gently. 'I wanted to tell you before you learnt from anyone else because I know it will come as a shock and will bring everything back.'

I gulp and nod. 'I know, Mum. I recognised Alison right away. And I think she recognises me.'

Mum looks flabbergasted. 'Then why on earth haven't either of you mentioned it?'

I swallow. I should have told Mum this years ago. I have no idea how she's going to take it now.

'There's something you don't know,' I say. I glance over my shoulder towards the house to make sure Alison is still inside. Then I tell Mum all about the part I played in Carol's death.

She looks shocked, and my heart plunges to my feet. I squeeze my eyes tight feeling the panic rising. This is why I didn't tell her.

Then I feel the warmth of her hands as she wraps them around mine, and I open my eyes. Her face is full of sympathy, her voice tender. 'Oh Lizzie, have you been blaming yourself for this all these years? It wasn't your fault, darling. You couldn't possibly have known what would happen.'

Relief gushes through me and for a moment I can't speak. When I find my voice again I say, 'I think Alison blames me for it though. She knows I was eating peanut butter sandwiches. I think she guessed at some point that the crusts were mine, or someone else saw me do it and told her. That's why she's trying to keep me away from you. And I think she's making you ill to get her own back. Because I was the one who caused her mum to die.'

Mum looks at me and I wait for the words 'Lizzie, darling, you're being paranoid again.' Instead she nods her head slowly.

'You might be right. After what you've told me things are finally making sense.' She raises her eyes to mine. 'Please don't tell anyone else about this, Lizzie. We need to think carefully what to do. I fear that someone is putting something in my food to make me feel drowsy.'

I gape at her. As I mentioned, I'd been suspecting that Alison was doing something of the sort, but now Mum thinks it too I'm positive that's what's happening. I hug her tight. 'I think you should come home with me. You'll be safer there.'

But I remember the peanut butter and the unlocked back door and how I suspected Alison of sneaking Mum's key to our house and letting herself in. It seems even more probable now.

Maybe Mum isn't her only target. Maybe Alison's trying to destroy both of us.

46

JUDITH

'Alison is making us a drink right now. I might be able to catch her red-handed.' Lizzie springs up and rushes over to the back door.

'What the hell are you putting in my mum's drink?' I hear her shout.

I grip the arm of the chair for support. So we were right. Sadness and fear wash over me. I liked Alison. I trusted her.

I grab my walker and slowly make my way over the grass, cursing myself for being such an invalid. When I reach the kitchen doorway I see Lizzie and Alison facing each other. Lizzie has her fists clenched by her side, looking furious, and Alison is holding a bottle of sweetener.

'This is my drink, and I always have sweetener instead of sugar,' Alison says icily.

'What's going on?' I stand in the doorway, supported by my walker.

'She's trying to hurt you, Mum. Just like we thought.'

'What?' Alison exclaims. She turns to look at me. 'You both think I'm drugging you? Why? Why would you think that?'

'Because she's so tired and woozy headed all the time, she feels like she's being drugged,' Lizzie replies before I can gather my thoughts.

'God, Lizzie, you're so paranoid. I can't believe you're accusing me of such a terrible thing. All I've done is care for your mum.' She looks at me with wounded eyes. 'I thought we got on. I thought you trusted me. Why on earth would I drug you?'

She looks so hurt and bewildered that I wonder if she's right and I've been swept away by Lizzie's suspicions.

'Because you want to get back at me! You're playing with my head and even trying to cause trouble between me and Nick.' Lizzie glares at her. 'And don't deny it, you're always messaging him to come over. I bet you're the one who bought the peanut butter, sneaked Mum's keys and put it in our cupboard.'

'What? This is ridiculous! Why would I do all that, Lizzie?' Alison demands.

'To get your own back on me for causing your mum's death,' Lizzie practically shouts the words out.

Alison looks incredulous. 'What do you mean?'

'Stop pretending that you don't remember me! I was at the amusement park when your mum died. I put my peanut butter crusts in your lunchbox. That was what caused your mum to have that fatal reaction.'

I can't believe that Lizzie has come out and said that. Alison is shaking, her mouth opening and closing like a fish out of water gasping for air.

'I'm sorry. Really I am. But I was a child and I didn't understand about allergies. I didn't know the consequences of my actions,' Lizzie says, her voice breaking. 'You'll never know how devasted I am about what happened, how I wish I could go back and put it right.'

Alison swallows and grips the worktop so tight her knuckles are white.

'It wasn't your fault my mum died, Lizzie. It was mine.'

47

LIZZIE

I'm so stunned that I can't move, can't speak. What does Alison mean that it was her fault? Does she think she should have thrown her crisp packet away? Maybe Carol had told her to empty her lunchbox and she hadn't got around to it, so Carol did it. That doesn't absolve me of any blame though, does it? They were my crusts. I should never have put them in Alison's lunchbox, I should have put them in the bin then her mother wouldn't have touched them and would still be alive.

Mum finds her voice first. 'What do you mean, Alison?' she asks softly. 'How can it be your fault?'

A river of tears streams down Alison's face. 'I wasn't pretending, I didn't recognise you, Lizzie. You've changed so much.' She takes a tissue out of her pocket and wipes her eyes. 'And I've never blamed you. You didn't know Mum was allergic to peanuts, but I did. I sat by you even though I knew you were eating peanut butter, and I should have emptied my lunchbox out into the bin myself. When Mum went into an allergic shock and I went to get the EpiPen, I dropped it. Those few extra minutes cost her her life.'

'You were a child! None of this was your fault!' I'm

outraged on her behalf that she's carried this guilt with her all these years. We've both been victims of the tragic events of that day, both carried the blame for it. Full of pity and remorse, I go over to her, wrapping my arms around her.

Mum places her hand on top of Alison's.

'Do George and Sheila know you feel like this?' she asks gently. 'I'm sure they would hate to think that you blame yourself. It was a tragic accident and you did your best to save your mother.'

Alison gulps back a sob. 'The thing is, she wasn't my real mum. I always felt that something changed when Mum died, something between me and Dad, but it wasn't until my eleventh birthday that I discovered that Carol wasn't my birth mum.' She licks her lips. 'My own mother was her best friend, Susie, she died of a drug overdose when I was two, and Mum... Carol... adopted me.' She looks into the distance as if remembering it all. 'That's when it all clicked into place, why Dad was so distant to me, he and Kenny were like a unit but I never felt that I belonged. Sheila was all over Kenny too, she fed me, but there was no love there. I think they all blamed me for Carol dying and resented me being there.' She paused, her eyes clouding over. 'They never said as much in words. But I felt they did. They closed ranks. I felt an outsider. I did everything I could to make myself useful, scared that they would send me to a home. Then as soon as I was old enough I got my nursing qualifications and went to live abroad.' She wiped her eyes again. 'I miss Carol so much, she was the only mum I've ever known. She treated me like her own.'

'That's very sad, dear, but I'm sure that George, Kenny and Sheila didn't intend to make you feel that way.' Mum's tone is kind, reassuring.

'Maybe not but that's why I was happy to stay and look after you. I felt it was my chance to belong.' She looks at Mum then me. 'I would never harm you. Never. How can you think I would?'

'I thought that maybe you were enjoying being part of the family unit and wanted me to need you a little longer,' Mum says softly. 'Making me dependent on your care would give you chance to do that.'

Alison shakes her head. 'That's a big accusation to make just because you're feeling exhausted after your fall. Which was only a week ago!' She's clearly shocked. 'How can you think that of me?' She turns to me. Her eyes are wide, her chin trembling. 'Nick told me how you suffer from anxiety and imagine all sorts of things. And I've sensed that you don't like me. Now I know why, it's your guilt. Seeing as you both think I'm some kind of monster who would harm a sick woman, I'll go. I'll book myself into a hotel and fly back to Spain tomorrow.'

Mum is watching her thoughtfully. 'I believe you, Alison. So please don't go. You're right, Lizzie and I have been so worried about my slow recovery that we've jumped to all sorts of silly conclusions. I hope that you'll forgive us and we can all put this behind us.'

Alison does seem really upset, and, like Mum, I'm inclined to believe her.

48

LIZZIE

'I expect my tiredness is simply that I'm older and taking longer to recover,' Mum says. She looks absolutely drained, this is all too much stress for her.

Alison nods slowly. 'I understand. I'm prepared to forget all about it.' She glances at me. 'If you are, Lizzie.'

'I guess Mum's right, sorry, Alison,' I say. I'm not actually convinced that Mum is right but I think enough trouble has been caused for one day, and if Alison isn't the one doping Mum I need her here to keep an eye on things. Our worries might make her extra vigilant.

Mum yawns. 'I'm sorry but I'll have to go and lie down for a little while.'

'Good idea,' I agree. 'I'm going back to Jodie's now, I don't want to leave the kids too long. I'll call you later to see how you are.'

Alison says, 'Let me help you to your room.' Then she hesitates and looks at me. 'Unless you want to, Lizzie?'

'Please.' I do want to, and not because I want to be the one to help Mum rather than Alison. I'm over that now. I genuinely believe that Alison is innocent and wants to help and it's her nurse training that's made her come across as overbearing. But I want to make sure Mum is okay. All this is a lot for her. I should have gone about things differently, not rushed in with my accusations.

'Are you all right, Mum?' I ask as I help her onto her bed. 'Do you need me to help you get undressed?'

She shakes her head. 'I'm not going to bed, I'll just have a rest here for a little while until George comes home.'

She looks so weary, her eyes almost closing. I kiss her on the cheek and leave her lying on top of the bed, and go back in to Alison.

'I thought you were trying to frame me,' Alison admits frankly, putting a mug of coffee in front of me. She looks ashamed. 'I'm sorry but I'm afraid that I told Nick that too. That's why I asked him to meet me yesterday.'

And Nick didn't tell me. I force my anger down, Alison is opening up to me and I don't want to ruin that.

'I could see that you were jealous of me being here, sleeping in your old room, looking after your mum. So I thought you wanted me gone.'

'And I thought you were pushing me out because you wanted to take my mum from me, like I took yours.'

'I just wanted to be part of the family, Lizzie, instead of feeling like an outsider again. I'm sorry if that made you feel left out.'

I understand that now. But there's one more thing I need to ask her. 'Can I ask you something? And it's really important to me that you tell me the truth.'

Her eyes meet mine and I do feel that I can trust her. 'Go ahead.'

'Exactly how close were you and Nick? Because the way you are around each other makes me think that you were really close.' I pause. 'And still are.'

She's silent for a moment as if considering her answer. I

listen to the clock ticking on the wall and wait. Finally she replies. 'That's something you have to talk to Nick about, Lizzie. But I can promise you one thing. I'm not after Nick, and I am sure that he isn't interested in me. Whatever feelings we had for each other are in the past.'

49

LIZZIE

Alison's words about Nick keep playing on my mind as I drive back to Jodie's. The way she said that I had to ask Nick made me think that something had gone on between them once.

It was a long time ago, I remind myself.

But why didn't he tell me?

And look how he jumps to do whatever she asks.

Because she's looking after your mum.

And how he confides in her.

Because they're old friends and he feels at ease with her.

Even so, I can't shake the feeling that there's still an attraction between them. And although Alison says she blames herself not me for Carol's death, that doesn't mean she doesn't fancy Nick. She said herself that she wants to belong to a family. Maybe she wants mine? But Nick would never betray me. He loves me. He's always been there for me, I remind myself. Maybe the attraction is only on Alison's side and he's struggling with how to deal with it, what with her being family now.

Or maybe it is all harmless. Alison is turning to Nick for help because she knows him.

Nick messages that he'll be home earlier than planned and will be back later this evening. I decide to wait until the kids are in bed, open a glass of wine and talk to him. Now I've told Mum and Alison, it's time I told Nick about my part in Alison's mum's death. Then he might open up about his past relationship with Alison. It would be good to clear the air and get things out in the open.

When I get back to Jodie's she's sitting in the garden rocking Freddie in his pram and watching the kids play.

'Mum!' Isaac waves and Grace runs over to hug me, but Mollie carries on playing. I sit down by Jodie. 'Hiya. Is Freddie a bit restless?'

'He's got a couple of teeth coming in,' she says.

'It's hard when they're teething,' I say sympathetically.

'How did it go with your mum?'

I fill her in.

'Wow! Who would have thought it! So it's all out in the open now and you trust Alison?'

'I don't like the way she and Nick are so cosy together, and he goes running when she calls. But yeah, I trust her with my mum.'

Freddie wails and Jodie reaches over and gives him his dummy before replying. 'Well you know Nick, he'll help anyone out. And he and Alison worked together years ago, so she's probably comfortable turning to him.'

'I think they were more than workmates.' There, I've voiced it, the doubt that's been tumbling round and round in my mind like washing on a spin cycle.

'Maybe, but it was a long time ago, Liz. We all have a past. Have you asked Nick about it?'

'Yes and he said there was nothing between them.' I want to believe Nick, he's my husband, my rock.

'Even if there was more it was years ago, it was before you and Nick even met. It's history,' Jodie points out.

'Exactly. So why deny it?'

'Perhaps he feels awkward because Alison is family now. Or maybe he's actually telling the truth and there wasn't anything between them.'

I mull it over. Alison worked at the company just before Dad died, a summer holiday job, Nick told me. She didn't even know that he'd died. It was Nick who found him, lying on the floor, an electric flex in his hand. He'd been electrocuted. Nick said that the electric socket was faulty and Dad had got a shock when he plugged in the photocopier. Nick turned off the electricity, called the emergency services, went to the hospital with Dad and stopped with him until we got there, but it was too late, Dad had gone. The electric shock had caused him to have a heart attack. Mum and I were devastated to lose Dad, especially like that. We couldn't believe he'd gone. And I couldn't help thinking that it was karma, that his life had been taken because I'd been the cause of Carol dying. The guilt ate me up but I couldn't tell Mum. I'd convinced myself that she would blame me and hate me. I was in a mess, trying to be strong for my mum.

'You and Nick always seem really solid to me.' Jodie's voice breaks into my thoughts. 'Anyone can see that he adores you. He has done ever since he met you.'

'I know,' I agree slowly. Nick really looked after us when Dad died, I recall, he came over frequently to see if we needed anything, helped organise the funeral, took over the running of the company. We owe him so much. I don't know how either of us would have coped without him. He thought that my trauma was grief, he didn't know that it was guilt as well. No one did. He was so kind and supportive. Gradually we got closer, and when he asked me to marry him I was so happy. I knew Nick was a safe pair of hands and would look after me. He's been a good husband and dad all these years.

He wouldn't cheat on me. I know he wouldn't.

'Mum, I'm hungry.' Mollie comes running over.

'Look, I'm going to get home and leave you to see to your kids, Rob will be home soon and you need to spend some time together. Thanks so much for last night. And looking after Isaac and Grace today.'

'You're welcome.' Jodie gets to her feet. 'Don't let Nick and Alison's past history come between you both, Liz. You two are good together. And don't get caught up in your own thoughts. I know how you are when you get anxious. Remember, I'm here if you ever need to talk.'

'Thanks, Jodie. And me for you.'

Jodie is the best friend anyone could wish for but she's never really understood my trauma about what happened to Alison and Kenny's mum. And I'm sure she thinks I'm overre-acting now.

I'm glad to be back in my own house. The kids are too. They rush outside to play, and I unpack our overnight bags and put the clothes in the laundry basket. Nick will be home later so I'll leave the washing until tomorrow and add his to it.

He messages me to say he's on his way.

Love you. Can't wait to be back home.

I can't wait to see him either. But I can't forget the way Alison looked when she said I had to talk to Nick, it made me feel that he was keeping something big from me.

I can trust him, can't I?

50

JUDITH

I try to rest but too many thoughts are swimming around in my head. I'm stunned to learn that Lizzie has been struggling with this terrible guilt all these years. I wish she'd told me. She said that Nick doesn't know either but promised that she's going to talk to him when he gets home from Leeds. And poor Alison, blaming herself. I don't like to betray a confidence but I think I should tell George about it, he would hate to think she feels that way, I'm sure. Carol might not have been Alison's real mum but I'm quite certain that they would all feel horrified if they knew how she felt, and that none of them blamed her or had tried to push her out.

I hear the doorbell ring and listen as Alison opens the door. 'Hi there,' she says cheerily, then I hear Kenny's voice. 'How's the patient today?'

'Getting a lot stronger. She'll soon be out and about again,' Alison replies.

She's right. I am getting stronger. I reach for my crutches and hobble into the kitchen.

'Hello, Kenny.'

'Well, it's good to see you getting around.' He's holding a

bunch of flowers and a bag from the supermarket bakery. 'Bought something to cheer you up.'

'Is that a custard slice in there?' I ask. Kenny always brings me a custard slice, he knows it's my favourite. Funny as it's George's favourite too. It's one of the things we quicky discovered that we have in common.

'You've guessed it.' He puts everything down on the table then walks over and gives me a kiss on the cheek, wraps his arm around my shoulder and leads me to the table. 'Shall we have a cuppa and tuck into our cakes? There's one for you too, sis. And for Dad,' he tells Alison.

She picks up the bunch of flowers. 'Thanks, I'll have mine later. Stick the kettle on, will you, it's full. I'll just put these in water.'

Something occurs to me. 'Alison, don't the flowers aggravate your hay fever?'

'Certain types do, like daisies and sunflowers, but not all.'

Kenny helps me sit down then flicks the kettle on. 'How are you doing, my lovely?' he asks as he takes mugs and two plates out of the cupboard and lays them on the worktop. He looks over his shoulder at me. 'You are looking much better.'

'I feel it, thank goodness. I was worried that I was going to be laid up forever.'

'Not you. You're too much of a fighter.' He turns back, grabs two cake forks out of the drawer then brings them and the plates over to the table. Opening the bag he takes out a custard slice and places it on a plate then hands it to me with a cake fork. 'Tuck into this, that will soon cheer you up.' He puts a Belgian bun on the second plate, leaving the remaining cakes in the bag.

'You're miles away,' Kenny observes as he sits down opposite me. 'Everything all right?' He taps the side of his nose and winks. 'I'm very good at keeping confidences if you need to offload about anything.'

I smile at him. He has such a relaxed, easy manner that I

imagine lots of people do confide in him and I'm tempted to but I think I should speak to George first.

'I was thinking how much has happened this last week and how glad I am to be back on my feet, even if it is with the help of crutches,' I tell him.

'I know it's been hard for you, but you've done really well. You could have broken your neck, falling down the stairs like that. You could have died.' He shudders and a shudder runs through me too. He's right, I'm lucky to be alive.

'Don't push things. Rest and let yourself heal. There's plenty of time to go to Prague. Another few weeks and you'll be running around again.'

'I'm not sure that I ever actually ran around,' I say with a grin. I'm so glad he's popped in. He's cheered me up no end.

Alison comes in with the vase of flowers. 'Shall we leave them in here, Judith? They make the place look cheerful.'

Kenny raises an eyebrow. 'Have you two had a fall out?'

'Goodness no, why would you say that?' Alison asks.

'Well, you were calling Judith "Mum" last time I was here.'

Alison looks a bit awkward. 'I know and I shouldn't have. It's a bit too soon and upsets Lizzie.'

'I'm sure she wasn't upset about that,' I butt in, although I know she was.

Kenny looks from one to the other of us. 'Am I missing something? Has something happened since I last visited?' He puts his head in his hands and feigns an excited expression. 'Come on, spill. I'm all ears.' He zips his finger across his mouth. 'And I promise not to tell.'

Alison picks up the magazine and playfully swipes at him. 'Nothing's happened, you idiot. But Lizzie is an only child and it's only natural that she feels it's a bit strange when an over-friendly newcomer to the family starts calling her mother Mum.'

'Well I have to admit I thought it was a bit too much too

soon.' Kenny cuts a slice out of his Belgian bun. 'That's our Alison though. She's used to putting her patients at ease and I guess that's what she was trying to do with you.'

'I was. No offence meant.'

'And none taken,' I reply. I feel so comfortable with them both, as if I've known them for ages.

We chat for a while then Kenny has to go. 'I've a shift soon but I'll come and see you again.' He kisses me on the forehead. 'Take it easy.'

'I will,' I promise.

George will be home soon. What a day it's been, I think. But at least now everything is out in the open and we can all move forward, a united family.

51

NICK

I'm really concerned about Lizzie. Thank goodness I managed to wrap this site problem up in a couple of days, and that she stayed at Jodie's last night, I think as I drive home. So many worries are crowding for space in my mind – Ian's remarks, Lizzie's state of mind, Alison – that I almost don't see the lorry pulling out at a junction and have to stamp on my brakes. It was a close shave and makes me concentrate on the road instead of worrying over Lizzie.

It seems peaceful enough when I get in, there's something cooking in the oven, music playing and Lizzie greets me with a hug and a kiss. 'How did it go?'

'Okay, all sorted now.' We hug tightly for a while, then she eases away.

'The kids are playing in the garden, dinner will be about a quarter of an hour. It's breaded chicken, chips and beans.'

'Great. I'll go and grab a quick shower and get changed.'

Isaac and Grace come running to greet me when I come back down from the shower. 'Daddy, you're back!' Grace says happily. I scoop her up and give her a big hug, Isaac smiles awkwardly, he thinks he's too big for hugs, so I wink at him and tousle his hair. 'Okay, son?' He nods and grins.

Lizzie is laying the table, so I get the kids seated and make a jug of orange cordial, putting it in the centre of the table, along with the bottle of tomato ketchup, salt and vinegar.

We chat pleasantly over dinner, then I clear away while Lizzie puts the kids to bed.

'I've put a bottle of wine in the fridge. I thought we could have a drink and a catchup when the kids are settled,' she says.

'Great idea,' I agree. I can't help feeling that she's concealing something from me though. I can't put my finger on it but something has happened since I went away. I'm sure of it. There's a sort of nervous energy about her.

I've cleared away and loaded the dishwasher by the time Lizzie comes down. I open the wine, pour it into two glasses and hand one to her. 'Let's take it into the lounge, it's comfier in there.'

She follows me and we both sit on the sofa next to each other. Lizzie stares into her glass, running her finger around the rim. I can see something is on her mind.

'What's up, Liz? Has something happened? Is your mum okay?'

She twists a lock of hair around her finger and looks at me with troubled eyes. 'I need to tell you something.'

I place my hand on her arm. 'Go ahead. You can tell me anything.' I brace myself for whatever revelation it is but her next words still blow me away.

'I'm responsible for George's wife's death.'

It was the last thing I expected Lizzie to say. I stare at her, my breath catching in my throat. She looks so earnest. She really believes what she's saying, but then she always does. When she loses her grasp on reality she is convinced that the crazy things she thinks in her mind are true and no amount of reasoning with her will change her mind. This is far-fetched though, even for her.

'Liz, Alison and Kenny's mum died years ago. You didn't even know her. How could you have had anything to do with her death?'

'I met them, I was on the same school trip. There were a couple of schools visiting the amusement park that day.'

I listen in astonishment as Lizzie blurts it all out, how Ally bumped into her, causing her to drop her ice cream, so Ally's mother bought Lizzie another one, how she and Ally and Jodie sat by each other for lunch, how she slipped her peanut butter crusts into Ally's lunchbox because Judith would be mad that she hadn't eaten them. How seeing Ally's mum die traumatised her for years. And finally, how she found out that she was the one who had caused her death.

'I didn't know it was me, not until what happened with Jamie. I didn't know that if someone is allergic to peanuts just touching something that has peanuts in it can kill them.'

Tears are spilling down her face.

No wonder she had a breakdown when that lad in her class almost died. Thank goodness she saved him, or I don't think she'd have ever got over it.

I can't believe that she's been keeping this in all these years, blaming herself. It must have been eating away inside her. And her mother marrying George and her meeting Alison again has brought it all back up. Poor Lizzie, she's so consumed with guilt that she's convinced everyone else blames her too and are out to make her pay. I wish she'd told me, but I can understand why she didn't. I know what it's like to carry guilt inside you for years, and to keep a secret from the one you love, scared that they will be horrified by what you did. This was different though, Lizzie was a child. Whereas I...

'Liz, you were a kid and it was an accident.' I kiss her on the forehead. 'I get that you feel bad about it but you weren't to know.'

'That doesn't change the fact that it's my fault she died. If I hadn't put those peanut butter crusts in Ally's lunchbox, she'd still be alive today. I've deprived Ally and Kenny of growing up with a mother. No wonder she's trying to worm her way in with mine.' She takes a tissue out of her pocket and wipes the tears from her eyes.

'Hell, Liz, you were seven. It's the sort of thing a lot of seven-year-olds would do.' I hug her tight. 'Is this why you had the panic attack at the wedding? Does Alison know what you did?' If she did, why hasn't she mentioned it to me, I wonder. 'And what about your mum?' I ask. Surely if Judith had known she would have reassured Lizzie that it wasn't her fault.

'Mum didn't know, but she does now.' Lizzie gulps. 'I thought that Alison was trying to push me out because of what I did, and that she was drugging Mum to make her sleepy, as payback.'

'Heck, Lizzie!' What on earth has been going on in her mind this past week since Alison came into our lives? I swivel to face her. 'This wasn't your fault. How were you to know what would happen?'

She nods. 'That's what Alison said.'

That staggered me. 'You've told her?'

'Yes, we all talked about it earlier. Alison said that she doesn't blame me, she blames herself.' I listen as she relates the conversation to me, hardly believing it when she says that neither Carol nor George were Alison's real parents.

I'm gobsmacked by all these revelations. And my heart is racing as I wonder what else Alison has told her.

'So you're all good now? No more hard feelings with Alison?'

Lizzie takes a sip of her wine then her eyes meet mine.

'No. And that's my secrets out in the open. Your turn now.'

52

LIZZIE

Nick pushes a lock of his hair back from his forehead. I can see beads of sweat glistening there. He's hiding something. I know he is.

'What do you mean?' he stammers. He's playing for time. What is it that he's scared I've found out?

Does he still have feelings for Alison?

I have to know. Whatever it is.

'I need to ask you something and I want you to be totally honest with me.'

He takes a sip of his wine, his actions measured. 'Go on.'

My eyes meet his. I hold his gaze. I want, need to see his reaction. I will see it in his eyes if he is lying.

'What exactly was your relationship with Alison? Did you sleep together?'

'What has she said?'

'She said I had to ask you. But that makes me think you did.'

He nods slowly. 'Yes, but it was only the once. And it was years ago, Lizzie. It's not important.'

'Then why didn't you just come clean? What are you trying

to hide?' I pause. 'Are you still attracted to her? Is that why you keep meeting up with her in secret?'

'Of course not! I love you!' He runs his hand through his hair. 'And I'm not meeting her in secret. I'm not trying to hide anything, but you were so worked up about thinking Alison was trying to push you out I didn't want you to start feeling insecure about me too.' He puts his wine down, moves closer towards me and lightly caresses my cheek with his fingertips. 'I love you, Lizzie. Always have, always will. Past isn't important.'

'It's not that I'm jealous, Nick.' I swallow, trying to find the words to explain how I feel. 'But ever since the wedding I feel like our worlds been tipped upside down. Mum's accident, and how weak she still is, and how Alison has completely taken over.' She hesitates. 'She's so much more glamorous and confident than me that I thought...'

He puts his finger on my lips to silence me. 'You're beautiful, Lizzie. And I adore you. Alison and I were friends for a short time years ago. That's all there is to it.'

'But Alison said to talk to you about it. As if there was something more.'

He shakes his head. 'There's nothing more. She probably told you to talk to me so I could reassure you, because you wouldn't believe her.'

That makes sense.

'I know that your anxiety has been sky high since the wedding, love. Now everything is out in the open do you think you can relax a bit?' Nick asks gently.

I want to. I really do.

'It's just so much has been going on.' I bite my lip. 'And someone has been posting one-star ratings and leaving bad reviews about my work. I've had a warning from my boss about it. I feel like everything's going wrong.'

'Liz, everyone gets bad reviews now and again...'

'I never have before. And there's the peanut butter. I'm not imagining that.'

'I thought we'd sorted that, agreed that one of the kids must have picked it up.'

Is he right? I have been in a state and I did take the kids to the supermarket before we came home. They do sometimes put things in my basket, especially Grace. I'd been wrong about Alison, am I wrong about this?

'Look, you haven't been yourself since your mum's wedding. You know you haven't. And I understand why, now that you've told me all this. You've been under tremendous strain all these years. And then when you realised who George's wife was, well, it must have really freaked you out.'

I can feel my eyes fill with tears.

'It did,' I acknowledge.

He takes my glass of wine out of my hands and puts it on the table. Then he wraps his arms around me and holds me tight.

'Can we put all this behind us, Lizzie? I hate seeing you under so much strain. Can you accept now that George's wife's death wasn't your fault and put it to bed?'

I nod. 'I'll try.' I snuggle into him. 'I'm so glad everything's out into the open now. No more secrets.'

He kisses me on the forehead.

'Me too.'

I cuddle into him and try to push all the doubts out of my mind. Mum is getting better and now that me and Nick have talked about things and shared our secrets, everything should be okay. So why do I still feel uneasy, and that Nick is holding something back?

53

The house is in total darkness. I stand outside the back door and listen carefully for a few minutes. Not a sound. Then I take the key out of my pocket and slip it into the lock, turning it slowly twice. I learnt that the other day, it's a double lock. I take the key back out, slip it back in my pocket and push the door open. I know the layout of the house well. I'm in the kitchen. The hallway leads to the stairs on the right then the living room. I'm not going in any other room though. Only the kitchen and maybe the hall.

I need to make sure that Lizzie is out of action for the next couple of days. I don't want her, or Nick, dropping in on Judith and spoiling my plans. Time is limited now. I have to move fast.

I go over to the cupboard and look at the canisters lined up. Tea bags, coffee, sugar. I hesitate. I don't want to harm the kids.

I open the cupboard and look inside, scanning the contents. Then I spot the ideal thing, a bottle of a well-known calming potion for adults. That has got to be for Lizzie. I open the bottle and see it's about two thirds full. I take the small container of liquid out of my pocket and pour it in, put the lid back on and place it back in the cupboard.

There's one more thing I need to do. She thinks that husband of hers is so perfect but she's wrong. He's hiding something, I don't know what it is, but I know it's there. I can see it in his eyes. I know how to tell when someone is putting on an act because I've been doing it myself for years. Well, this will make her think twice.

I've just finished when I hear a noise. Someone is coming downstairs.

Shit! I need to get out of here. I'm in such a hurry that I knock the tea towel onto the floor as I dash through the kitchen. I can't stop to pick that up now. I reach the back door in a couple of strides and I'm out, crouching down by the bunker. I don't even have time to lock the door when the kitchen light comes on. That was too close for comfort.

Whoever it is, they've probably come down for a drink. I'll stay where I am and lock the door when the light goes back off again.

I wait and wait.

Twenty minutes pass. The kitchen light is still on. I can't wait any longer. I have to go. With a bit of luck they'll think they forgot to lock the door.

I sneak down the path and climb over the gate. It's a good job they don't have a high fence. Or security cameras. They probably think this is a safe area. Big mistake.

They say most accidents happen in your own home.

SUNDAY

54

LIZZIE

I go to sleep snuggled in Nick's arms, feeling safe and secure. I feel happier now that things are out in the open between us. He's been so kind and supportive. As he's always been ever since he came into our lives. How could I have doubted him like that? I should have talked to him about everything before, Mum too. They've both always been so understanding. And poor Alison, to think she'd been carrying guilt all these years too. Maybe that's why she'd become a nurse, so that she knew what to do if anything like that happened again.

A few hours later I wake with a start. What was that? I listen carefully, all I can hear is the sound of Nick snoring softly. Maybe it was a cat.

A thought flashes into my mind. Mum's missing papers! I was about to tell Mum about them, and about what the customer said about George being in financial trouble, before I dashed into the kitchen to try and catch Alison doping Mum's drink.

Immediately my brain is wide awake. Was I right when I suspected that someone was drugging Mum? Was it George, making her mind hazy so she'll agree to sign her finances over to him? Has he already coerced her to alter her will?

I have to stop thinking like this. It's my anxiety again making me paranoid.

But sleep has gone now so I go downstairs to make myself a drink.

An eerie feeling creeps on me as soon as I open the kitchen door. I can almost taste danger. I flip on the light and look around. Everything seems fine but my senses are exploding, warning me to be careful.

I pad across the floor, my eyes scanning the kitchen. They rest on the tea towel lying on the floor. I frown. Why is it lying there as if it's been knocked over?

I stoop and pick it up. Everything else is in place. I flick on the kettle to make myself a cup of chamomile tea and sit at the kitchen table, savouring it and thinking over the events of the last week or so. I'm glad that it's all sorted with Alison now, and that I know the truth about her and Nick. I wish he had told me right away but it was a long time ago, and I'm not going to let it bother me. I'd jumped to conclusions so much, I must be careful not to do it again. And as for George, there must be a reasonable explanation. Mum told me that they had agreed to keep their finances separate when they were married and she was going to see the solicitor about it. She probably asked George to drop her will in seeing as she couldn't get about with her bad ankle. Or she asked him to fetch the papers for her so she could look through them. She couldn't get upstairs herself, could she? I'll talk to Mum about it when I next see her.

I finish my drink, my mind calmer now, and go back to bed where Nick is still snoring softly. The drink must have soothed me because the next thing I know Nick is opening the curtains and sunlight blazes into the room.

'Morning. Did you have a disturbed night?' he asks.

'A bit. I went downstairs and made myself a drink,' I tell him, yawning and sitting up.

'I don't like you going outside late at night though, Lizzie. I realise that you probably wanted some fresh air but you never know who's lurking about.'

I rub my eyes and yawn again. 'I didn't go outside. Why do you think I did?'

'You must have done, Liz. The door was unlocked and I definitely locked it when I went to bed. I always do.' Which is true, Nick is super security conscious. He always locks the doors and takes the key out so that the kids can't let themselves out while we're asleep.

The door was unlocked! I recall the feeling I had when I came down that someone had been in the kitchen. The tea towel lying on the floor as if someone had brushed past the drawer handle it had been hanging on and knocked it off.

'Someone came in.' I tell him about my feeling and the tea towel. 'It was lying on the floor.'

'That doesn't mean someone sneaked in, Liz. How could they? There's no sign of a break-in which means they used a key and no one has a key but us.'

'And Mum,' I point out. 'It's like the peanut butter. Someone has a key to our house and is sneaking around, Nick.'

'Liz, love, you need to stop jumping to all these conclusions.' Nick's voice is calm, soft. Patronising. 'Nothing has been taken. There's no sign that anyone's been in. You must have opened the door and gone out into the garden, half awake. You know what you're like when you get up in the night.'

I don't like the tone of his voice or the look he's giving me but I don't say anything because I'm scared that he might be right.

'Look, I'll take the kids out for a bit, you stay and rest,' he says. 'This week has been a big strain for you.' He kisses me on the forehead and goes out, shutting the door behind him.

I close my eyes and try to brush away the memory of the dark days when I had a breakdown, when I was imagining things, forgetting things, seeing danger all around us. Has Mum marrying George and bringing the past back up sent me spiralling again?

I hear Nick calling the kids, telling them to get ready as they're going to feed the ducks straight after breakfast. There's a small duck pond in the woods about ten minutes' walk from where we live and the kids love to go there. We always keep a bag of mixed grains in the cupboard to give them as bread isn't good for them.

I don't want to lie in bed while life carries on around me, like I did all those years ago. I'm going to face this and deal with it. I have to for my children's sake. I get up, grab my dressing gown and head downstairs shouting, 'I'll get the breakfast ready.'

I walk into the kitchen and look around. Everything is as it should be. The tea towel is folded and hanging through the handle of the drawer, as I left it. One of us must have knocked it off last night and didn't notice. After all, as Nick pointed out, nothing's been taken or disturbed. A spooky feeling and a tea towel lying on the floor isn't much to go on.

And the unlocked back door.

I take out two bowls and shake the kids' favourite cereal into each one, then fill a jug with milk. I've just put it all on the table when Isaac and Grace run in, washed and dressed, their eyes sparkling with excitement.

'Morning, you both look happy.' I hold out my arms and they both rush in for a hug.

'Daddy's taking us to feed the ducks,' Grace tells me, then her eyes rest on my wrist. 'Mummy, your bracelet is making you bleed.'

Isaac looks down at it, his eyes troubled. 'You need to take it off, Mum.'

Yes, I do. Look at the example I'm setting my children, I need to find another way of coping. 'I will. I'm going up for a shower now and I'll take it off and put it away.'

'Are you coming with us, Mum?' Isaac asks, his eyes watching me warily. He's a sensitive little boy and seems to always detect if there's something wrong. Gracie is more care-free, she's already tucking into her breakfast, eager to be gone.

I give him a reassuring smile. 'No, I'm going to get a couple of jobs done, but we'll all have a game of skittles in the garden when you come back. How's that?'

A big grin spreads over his face and he nods. 'Can I be on your team?'

'I want to be on Mummy's team,' Gracie protests.

'What's this? What are we having teams for?' Nick walks in, dressed in his new jeans that fit snuggly around his hips and a black tee shirt. He looks good. He walks over and puts his arm around my shoulder, pulling me into a hug. 'What are you planning?'

I feel my spirits lift. Nick and my family mean everything to me. 'I promised we'd play skittles with them when you come back.'

'That's a great idea,' he agrees enthusiastically. 'Now eat up, kids, those ducks are waiting to be fed.'

He opens the cupboard and takes out the muesli. 'Want some?'

'No thanks. I'll have a coffee and take it up to the bathroom while I shower. I'll eat something later.'

'Please make sure you do.' His eyes rest on my face and I can see the concern in them. When I get stressed I find it diffi-cult to eat.

'I will,' I promise. I make us both a coffee and kiss the kids. 'Have a good time, I'm off for a shower.'

They're too busy chatting about how many ducks they think will be at the pond to reply but Nick blows me a kiss.

. . .

I'm in the shower for a while, taking my time to lather with the relaxing spa shower gel the kids bought me for a birthday present earlier this year, enjoying the warm water cascading over my body. It was one of the calming techniques I'd learnt over the years, to focus on things, be in the moment. I feel a sting as the shower gel runs into the welt on my wrist where my band has been.

When I'm dressed I collect the laundry basket and take it downstairs to load up the washing machine. I see Nick's jacket hanging on the banister in the hall. It's a lightweight summer jacket and there's a smudge on his sleeve. I'll stick that in as well, I decide, picking it up and dropping it into the basket.

I know what Nick's like for shoving things in his pocket so I check through them before putting it in the machine. His pockets are empty apart from a receipt from the local supermarket. I glance at it as I go to put it in the bin and stop in my tracks. Top of the list is a jar of peanut butter.

My legs almost collapse underneath me, and I reach out and grab the banister for support, my eyes still focused on the piece of paper in my now-trembling hand.

Nick. It was Nick who bought the peanut butter and put it in the cupboard, then denied it, tried to make me think it was me. Why? He knew what this would do to me.

I sit down on the bottom step before I collapse. Nick is the one person I thought I could rely on. He's been my rock, my support, always there to lean on. Why would he do this to me?

55

NICK

The kids have a great time feeding the ducks and we make a detour to the park on the way home. I want to give Lizzie time to herself, hoping she will be able to relax and see that she's overthinking all this. When we get back home there's washing on the line, and the skittles are out in the garden, ready for our game.

'Mum, we're back!' The kids run into the house, shouting. I follow them. I can see by the strained look on Lizzie's face that something is wrong.

'What's happened? Is Judith okay?' I ask.

She nods, but her eyes don't meet mine. 'I'll tell you later.'

This doesn't sound good.

We play a couple of games of skittles with the kids, as we promised, but I can see that Lizzie's heart isn't in it, and I feel on edge myself. Whatever's happened, she doesn't want to talk about it in front of the kids, which is fair enough but means that it's something serious.

Finally the kids are bored and run inside to play a computer game together so I turn to Lizzie. 'Now will you tell me what's wrong.'

She reaches into her jeans pocket. 'Want to tell me what this was doing in your jacket pocket?'

I glance at it. Then my eyes widen when I see that it's a receipt for a jar of peanut butter. I shake my head. 'What the hell, Liz, this isn't mine!'

'Just jumped into your pocket, did it?' She folds her arms across her chest, her lips trembling.

'Lizzie, I promise you that I didn't buy it. Why would I? I don't know how it got into my pocket but I promise that it wasn't me.' I can't believe this. It's like I'm in some sort of nightmare.

'Why are you lying to me? The evidence is right there in front of your eyes. Are you playing me, Nick? Trying to make me think I'm having a breakdown?'

She can't really think that! But I can see how bad it looks. I grab her hand in mine.

'Liz, I don't know how that receipt got in my pocket, but I swear to you on our kids' lives that I didn't buy that peanut butter.'

I don't like swearing on the kids' lives and she knows it. We both said we would never do that. Surely she has to believe me now.

'So how did it get there?'

I shake my head again, bewildered. 'I have no idea.'

'Unless!' Lizzie's hand goes to her mouth. 'You found the back door unlocked this morning, Nick. And I told you that I had an eerie feeling when I went down for a drink last night. Someone must have sneaked in and put the receipt in your jacket pocket.'

I'm struggling to take this in. 'Who would do that? And why?'

'I don't know but it's the only thing that makes sense. Whoever it was wanted to frame you, Nick.' The colour drains from her face. 'Someone has access to our house and I'm scared that we're all in danger. I think we should call the police.' She's trembling now.

'And say what? Nothing's been taken. We've no proof that anyone has sneaked in or done anything.'

'Why are you so willing to sweep this under the carpet?' she demands. 'Nick, this is serious. Someone has sneaked into our house twice now, and they must have heard me come down last night and legged it, leaving our back door unlocked. What would they have done if I'd walked in on them? Or if it was one of the kids who came down?' She gulps. 'Aren't you even the slightest bit interested who that person is?'

There's only one person I think can be responsible for this and that's Alison. But if it is her then the last thing I want is the police involved.

'I am, of course I am. But let's not jump to conclusions, Liz. There might be a reasonable explanation for this.'

She glares at me. 'You think it's me, don't you? You think I'm having a breakdown again and doing things I don't remember! How bloody dare you put this on me!'

She storms out and I hear her go upstairs.

I groan. I don't want to do this to Lizzie. But I need a bit of time to deal with it.

I open the messages on my phone and reread the one that pinged in earlier when I was at the park with the kids.

I want five thousand by the end of this week.

Or I'll tell everyone it was you who killed Arthur.

I'll be in touch with instructions where you have to leave it.

56

LIZZIE

'Mummy, why are you shouting?' Grace comes out of her bedroom, worry etched all over her little face. Me and Nick always try not to argue in front of the kids, but I was so mad I hadn't kept my tone down.

I go over to her and pick her up. 'It's nothing, darling, just a silly little squabble like you and Isaac sometimes have.' I kiss her cheek. 'It's all over now, you go and play.' She squirms out of my arms and runs back into the bedroom. I glance over at Isaac's room, his door is firmly closed – probably to keep Grace out while he builds his Lego. I don't think he heard anything or he would have come out to see what was going on too.

I go into our bedroom and sink down onto the bed, I don't know what to do. I'm at my wits' end.

Nick comes up a few minutes later with a coffee. 'I have no idea what's happening here, love. But I'm working on a new project that's computer-based so I'll work from home this week. Why don't you call in sick and take a couple of days off. Give yourself a chance to chill out a bit. I'll look after the kids.'

Is he trying to say that I'm responsible for all this? That I'm going crazy?

Am I? Is there a simple explanation to it all? Do I really think that Nick, my husband, would do this to me? My head is throbbing and I don't trust my thoughts anymore.

'Maybe you're right. It would be good to have a couple of days off.'

'Try to rest. Everything will be okay. You've been under such a strain.'

I close my eyes. I don't want to talk to him. As he closes the door my mind goes back to that dreadful time after Jamie, the boy in the class I was teaching, almost died.

I was a mess. I wasn't sleeping. I couldn't focus on anything. I wasn't fit to look after Isaac. I squeeze my eyes as I remember the day I put Isaac out in the garden in his pram to sleep and forgot about him. Then thought someone had taken him. Another day I was watching a film when Mum came round and Isaac was screaming his head off in his cot upstairs, long overdue for a feed and with a nappy that needed changing. I was so sleep-deprived, so riddled with guilt that I barely got through each day. I left doors unlocked, put food on the cooker and let it overboil. Left the iron plugged in and switched on, forgot to put the shopping away and left it on the kitchen table to thaw. Whole hours were lost.

Am I doing that again? Did Alison coming back into my life drag everything back up, make me have another breakdown?

I try to process it. Is it really all in my head?

I shake my head. That receipt is real. The jar of peanut butter is real.

Even if the kids picked up the peanut butter in the supermarket, how did the receipt get in Nick's pocket?

And why, when he was the one who found the back door open, and he's the one who's being framed, isn't he as concerned as I am?

It's almost as if Nick doesn't want me to believe it's true. As if he's hiding something.

57

NICK

My first thought is that the anonymous text was Ian. He'd made a point of saying how much I'd benefitted from Arthur's death when I bumped into him at Leeds. But I don't see how it could be him. He wasn't in the office the day Arthur died. Only Alison and I know what happened that night, so it has to be Alison who sent me the text, she must have another phone that she's texting me from.

Did Alison buy the peanut butter too? And did she sneak into our house last night and slip the receipt in my pocket? It would be easy for her to get hold of Judith's key and do that.

When Lizzie and I had our heart to heart, promising each other that there would be no more secrets, I felt bad because there's one secret I'll never tell her. I can't. It would destroy her, and our marriage. At the time, Alison and I vowed to never speak about it again, but that was easy when we thought we'd never be seeing each other anymore. Now it seems that Alison wants paying to keep that promise.

Everything is falling apart around me and I'm desperately trying to keep it all together. Lizzie is struggling, and the way she's going she will lose her job, and things are getting difficult at work too. We've lost a couple of tenders just lately and profits are going down. Then there was that emergency at the site in Leeds, which was far more serious than I let Lizzie and Judith know. And lost us a potentially lucrative contract.

I wish that Alison would go back to Spain and then I could forget all about this nightmare. I wish that Judith had never met George. Everything has gone wrong since they got married.

The business started getting into difficulties before then, though, I have to admit. I ponder for a moment, trying to recall how long. Just after Judith met George. And that couldn't be anything to do with Alison, as she was living in Spain.

But this text must be from her. Pay-as-you-go phones are cheap enough, she might have got one so she could text me anonymously.

I have to deal with this situation before it gets worse. I need to meet up with Alison and find out what she's up to because if she reveals everything she knows about me then my whole world will come crashing down.

Lizzie will never forgive me and neither will Judith. But it was a tragic accident, one that I couldn't possibly have foreseen, and the consequences of which I've had to live with ever since.

My mind goes back to that dreadful day.

58

NICK

Nine Years Ago

I liked Alison straight away. She was pretty, good at her job, and fun. We were both in our early twenties, the youngest two in the company, and soon got into the habit of bantering with each other whenever we met, then sharing our breaks together. We chatted about everything, our hopes, our dreams. I wanted my own company one day. Alison wanted to be a nurse but planned on having a gap year first. She wanted to travel, see a bit of the world, she said. I admired how confident she was. We got closer and closer as the weeks went by.

Soon it was Alison's last day, she was off travelling the next day with some mates, so we decided to have a drink together after work. George had left early and asked me to lock up. As I unplugged the photocopier I felt a small electrical shock run up my arm. We'd been having a bit of trouble with that extension cord the past couple of days. It must be faulty, I thought. We were closed for the weekend and no one was likely to use it, but even so I'd better put a warning sticker on it. It was company procedure and someone might come in early on Monday morning and go to use it.

'Are you ready?' Alison asked.

I looked around to see her leaning seductively against the doorpost, the top couple of buttons on her blouse undone, handbag slung over her shoulder and holding a bottle of wine in her hand. My pulse raced.

'Everyone's left,' she said. 'So I thought as the office is empty we could say our farewells here.'

My car was parked outside but I could get a taxi home and pick up the car tomorrow. I didn't live that far away. Alison was hot, and we were both single, so yeah, it was a temptation I wasn't going to resist.

'Sounds good to me,' I said, walking slowly over to her with what I hoped was a sexy grin on my face. She leaned forward, loosened my tie a little and pulled me to her. We kissed in the doorway, the kisses getting more and more urgent.

'Let's continue this somewhere more comfortable,' she murmured, grabbing my hand and leading me along the corridor to the meeting room. It was the poshest room in the office, with a long wooden table, padded chairs, and – more importantly – a comfy sofa.

I don't know how long we were in there. The sex was hot, as if the fact that we wouldn't see each other again had unleashed something in both of us, allowed us to be as uninhibited as we wanted. Finally, our lust sated, we helped ourselves to a drink from the water machine and pulled our clothes back on.

'I think that's the wildest thing I've ever done,' she said.

I grinned. 'It's a memorable way to say goodbye!'

Still flushed with excitement we walked out, hand in hand. Then Alison remembered that she'd left her handbag in the office, she'd put it down when we were kissing.

So we went back. The door was half open, I thought I'd pulled it shut but we had both been rather distracted. I pushed it open further and then gasped in horror when I saw a body sprawled out on the floor.

Alison put her hand over her mouth, her eyes wide with shock. 'It's Arthur.'

I ran over to him and my blood ran cold when I saw the plug to the photocopier in his hand. He must have gone to plug it in and got an electric shock. It was my fault. I should have unplugged that extension lead and put a warning sticker on it, I knew it was faulty. Nausea swam in the pit of my stomach.

'It looks like he's had an electric shock. Don't touch him until we've turned off the power!'

I couldn't move. My legs had turned to stone while my eyes were fixed on the motionless body in front of me. Had my negligence killed him?

I watched in horror, frozen to the spot, as Alison used a wooden chair to move Arthur away from the plug then bent down to check him over.

'Nick, call 999! He's breathing but he needs an ambulance!' she shouted.

Thank God! I pulled myself together and dialled for an ambulance, my mind racing. No one knew about the faulty extension cord but me. I had to keep quiet about this or I would be in big trouble. This was a major health and safety issue that could have massive repercussions for me.

'We need to get our story straight about what we were doing here so late,' I told her.

'Why?' she asked, puzzled. 'We didn't have anything to do with this.' She looked shocked. 'Nick, you didn't know that extension cord was faulty, did you? You were working in here.'

'I was about to unplug it and put a warning sticker on it when you came in,' I confessed. 'I thought everyone had left for the weekend so it would be okay. I didn't know Arthur was going to come back.'

She started to shake. 'And then I distracted you...'

'Look, no one needs to know that you were here. He's alive and you have a flight to catch so you go. I'll say that I was working late and saw the office door open, then found Arthur lying on the floor.'

She got to her feet. 'Are you sure? I could do with going now, I'm running late as it is.'

Alison left a little before the ambulance arrived. Arthur was still conscious when he was taken to hospital. The police took a statement from me but it all seemed straightforward. Arthur had received an electric shock from the faulty extension. It was only a mild shock, not enough to kill him, but it had caused him to have a heart attack.

He died a few hours later in hospital, with Judith, Lizzie and me by his bedside. I'd never met either of them before but I recognised them straight away because Arthur kept a family photo in a frame on his desk. They were distraught, obviously, and I tried to comfort them. Alison phoned me from France the next day and was shocked when I told her that Arthur had died from a heart attack. We never had contact again.

I told Judith and Lizzie what a good boss Arthur had been to work for, and I helped them to arrange the funeral. They were so grateful and I felt so guilty that I got into the habit of popping in now and again to check on them, doing odd repair jobs, helping with paperwork.

Judith was quietly determined to hold it together, Lizzie was fragile. I hated myself for the part I had played in Authur's death and was determined to make it up to them in any way I could. Gradually, I realised that my feelings for Lizzie were getting stronger. I wanted to look after her, take all the troubles and anxiety away from her, so I asked her to marry me and she instantly agreed. I love her so much, my family means every-thing to me.

I worked hard to build up the company so that Judith wouldn't have to ever struggle financially. Arthur was insured, thank goodness, so the mortgage was paid off and there was a bit in the bank but I didn't want Judith to ever have to worry about money.

After a couple of years my hard work was acknowledged and I was given a promotion. Gradually I worked my way up to being the Construction Manager. I look after the business as if it's my own. I look after it for Judith and Lizzie, I am so grateful for them and every day I try to do the best I can for them, to make up for what happened.

And now Alison has come back and is trying to destroy it all.

Well, I won't let her. I'll do whatever it takes to keep Lizzie and my family safe.

59

NICK

I text Alison and tell her that I need to talk to her alone, suggesting that we meet at the row of garages behind the shops.

She replies that she'll be there in ten minutes.

'I'm going to the shop for a paper,' I call to Lizzie then hurry out before she can question me further.

When I reach the garages, Alison is already there, pacing around.

'What's this all about, Nick?' she demands when she sees me walking towards her. 'You're taking a big chance, Lizzie is already suspicious about us.'

'I don't like going behind Lizzie's back like this but I need to talk to you.'

'What about? The big secret that you're keeping from her?'

I gasp. 'So it is you! You're blackmailing me.'

Her mouth drops open and it's a second or two before she gets any words out. 'What the hell are you on about?' The realisation dawns in her eyes. 'You're being blackmailed? About Arthur's death?'

She looks genuinely shocked but she's got to be faking it. It can't be anyone else but her.

'Stop lying, I know it's you.'

She shakes her head. 'You're barking up the wrong tree here, Nick. It's not me. I've had years to blackmail you over this, if I wanted to. Why would I now?'

'I don't know but everything has been a mess since you arrived.'

She jabs a finger at me. 'George marrying Judith seems to have opened a can of worms but none of this is anything to do with me. Maybe you should just confess the truth to your wife, and mother-in-law.'

'Why are you doing this? You promised to never breathe a word about what happened,' I remind her.

'And I haven't. Someone else obviously knows your secret. Maybe they've been watching you all these years and think that you've benefitted very well over Arthur's death, Nick.'

My blood runs cold. 'What are you insinuating? You know it was an accident.' God, it would have only taken me a couple of minutes to pull that extension cord out and put a warning sticker on it. Why didn't I do it?

'I don't like being accused of blackmail, Nick. I've kept your dirty little secret all these years, but now it seems that someone else knows about it.'

'It was your fault. You came on to me!' I remind her. 'I was about to go and get a safety sticker, but you distracted me. Everyone had gone home. I didn't know Arthur would be coming back. Or that he would plug in the photocopier.'

'Why blame me when I didn't even know that the extension was faulty?' Her gaze levels with mine. 'It seems to me that someone else was there that day. They've seen how you've benefitted from Arthur's death, worked your way up, practically run the company. Quite a coincidence I'd say.'

What the hell is she getting at? 'I did it for Judith and Lizzie so they would be secure,' I say furiously.

'Really? Well it all seems a bit too convenient to me. Maybe your blackmailer thinks so to. Maybe they wonder if you knew that Arthur was coming back to do some photocopying. You could have known that he had a bad heart and an electric shock would cause him to have a heart attack.'

'How dare you insinuate that I plotted to cause his death? I admired Arthur. I enjoyed working for him. What would I have to gain from that?'

'Exactly what you've got, Nick. His company, his daughter, and his wife eating out of the palm of your hand.'

I stare at her, rage coursing through me.

'I think you should tell Lizzie and Judith the truth before someone else does.'

She turns to walk away, and I grab her arm.

'You'd better not be trying to blackmail me, Alison. If you are, you'll be sorry.'

She throws me a look of utter contempt, shakes her arm free and walks off.

I watch her go, anger simmering inside me. I was right. She's the one playing with us, sneaking into the house and putting peanut butter into the cupboard, slipping the receipt into my pocket. Who knows what she'll do next, especially now she and Lizzie are all pally.

I need to put a stop to this before I lose everything.

60

LIZZIE

Where the hell has Nick gone now? It had better not be to meet Alison again. I am sick of their secret trysts.

I want to trust Nick, I really do, but things don't add up and my instincts are telling me that he's hiding something from me.

'Mummy.' Grace opens the door. 'I'm thirsty.' Her face puckers as she looks at me. 'Are you crying, Mummy?'

'No, darling, I poked my eye. Silly me!' I stand up and paste a big smile on my face. I've got to keep it together for my children's sake. Whatever is going on I have to be strong and deal with it. I hold out my hand. 'Come on, let's go and get a drink.'

She runs over and clasps my hand, beaming up at me, and I feel the strength building in me. I will do anything to keep my kids safe.

I knock on Isaac's door then open it. As I thought, he's building his new Lego Batmobile. He looks up, triumph in his eyes. 'Look, I've almost finished it.'

'Well done. That's brilliant. I'm going down to make Grace a chocolate milkshake. Do you want one?'

'Please.' He gets up. 'And some crisps. I'm hungry.'

We all make our way downstairs and into the kitchen. The

kids get themselves a bag of crisps and I make them a milkshake, listening to them chattering away happily. I'll do anything to keep them this way. To stop them turning into a nervous wreck, like I was.

Where's Nick gone? He's been ages. My anger builds. Is he meeting Alison? Have they revived their relationship? If anyone had told me a couple of weeks ago that I would be doubting Nick's loyalty, I would have scoffed, told them that I trusted Nick with my life. Now though I'm not too sure. Something is off, I know it is. I can feel anxiety building up in me and try to push it down. I give the kids their milkshakes then turn back to the cupboards and take out my bottle of calming liquid. I unscrew the top ready to pour some out.

'Are you okay, Mummy? Why are you taking your special medicine?' Isaac asks.

I turn around and see his troubled eyes watching me.

What am I doing to my kids? I thought I had it together but now I'm back to anxiety bands, panic attacks and calming medicine which will make me feel doped up. I'm stronger than this.

'I'm fine, darling. And I'm not taking my medicine. I'm pouring it away because I don't need it anymore.'

Isaac's face lights up. I turn back to the sink and pour the medicine down it, wash the bottle out and put it in the recycling bin.

'Well done, Mum,' Isaac says in delight.

I'm proud of myself. I can do this. Then a message pings in. I bet that's Nick telling me that he's on his way home. I take my phone out of my pocket but it's a withheld number. Curious, I open it up and gape at the message.

Don't trust your husband. It's his fault your father died.

I hold on to the sink, my head reeling. Who has sent this

and what do they mean? Nick tried to save my dad. He called an ambulance for him.

I almost gasp aloud as thoughts crash into my mind.

Is this all tied into everything that's been going on? Is this message from the person who came into our house and left the peanut butter, then came back and put the receipt in Nick's pocket?

Has Nick had a message too? Has he gone out to meet this person? Is he in danger?

61

LIZZIE

I think back to what the doctor had said when Dad was taken to hospital. The extension cord was faulty and when Dad had plugged the photocopier in it had given him an electric shock. Only a mild one, but he already had angina – something he hadn't told Mum or me about – so it was enough to give him a heart attack. One that he never recovered from.

How could Nick have anything to do with that? Dad was supposed to be away at a conference, he'd come back for his notes and for some reason had decided to photocopy something.

That mystery messenger is trying to cause friction between us. Maybe that's what all this is about, everything that's happened, it's as if someone is trying to push us apart.

Could it be Alison? Does she still hold a torch for Nick? I accept that I was wrong when I thought she was trying to get her own back on me for her mother's death. Wide of the mark, in fact. But there had been something between her and Nick all those years ago, and she's alone, no real family. And she's admitted that she was over-pally with Mum because she wanted to be part of the family. Maybe she sees our happy life and wants the same. Maybe she wants to take Nick from me.

I decide to talk to Nick about it tonight, show him the message. Whatever is going on I have to be strong and face it, for our kids' sake.

When Nick comes in a little while later he looks agitated.

'Where did you get to?' I ask.

'Just for a walk, I needed to clear my head.'

It doesn't look as if he's cleared his head. He looks really strained. 'Want a cappuccino?' I ask, filling up the water tank of the coffee machine.

'Yes, please.' He nods. 'I'll pop up and say hello to the kids.'

When he comes back down I pass him his coffee, and we both take our mugs into the lounge. I wonder what Nick would say if I told him about the text. We said we wouldn't have any more secrets from each other, and here I am, keeping another one. If I don't show him and he finds out later, he will think I didn't tell him because I believed it.

I don't. Do I?

I study him thoughtfully, his gaze fixed on his cup. Then I reach for my phone and open the message. 'This came when you were out. It's from a withheld number.' I hold it out so he can read it.

He slowly lifts his head and his eyes shoot to my phone screen. They widen and the colour drains from his face. 'What the hell? Who sent this?'

'I don't know, but it's someone who has my number. I wasn't sure whether to tell you but we said no secrets.'

He looks really shaken up. 'I don't know what's going on here, Lizzie. Why would anyone say such a terrible thing? Especially now, your dad's been dead nine years.'

'It's one thing after another since Mum and George got married. I feel like our life has been turned upside down,' I tell him.

He runs his hand over his face. 'You think it's connected? But if it is, who's responsible for this and what are they hoping to achieve?'

I consider it. 'If you think about it, it's only been since Alison came back from Spain that all this has happened.' I chew my bottom lip. 'You don't think she still fancies you, do you, and she's trying to split us up? Has she made a pass at you?'

'God no,' he says emphatically. 'Honestly, Liz, it was one night years ago. A sort of goodbye thing. Alison went off abroad and I never saw or heard from her again until the wedding. I had no idea she was George's daughter.'

I believe him. 'Well, someone is trying to cause trouble. First that receipt in your coat pocket and now this.'

Nick reaches out and squeezes my hand. 'We can't let them, Lizzie. We need to stick together.'

'You're right.' I nod. 'We have to find out who's doing this, Nick. We don't know how far they will go. They've sneaked into our house...' I shudder at the thought that we might all be in terrible danger.

Suddenly my phone rings and we both jump with shock. I look down at the screen. It's George.

'I hope nothing else has happened to Mum.' I press answer, and George's voice says shakily, 'I thought I'd better tell you, love. Alison has had an accident.'

62

LIZZIE

'Oh my God! Is she okay? What happened?' I ask, my voice shaking.

'Lizzie? What is it?' Nick has got up now and is standing by me. I put George on loudspeaker so Nick can hear too.

'She went out for a walk earlier and didn't return home. Later, we had a call to say that someone found her by the garages, lying on the floor unconscious. It looks like a heel of her shoe broke, causing her to trip, and she hit her head on a brick. She's all right, apart from a few bruises. She isn't hurt but she has mild concussion, so they want to keep her in for observation, at least overnight.'

I can't take it in. Another thing that's happened that's an accident. It's all too much of a coincidence.

'What was Alison doing by the garages?' I ask Nick when George has ended the call. 'This all sounds very suspicious to me. You don't think she was meeting someone and was attacked, do you?'

'Wow! That's a big leap of imagination, Lizzie,' Nick says quickly. 'Perhaps she took a walk to the shops – the shortcut is down the side of the garages remember? And the pathway is very uneven with lots of cracks. Her heels might have got stuck in a crack and broke, causing her to trip. I'm sure the police would say if they had any suspicions otherwise.' He rubs the patch of skin between his eyebrows, looking agitated.

He's right. But it still seems a bit off to me. And it means that there's no one to look after Mum, I suddenly realise. I'm still not convinced that someone isn't drugging her, the exhaustion she's suffering seems too much. Mum even thinks so, too.

Thoughts hurtle into my mind. What if George is the culprit? I know he's in financial trouble. Mum planned to see the solicitor when she came back from Prague, to update her will and make it clear that the sole beneficiary was me, but because of the accident she probably hasn't been able to do that yet. Without it, would George, as her husband, be the beneficiary?

Kenny is too young to remember me, and doesn't know the truth of that day, so has no motive. What about Sheila? She was the matriarch of the family until Mum came along, now the family is split. Kenny is moving out soon, too, so does she feel that Mum has deprived her of the only family she has?

I make up my mind.

'Nick, I have to go and stay with Mum until Alison is out of hospital. I can't leave her there alone.' I jump up, ready to get my things and go.

Nick looks surprised. 'She isn't alone. George is there and I'm sure Kenny will drop Sheila over to stay with Judith if he can't get cover for the shop.'

'She needs me! I've got to be with her, Nick. And you're working from home so you can look after the kids, can't you?' I tell him. 'It's only until Alison comes out of hospital.'

He frowns, clearly not liking the idea. 'Are you sure that's necessary? I'm worried about you, you're struggling as it is. I'd prefer you to be here where I can look after you. The kids need you too.'

'They have you,' I point out. 'And Mum's practically immobile. She can hardly do anything for herself.'

I can't bear the thought of Mum being helpless with no one to turn to. I don't trust George, Kenny or Sheila and I know Nick thinks I'm being paranoid. He's always irritatingly logical.

'I understand that you're concerned, but I'm worried about you, Lizzie. You're coping with enough.'

He doesn't say *you're losing the plot* but I'm sure that's what he's thinking.

'I have to do this. Mum needs help with intimate things. I've got to go.' I can feel the panic welling inside me. 'If I don't go, I'll only fret more.'

He nods reluctantly. 'If you feel you must then of course I won't stop you. I wish I could come over with you, but the kids are in bed asleep.'

'I'll speak to the kids on FaceTime in the morning, explain to them that I need to look after Nanny. They'll understand.'

I hurry upstairs to pack a few things, fear giving flight to my heels. Too much is happening. I need to make sure Mum is all right.

I grab my overnight bag and start putting my nightwear, change of clothes, makeup and a few toiletries in it.

When I go back downstairs, Nick hugs me. 'Phone me and let me know how everything is. And if you need me, call me. Anytime. Even if it's in the middle of the night. Promise?'

'I will. Thank you.' I wrap my arms around him and he holds me close. Then I grab my overnight bag and set off for Mum's.

As I pull up in the drive I pause for a moment, staring at the house where I grew up. It looks quiet and peaceful, but danger could be lurking inside. I know I've made the right decision to stay with Mum, though I'm worried about Isaac and Grace, too. What if someone sneaks into our house again?

I shake my head. They won't. I think the reason they did that was to frame Nick, to cause trouble between us both, which hasn't worked. And maybe it was Alison, I'll ask her when she comes home. Besides, Nick is there and he adores the kids. He won't let anything happen to them.

Whereas Mum has no one to look out for her, and I can't risk anything happening to her. I've already lost my dad. I'm not going to risk losing my mum too.

63

LIZZIE

George comes out of the living room and blinks in surprise as I walk in, carrying my overnight bag. 'Hello, Lizzie, have you come to stay?'

'Yes. I'm going to look after my mum while Alison is in hospital,' I tell him. 'Then you won't have to worry about her while you go to visit Alison or to work.'

'That's very kind of you, dear, but there's really no need. Sheila is coming over tomorrow to help. You have enough to do and your children need you.'

'Nick is working from home for a few days so he can look after the kids,' I say.

George frowns. 'Lizzie, dear, I know you're worried but I assure you that we can cope.'

'I won't rest knowing that Mum hasn't got anyone to help her with personal stuff.'

George sighs. 'If it makes you feel more at ease, that's fine by me, Lizzie. The last thing I want is for you to be worried about your mum. Judith's in the lounge, why don't you go and chat to her. She'll be delighted to see you.'

'Thank you.' I stand my bag under the coat rack and go into the lounge.

Mum is sitting on the sofa, and like George, looks surprised to see me.

'Lizzie, is everything okay?' she asks. 'George said he told you about Alison. Is that why you've come?'

I want to tell her everything, but I can't with George here. Thankfully he pops his head around the door and says, 'I'll go and visit Alison while you're here, Lizzie. I was going to leave it to Kenny and Sheila but I'd like to check on her myself. I'll only be a couple of hours and it will give you and Judith time to have a catch-up.'

I'm glad for the chance to talk to Mum. I want to tell her everything that's happened, see if she thinks I'm being over-dramatic, like Jodie and Nick do. I'm not going to tell her about the text message though. I don't want to upset her by bringing up Dad's death again. And it feels disloyal to Nick.

'It's good of you to come and sit with me, love. But I'm okay, honestly. And those kiddies will be missing you,' Mum says. She gives a little yawn.

'I'll probably be back home by the time they come out of school tomorrow, as George said that they're only keeping Alison in overnight.' I pause. I've got to do this. 'Mum, I need to talk to you.'

'What is it?' Her eyes sharpen. 'Has something else happened?'

'I don't know if it is anything but a couple of days ago, when I had the key cut, I came in and you were asleep so I went to the bathroom upstairs.' I can't bring myself to confess that I was snooping. 'And I saw your bedroom door open and your docu-ment file on the bed, as if someone had been looking through it.' I can feel my cheeks flush. 'I know that I shouldn't have gone in your bedroom but I was worried, so I checked the file and your will and insurance were missing.'

Mum nods. 'I had an appointment arranged with my solic-itor on Thursday, when we were due to have returned from our honeymoon, to update my will after our marriage. I told you that George and I have agreed to keep our finances sepa-rate. As I couldn't go to the solicitors myself I asked George to pop my will in for me. You will remain the beneficiary of my life insurance too, so the solicitor needs both documents.' She frowns. 'I'm not sure what you're trying to suggest here, Lizzie.'

I bite my lip. I don't want to say the rest but I have to. 'George isn't as financially secure as you think, Mum. One of his customers told me that he was in so much debt before he met you that he was going to have to sell his shop. And the house belongs to Sheila, not him.'

Mum sets her mouth in a firm line. 'Lizzie, I can't believe you've been gossiping about George to one of his customers.'

'I wasn't, she offered the information.' I take the plunge. 'And you have to admit that lots of things have gone wrong since the wedding. You are getting weaker instead of better.'

'Are you suggesting that George is making me ill? Putting aside the fact that George would never do such a thing, what would he gain from it? He won't get any of my money if I die, you will.'

I guess she's right, George has no motive if he's not gaining financially from it.

'Something's going on, Mum.' I tell her about finding the jar of peanut butter in the cupboard, and the receipt in Nick's pocket. 'Someone has a key to our house and is sneaking in. And look what's happened to Alison. What if she didn't fall? What if someone attacked her?'

Mum's eyes widen. 'Who on earth would do that and why? Besides, Alison told the police she tripped because the heel of her shoe broke.' She shuffles in her seat. 'I think you're letting your imagination get a bit carried away with you, Lizzie.'

Which is what Nick thinks too. But something isn't right, all my senses tell me so.

Mum pushes herself up and reaches for her walker. 'I need to go to the loo. I'll put the kettle on then and make us a cuppa.' Which is code for conversation finished.

'No, I'll do that,' I tell her. She's still unsteady on her feet and I don't want her spilling boiling water over herself.

We're sipping our tea when George returns from the hospital. 'How's Alison?' Mum asks.

'Not bad. She's got a big bump on her head, she hit it with some force apparently but the doctor thinks she'll be home tomorrow.'

'She could have been killed.' I still can't help worrying that this might not have been an accident. But then surely Alison would remember if someone had pushed her.

George nods. 'She was lucky. She will be okay though, after a few days' rest.' He sits down and twists his hands together anxiously. 'Alison's accident has given me quite a shock.' He puts his hand to his chest. 'My old ticker is racing a bit. I must say that I'm relieved you're here, Lizzie, to keep Judith company.'

He leans back in the chair and closes his eyes wearily.

'Why don't you go to bed, love? You look done in. Lizzie will help me into my room,' Mum tells him.

He does look shattered. His skin is pale and he's heavy under the eyes, and I wonder if I'm wrong about him. Wrong about all of them.

'I think I will, if you don't mind helping Judith get ready, Lizzie.'

'Of course not. You must be shaken up about Alison.'

'I am a bit.' George gives Mum a hug goodnight. As they

wrap their arms around each other I think of Nick. I miss him. And the kids.

I don't feel easy leaving Mum down here by herself. Maybe I'm imagining it all, as everyone thinks, but I want to make sure my mum is safe. 'I'll sleep on the sofa in the conservatory for tonight,' I say.

George looks at me in concern. 'You won't be very comfortable there, Lizzie. Why don't you take Alison's bed in your old room?'

'I prefer to be down here in case Mum needs me. I'll be fine, don't worry,' I tell him.

I fetch Alison's light duvet and pillow and put them on the sofa. I'm glad that Nick and Alison took the wicker one outside, this one is much more comfortable.

'Shall we have another drink before we turn in?' I ask Mum when George has gone up to bed. 'Do you fancy hot chocolate?'

'That would be lovely, I'll go to the bathroom and get ready for bed. Do you mind bringing it in to my room?' she asks.

'Of course not.'

I warm some milk up on the hob, make two mugs of hot chocolate, put some marshmallows in a bowl and take them in to Mum's room.

We have our drink together then Mum settles down to sleep. I put a glass of water within her reach in case she wakes in the night and is thirsty. I've poured one for myself too. I take it into the conservatory and lie down on the sofa in there. I think of my comfy bed back home, and Nick. I miss snuggling up to him.

As if he can sense my thoughts, he phones me. 'Hello, love, how are you doing? Is everything okay at your mum's?'

I'm so happy to hear from him. 'Everything's okay. Mum's asleep now. I'm glad I came, George looks shattered. I think Alison's accident has really shaken him up.'

'It's a lot for him, especially not long after Judith's fall. It's a lot for you all.'

It is. 'How are the kids?' I ask.

'Fast asleep. Everything is fine here, don't worry about us.' He pauses. 'I love you, Lizzie. If you need me call. Anytime. Even in the middle of the night. Promise?'

'I promise. I love you too.'

When our phone call has ended, I curl up on the sofa and wrap the blanket around me, thinking how much I miss Nick and the kids. I wish I could go home, that we were all together again, but I can't until it's safe. And right now, I don't feel that it is. Exhausted, I snuggle down into the pillow and close my eyes.

I don't know how long I've been asleep but something wakes me. Something that makes my eyes snap open and my ears prick, on full alert. I sit up and reach for the light, switching it on. *What is it?*

I can smell something. Smoke! I can smell smoke. I jump off the sofa in panic.

Oh my God, something is on fire!

MONDAY

64

LIZZIE

Mum! I've got to get to Mum. The back room is right next to the kitchen, it won't take long for the smoke to get in there and she's so weak it will overcome her in no time.

I run over to the door. I can hardly see through the glass because of the smoke. I need something over my mouth. I reach for the vest top I wore yesterday that I draped over the arm of the sofa, pour the remaining water from the glass I filled last night onto it and tie it around my mouth then open the door into the back room. I can barely make out Mum but I hear her coughing and make my way in that direction.

'Lizzie...' She coughs again 'What's happened?'

'There's a fire, we've got to get out!' I need to wake George too, if he isn't already awake, and call the fire brigade but in my rush to save Mum I left my phone in the conservatory. I can't shout him, my mouth is covered with the wet vest top, I'll get Mum out then I'll call him.

'Lean on me,' I say as Mum tries to get out of bed. There isn't time to put her boot on or grab her walker, I'm going to have to support her. And she needs something around her mouth to protect her from the smoke. I whip the pillowcase off while Mum struggles to sit on the end of the bed, use her glass of water to wet it and tie it around her mouth. It's not ideal but it's better than nothing.

Smoke is seeping under the door and billowing into the room. I'm guessing that the fire is in the kitchen. We have to escape through the conservatory. Once Mum is outside I'll try and get my phone and call for help. And I must wake George somehow.

'Save yourself, Lizzie. Get out! I'll slow you down,' Mum wheezes as I wrap my arm around her waist and lift her out.

'I'm going nowhere without you.' I'm standing on the side of her fractured ankle, so that I can take the weight. 'Lean on me and we'll soon be out of here.'

Mum puts her arm around my shoulder and we set off.

It's an arduous process, baby steps, coughing and spluttering, but gradually I help her back into the conservatory. It's too full of smoke now to see my phone and I can't stop to look for it. Mum is like a dead weight and seems barely conscious. We inch our way across to the French doors and I open them out into the garden. Fresh air rushes in. A couple more steps and I can seat Mum on one of the wicker chairs. She removes the pillowcase from her mouth and starts coughing, huge coughs that wrack her body. I'm worried about her but I've got to wake George and get him to call the fire brigade.

Mum is obviously thinking the same thing. 'George,' she croaks.

I haven't got my phone and I'm not running back into that house, we were lucky to get out of it. Mum and George's bedroom is overlooking the back, so I shout George's name as loud as I can and look around for a stone to throw at the window. Then suddenly the back door bursts open and George comes out, his face black, his dressing gown untied, brandishing the fire extinguisher. Mum keeps one on the landing upstairs and one in the kitchen. Thank goodness! The fire had obviously woken him up and he'd grabbed the fire extinguisher on the way down.

'Judith! Darling! Are you all right?' He puts the fire extinguisher down and runs over, kneeling down beside Mum and hugging her.

'Oh, George!' She clings onto him, sobbing, and as I watch them I wonder how I could have possibly thought that George was harming my mum. It's clear that he dotes on her.

'We need to call the fire brigade,' I tell him.

'No need, I've managed to put the fire out,' he replies. 'Leave them to deal with more urgent cases.' He stands up. 'Thank you for getting Judith out. I was so worried about her.'

'I think she should see a doctor. The smoke could have damaged her lungs.'

'I'm perfectly all right, Lizzie. There's no point in us all hanging around in A&E for hours,' Mum says.

'I really think you should go and get checked over,' I tell her. 'Smoke inhalation can be dangerous.'

'Seriously, my chest feels fine. Let's see how I am tomorrow,' Mum insists.

'How bad is the kitchen?' I ask George.

'I put it out in time to avoid any real damage, thank goodness. Everywhere is black though, we will need to completely redecorate the kitchen and probably the back room too.'

He looks at me and I can see the accusation in his eyes. 'The hot plate on the cooker hadn't been turned off and the tea towel fell on it and caught alight. That's what caused the fire.'

It's clear what he's saying. I warmed up the milk to make our hot chocolate and he thinks that I didn't turn the cooker off. But I did.

Didn't I?

I start to shake as I think how we could have been killed while we slept. The smoke would have killed us before the flames did.

65

NICK

It's pitch black when I'm woken by the ring of my mobile. Half asleep I instinctively reach for it then sit up, instantly awake when I see the caller is Lizzie. My eyes dart to the clock on my bedside table. Three fifteen. My heart races. Why is Lizzie phoning me at this time? Something must have happened. I press answer and shuffle myself upright. 'Lizzie?'

Half-sobbing, she tells me how there's been a fire in the kitchen, they're all safe. 'George put it out in time.' Her voice breaks.

'Oh my God, Lizzie. Are you all okay? You could have...' I don't finish the sentence. I can't bear to think what could have happened if Lizzie hadn't woken up and got her and Judith out of the house before the fire took hold. And if George hadn't heard the commotion and managed to put the fire out.

'Yes, just a bit of smoke on our chest. Thank goodness George got to the fire extinguisher. Will you please make up the sofa for Mum? I'm bringing her over now.'

I'm not sure that sleeping on the sofa is the best place for Judith when she has a fractured ankle but I can hear the panic in Lizzie's voice. And I'm desperate to see her and make sure she's safe, but the kids are fast asleep in bed and I can't leave them.

'What about George?'

'The upstairs is fine, but the back room has been smoke damaged. Mum can't sleep there. I'll be home in a few minutes,' she adds.

'Okay. Drive carefully,' I tell her.

She ends the phone call, and I get out of bed. Shoving my feet into my slippers I go out to the linen cupboard in the hall and take out a spare throw and two pillows. It's warm, Judith won't need a duvet. There's no sound from the kids, thank goodness, so I carry the bedding downstairs and put them on the sofa. Then I walk into the kitchen and put the kettle on. I'm guessing everyone will want a hot drink. I feel numb, like I'm in a dream, the image of Lizzie and Judith trapped in a burning house going round and round in my mind. I should never have agreed to Lizzie staying there. But then she insisted, so how could I have stopped her?

I go to the front door and open it just as Lizzie's car pulls into the drive. I walk over to the driver side and hug her as she gets out. She clings to me for a moment, her whole body trembling.

'Let me help your mum out,' I say.

Lizzie is there before me, opening the passenger door, then we both help Judith into the house, sitting her down on the sofa in the lounge. She looks shaken up. Obviously.

'George. I shouldn't have left George.'

I kneel down beside her. 'It's only for tonight. We can see what damage has been done tomorrow and then sort out for you to go back.'

'She's not going back,' Lizzie says firmly.

We both look at her.

'Mum could have died today. I want her with me where I can keep an eye on her.' She sits down, shaking.

I look over at Judith who is practically falling asleep. 'Your mum needs to sleep, Liz. Let's get her comfortable and we'll talk in the kitchen.'

We settle Judith down on the sofa, she closes her eyes as soon as she lies down, and we go into the kitchen where I make us both a coffee, adding a little shot of brandy for the shock.

Lizzie is sitting down at the table, her head in her hands. She's covered in smoke dust. She needs a shower, I think. Judith does too, but the poor woman looks too exhausted.

I sit down by Lizzie and put one of the mugs in front of her. 'Do you know how the fire started?'

'George said the cooker hob was left on and a tea towel fell onto it.' She raises anguished eyes to me. 'He's trying to blame me because I made Mum some hot milk before she went to sleep. But it wasn't me. I turned that cooker off. I think someone sneaked into the house and started the fire.' She stares at me defiantly. 'Just like someone has been sneaking into our house. We're all in danger, Nick. We need to call the police.'

'And tell them what? That a fire broke out because the hob was left on and a tea towel fell on it?' I ask her.

'What about all the other things? What about someone breaking in here?'

'We have no proof,' I remind her.

'There's that message on my phone.' She picks up her phone and tries to find it. 'It's gone!' she says.

I know it's gone. I deleted it yesterday when she was in the bathroom. I hate to do this to her but I can't have her showing that text to anyone. As for the fire, I know how Lizzie gets when she's anxious. How forgetful she is. It makes more sense to me that Lizzie accidentally left the cooker ring on just like she left the iron on the other day than that someone sneaked into the house, turned on the hob, arranging the tea towel in such a position that it would fall and catch fire.

Lizzie is quiet as she sips her drink, lost in her thoughts. I'm glad of the silence so that I can examine my own thoughts. I'm scared to look at them, to bring them out into the open, but I have to. So many things have gone wrong since Judith and George got married. They can't all be coincidence. Could Lizzie be responsible? Could her agitation and worry over her mum marrying the husband of the woman whose death she feels responsible for have sent her spiralling?

She's not responsible for my blackmail message though, is she?

66

LIZZIE

'I think it's best not to tell Isaac and Grace about the fire, and I'll keep them out of the sitting room so they don't disturb Judith,' Nick says when the alarm goes off a few hours later. 'You rest and I'll take them to school.'

I nod, exhausted. 'Thanks.' Within seconds I'm asleep again.

It's almost midday before I can drag myself out of bed, shower and go downstairs. Mum is up, dressed and sitting on the sofa, talking to Nick.

'How do you feel, Mum?' I ask her, sitting down beside her and putting my arm around her shoulders. 'You must have inhaled a lot of smoke.'

'A bit chesty but nothing to worry about,' she replies, her voice a little raspy. 'Thanks to you for saving me.' She puts her hand on mine. 'You were very brave. I bet you're feeling a bit rough today.'

'A bit chesty, like you, but otherwise fine,' I tell her.

'You were both very lucky,' Nick says. 'This could have been a terrible tragedy.'

We're all silent for a moment as the enormity of the danger

we were in hits us. Then the ring of the doorbell makes us all jump. Nick goes to answer the door and returns a few minutes later with George.

'Judith darling, how are you?' His voice is full of emotion as he sits down on the other side of Mum. I move along a bit, leaving them to hug.

After asking how we both are George tells us that the insurance company have already sent an inspector out, and they have confirmed the cause of the fire as accidental. The look he gives me when he tells me this leaves me in no doubt who he blames.

'They're arranging to have the cupboards replaced and the kitchen and back room repainted.'

'Mum had better stay here with us until it's all finished,' I say. 'It's not good for her to be amongst all that.'

'I want my wife with me,' George replies firmly. He takes a seat by Mum. 'Alison is coming home today, darling, and between us we'll be able to help you up the stairs, you can sleep in our bed again,' he says, holding her hand and gazing at her adorably. 'Sleeping on the sofa like this is no good for you.'

'I think Mum is safer here,' I tell him.

To my dismay Mum pipes up, 'I want to go home with George, Lizzie. I think I can manage the stairs now. And you have the children to think about. You don't really have room for me here.'

'If you can manage the stairs, I can put the kids in together and you can have Isaac's room,' I tell her. Both kids have a pull-out spare mattress under their beds for when they have friends to stay over, so it won't be a problem for them to share.

Mum is adamant though. I am terrified of her going back home, the only comfort I have is that Alison will be there too.

'It's only natural that your mum will feel more settled in her own home,' Nick says. 'I know you're worried, Liz, but you need to look after yourself too. You went through a terrible ordeal last night.'

Kenny and Sheila arrive then. George has obviously told them what happened, so they've come straight to our house.

'Are you all right, dear? What a horrific experience,' Sheila asks Mum. 'Don't worry, we'll all look after you. Now, let's get you home and comfortable.'

'We can all look at the wedding photos together, Sam's just emailed them over to me,' Kenny adds.

'I'd like to see those,' I say.

'We'll check them all and Judith will send you a selection when she feels stronger,' George tells me. 'Now come on, love, let's get you home.'

I'm outnumbered. Again. And all I can do is watch them help my mum into the car and drive off.

Everyone obviously thinks that I'm responsible for accidentally starting the fire and that Mum is safer away from me.

'Don't take it personally, it's only natural that Judith will want to go home,' Nick tries to reassure me. 'Now I'll go and get the kids from school, you put your feet up and relax.'

I can't relax. I keep going over and over last evening. I'm sure that I turned off the cooker. I forgot to turn off the iron the other day though, didn't I? When my anxiety is really bad, I sometimes get confused and forget things. Could that have happened this time?

I feel so bewildered. I'm doubting myself. I need to get away for a bit, put a bit of space between me and Nick with his watchful eyes and unspoken accusations. I need to get my head together.

I text Jodie.

Can I stay with you for a couple of nights?

Sure. Are you bringing the kids?

I know that there is no way Nick will let me take the kids. Besides, I need space and they have school.

'No, Nick's working from home, so he'll be there for them. I need a bit of time to myself, to clear my head.'

Her reply shoots back.

Come whenever you're ready. I'll make you a bed up.

Nick is back with the kids now, they're full of chatter about school. I wait until they've gone up to their rooms to play then tell Nick that I'm going to Jodie's for a bit. He doesn't even try and talk me out of it. He merely nods and says that maybe a couple of days away to rest will do me good.

I say goodbye to the kids, telling them that I need to go and help Jodie then pick up my bag and walk out to my car, my heart breaking inside. I've never felt so lonely and so helpless. I feel like I'm losing my family, my mum, my mind.

67

LIZZIE

Jodie embraces me when I arrive. 'You look exhausted. I've put you in Millie's room, she's at her dad's this week. Hopefully Freddie won't keep us awake.' Kyle, Jodie's ex – and Millie's dad – lives ten minutes' drive from her, so they co-parent. 'Go and get some rest, then when you're refreshed we'll open a bottle of wine and you can tell me what's going on.'

I'm so grateful for her unquestioning reply that tears spring to my eyes. 'Thank you,' I whisper.

I'm bone tired, weary enough to ignore all the noise in my head and as soon as I lie down on Millie's bed, I fall asleep. When I wake the room is in darkness. How long have I been lying here? I look at the clock and see that it's gone six. Four hours. I've slept all afternoon. I get myself out of bed, freshen up and get dressed then go downstairs. Jodie is on the phone. She looks up as I come in.

'She's here now, Nick, did you want a word?'

Nick? I frown. *Why is he calling Jodie?*

'Nick wanted to check how you were and thought you might be sleeping, so called me.' She hands me her phone. I take it. Jodie gets up and goes into the kitchen, leaving us to talk in private.

'Nick? How are the kids?'

'They're good. So is your mum. I don't want you to worry about anything. Concentrate on yourself. Rest. Take it easy.'

Get your mind straight again, I inwardly finish for him. 'I will, I'll be back in a couple of days,' I tell him.

'I love you,' he says. 'Never forget that.'

'I love you too,' I reply. I feel like we're both going through the motions, that we're drifting further and further apart and there's nothing I can do to stop it.

Jodie comes back with a bottle of rosé and two glasses. 'It's low alcohol but I thought it still might cheer you up,' she says. She fills both glasses and hands me one. 'Now, tell me what's been going on.'

She listens attentively, without interrupting, as I fill her in. When I've finished she takes a hold of my hand. 'Geez, Lizzie, that's a heck of a lot to deal with. And a really scary situation last night. You both could have died. Are you okay?'

I don't trust myself to answer so simply nod and take a gulp of my wine. When I've composed myself I say, 'Nick and George think it was me who left the cooker on, Jodie. I've been a bit confused, forgetting things.'

She squeezes my hand. 'It's not your fault, it was an accident. There's been a lot going on which has brought up some deep trauma for you.' Her voice is laced with sympathy. 'Nick understands. You'll both sort it out.'

I stare down into my glass. 'He's trying to be supportive, but we're kind of dancing around each other. I feel like he thinks I'm going to have a breakdown, so he doesn't trust me around the kids. He's working from home this week, supposedly to support me but I think it's because he doesn't want to leave the kids alone with me. He's never forgotten how I was when Isaac was small. And now he thinks it's all happening again.'

Jodie fixes me with a serious look. 'Liz, you had a break-down, and no wonder after what you went through. That was years ago. It's not happening now. You're anxious and worried about your mum, and who wouldn't be? It's been one thing after another since she got married. And last night you could have both died.' She pauses. 'I don't know what to think of all this but if you really believe that someone has been sneaking into your house then you need to go to the police. But you need strong evidence to convince them. Have you got any?'

That's one of the reasons I love Jodie so much, she says it as she sees it and she always has my back. I don't have strong evidence though. Or any evidence at all. Even the warning text has disappeared from my phone. I must have deleted it.

I shake my head. 'Only my gut feeling that all these things aren't coincidence. And that jar of peanut butter and receipt. That wasn't me, I know it wasn't.' I wipe the back of my hand over my eyes. 'None of it adds up, Jodie. And I hate to think that Mum is alone with no one to help her. I should be with her.'

'Why don't you phone Judith and see how she is? That might put your mind at rest.'

I nod. 'I will. And I've just remembered that Alison's coming home today, she'll be there to look after Mum.'

But when I call Mum but there's no answer, so I call Alison but again no answer. *What's going on?*

I phone George next. 'Lizzie, what can I do for you?' he asks wearily.

'Oh, hi George. I wondered how Mum is, can I talk to her?'

'She's asleep, Lizzie, and I don't want to disturb her. Why don't you phone back tomorrow?' Is it my imagination or is he being unusually abrupt?

'Can I speak to Alison then?'

George sighs. 'Alison is still in hospital, Lizzie, they've kept her in another night. Please phone tomorrow at a reasonable time. I'm going to bed. Last night was a terrifying experience for us and has left us feeling exhausted.'

He ends the call.

I look at Jodie. 'Talk about fobbing me off.'

'They probably are shattered, Liz, and you must be too. Why don't you get a good night's sleep and drive over to see your mum tomorrow?'

I try to sleep but I can't, I toss and turn for hours. There was something about George's attitude that was really off. He's never been that cold to me before. I bet it's because he blames me for the fire but it wasn't me.

Suddenly, I sit up as the realisation that if it wasn't an accident, dawns on me, that someone started the fire on purpose. Someone tried to kill us. It couldn't be George because he put out the fire, so someone else sneaked in. Like they sneaked into our house. I have to go back and stay with Mum until Alison comes home. I'll never forgive myself if anything happens to her.

TUESDAY

68

Tonight's the night. I can't wait any longer. They want their money and they're getting impatient. I need to be single-minded and do what I have to do. There's no time for sentiment. She didn't care that I was left without a mother at such a young age. This is payback.

I park my car around the corner and walk to the house. It's in total darkness, no lights are on. Everyone's in bed. I stop outside the front door and listen. All quiet.

Do I go in the front door or the back? I've thought about this all the way over here. The back is the best. It's easier to sneak in and out that way.

I climb over the gate, unbolt it so I can make a quick getaway then creep over to the back door. I'm wearing trainers so that I don't make any noise, and gloves so that I don't leave any fingerprints. Although the police would expect my fingerprints to be here, wouldn't they?

I take the key out of my pocket and open the back door, pausing to listen. There's no sound. I gently push the door open and creep inside. I can smell the smoke in the kitchen. That plan that went wrong. This one isn't going to fail.

I go into the back room, it's dark and it takes me a while to focus. I see the shape of the bed and carefully make my way over to it, picking up a cushion from the chair as I do so. I stand over her for a while, watching her breathe. She's fast asleep. She won't feel a thing. Then I hold the cushion in front of me and bring it down over her face.

'What the hell do you think you're doing?' a voice roars from behind me.

I panic and swing around, my hand reaching for the nearest thing. The table lamp. I bring it down on their head. There's a scream and a thud.

69

LIZZIE

I'm almost at Mum's when I see a shadowy figure running out of the front door of her house. For a moment I think it's Nick and call to him, but the person carries on running, bolting around the corner, the opposite direction from where we live.

Is it a burglar?

I increase my speed, pulling up outside the house, then run inside. 'Mum!' I shout. 'George!'

One of them must be awake. One of them startled the burglar or he wouldn't have run for it empty-handed like that.

I hit the light switch in the hall and make my way down to the back room – the door is wide open. Cautiously I step inside, my hand flying to my mouth at the horrific scene inside. George is lying sprawled out on the floor, blood pouring out of a gash in his head. On the carpet beside him is the table lamp, splattered with blood. The burglar must have hit him with it. In bed, almost comatose, is my mum. Lying on the floor beside her is a cushion. My blood turns to ice and my body trembles so much I have to grip the doorframe for support.

What the hell has happened?

Who was running from the house?

My feet feel like blocks of lead as I walk over to Mum and feel her wrist for a pulse. It's quite strong, thank God. Slowly I kneel down and feel for George's pulse. It's there but very faint.

'What's going on here?' a voice asks behind me, and the room blazes with light.

I look up and see two police officers.

'Someone phoned us to report a disturbance. We were driving past and saw the front door open,' one of them explains.

I get to my feet. 'Someone has attacked my stepfather. And my mother seems to be drugged,' I reply, my voice shaking.

'Are you the only people in the house?' the taller police officer asks.

'Now yes, but I've only just arrived. I saw someone running away from the house, they left the front door open,' I stammer.

'Do you often visit your mother in the middle of the night?' the taller policeman asks as the other one bends down to check George. My breath catches in my throat. *Please let George live.*

I suddenly realise how suspicious it looks for me to be standing here in the middle of the night, with blood over me. George's blood. I wish I hadn't come now. I should have stayed at Jodie's.

'I was worried about my mum. I think someone is trying to harm her. There was a fire here yesterday...'

Paramedics arrive, and another police car. The house is rapidly swarming with police.

'I think you'd better come to the station with us and make a statement,' the police officer says.

'Someone was running away. Someone broke in,' I tell them.

'You can tell us all about it at the station,' he says. He looks around. 'Is there a door camera or any kind of security camera here?'

'Mum didn't like them. She felt that she was being spied on,' I say. The times I'd asked her to get a doorbell camera for security reasons. Nick always supported her too. He didn't even want a doorbell camera at our house.

Theories are spinning around in my mind. *Who has done this? Who had such a grudge against George that they would want to kill him?*

Maybe the same person who attacked Alison, because I'm not convinced that was an accident.

Was that the same person who's been targeting us, sneaking into our house?

If only I'd got a better look at whoever was running away.

Then I recall how my first thought was that it was Nick.

God, no. It couldn't be!

But Alison hinted that he was hiding something. And there was that anonymous text I got about asking him what really happened when my father died. And he didn't protest about me going to stay at Jodie's, it was as if he wanted me out of the way.

I shake my head. It couldn't be. I don't believe it. I won't believe it.

70

NICK

I put the phone down, my hand shaking. I can hardly take in what Jodie told me. George has been attacked by an intruder, and Lizzie is down at the police station being questioned. 'Lizzie wanted me to tell you,' Jodie says. 'She's in pieces, Nick.'

I can't understand why Lizzie phoned Jodie instead of me. Surely I should have been her first port of call? And why is she being questioned? I asked Jodie that and she replied that she presumed it was because Lizzie was at the scene of the crime.

I can't get my head around it. Who would want to kill George? I want to go to the police station and see Lizzie, but the kids are asleep and even when they wake I can't really take them with me, can I? I'll have to wait until they are at school. I realise for the first time how frustrating it must be for Lizzie to not be able to go and check on her mum when she wants to. To be so close yet unable to pop in.

Suddenly a message pings in. It's from Jodie.

I've just thought, do you want me to come over and sit with the kids while you go to the station and see what's happening? It's no problem. I'm awake anyway feeding Freddie, and Millie is with Kyle.

I reply straight back to say I'd be really grateful if she could do that, and she texts that she'll be here in ten minutes.

I have a quick shower and pull on jeans and a top. The kids will be awake in a couple of hours but they'll be fine with Jodie, they're used to her. She's like an aunt to them.

I've just got downstairs and am grabbing a drink of water when Jodie messages:

I'm here.

I open the front door.

'I didn't want to ring and wake the kids,' she whispers as she follows me inside, carrying Freddie in his car seat.

'This is really good of you,' I say.

'Lizzie is my best friend. I'll do anything to help her.'

One thing is bugging me. 'I thought she was staying at yours? What was she doing at her mum's house at this time of night?'

'She was at mine. We both went to bed. The next thing I know I'm woken by a phone call from Lizzie, saying someone has attacked George and she's at the police station. She swears she didn't do it. And I believe her.' Jodie fixes me with a hard stare.

I fidget uncomfortably. 'Are the police accusing Lizzie?'

'No, not yet, anyway. But from what Lizzie told me she thinks you will. Or George's family.'

'Look, I'm worried about Lizzie, yes, but I don't think she would attack George. She would never hurt anyone on purpose.'

'Are you saying she might have done it accidentally?'

I think about it. 'Maybe,' I say reluctantly. 'I think Liz is having some kind of breakdown, Jodie. She's got this idea that someone is out to harm her mum.'

Jodie settles Freddie's car seat by the sofa then looks up at me. 'I know and I pooh-poohed the idea too, but now, well, considering the events of tonight, I'm thinking that she could be right.'

We stare each other out for a few seconds. I'm the one to break it. 'I'd better go. Thanks again, Jodie.'

I head out to the car, Jodie's words going over and over in my mind. Why did Lizzie sneak out in the middle of the night and go to her mum's? Did she attack George, convinced in her anxious state that he was harming Judith? I wonder if anyone has told Kenny, Sheila and Alison. I decide to wait until I get to the hospital and see what the situation is, then I'll notify them.

As I pull up in the police car park, my phone rings. It's Alison.

'George has died,' she stammers, her voice shaking. 'They couldn't save him.'

71

ALISON

We all stare down at Dad's lifeless body, none of us speaking. I can't believe that he's dead. The doctor said that the blow to the head was too hard, and Dad was too old. He had no chance of surviving. If only they hadn't kept me in hospital another night for observation. If I'd been home, I might have been able to prevent this and George, the only dad I've known, would still be alive. Kenny looks ashen. His eyes are fixed on George, and his body trembles as he stammers, 'He can't be dead. He can't be.' Then he turns and bolts out of the room.

'Poor lad. It's all too much for him.' Sheila reaches for George's lifeless hand and holds it, tears pouring down her cheeks. 'I can't believe someone would do this. George would never hurt a soul, he was such a good man.' Her body wracks with sobs.

She's wrong, George isn't a good man but he didn't deserve this brutal death. I can't tell her that though, she would never believe me and at the moment I can't prove anything. But I will soon. I have to speak up for Lizzie. I can't let her take the fall for all this, even though by speaking up I'm destroying what family I have left.

My phone pings, and I take a look at the message that has just come in from Nick. He's on his way to the police station to see Lizzie. He'll come to the hospital afterwards.

I close the message without replying. *I'm sorry, Nick, but I can't protect you any longer.*

'I have to go,' I tell Sheila.

I walk outside the hospital room, where a police officer is waiting. There's no sign of Kenny. I'm guessing he's gone home.

The officer looks up at me. 'Are you all right, miss?'

I nod slowly. I want to tell him what I know so that they'll release Lizzie but I have to make sure first. I walk outside and get in my car.

72

It's all gone wrong.

I've got to get away before anyone realises what I've done. I grab my passport and throw a few things into a backpack. I'll have to travel light. I've already transferred a lot of money from AT Construction company accounts into my bank account, and that will tide me over for a while. I've been doing it slowly for months. There's not much I can't do with computers.

I zip up the bag and look around the lounge. The place which has been my home for years. It's all her fault. She's ruined my life and now she's going to get off scot-free, all because I made one stupid mistake. I'd planned all this so well, and it's been going like a dream, if only I'd been quicker with that cushion. If I hadn't grabbed that lamp. Tears well in my eyes and a lump fills my throat at the knowledge that he's dead. And it's all my fault.

There's nothing I can do now. I have to get away. I turn towards the door but as I reach for the handle it opens.

'Going somewhere?'

73

LIZZIE

I've been at the police station for hours, questioned and questioned until I'm not even sure what I saw anymore. George is dead and I'm terrified that I'm going to get the blame for killing him. I realise now that I've calmed down that it couldn't have been Nick who I saw running away, he was home with the kids. Besides, Nick would never do anything like that. Neither would I, but I'm scared that Nick will believe it's me. He will think I've finally flipped. That maybe I walked in and saw George bending over Mum to kiss her goodnight and thought that he was going to hurt her, so picked up the first thing I could put my hands on. Nick is always scared of what I will do when I have my anxiety attacks. He should know that I would never hurt anyone, let alone kill them. My whole life I have been tormented by the guilt I feel at causing Carol's death, so how could I deliberately cause another?

The policewoman told me that my mum is okay. I'm right and she's been drugged. They're running tests but they are pretty sure that it's antihistamine, which is what I always suspected. Even though I suspected it, the knowledge that I was right hits me like a sledgehammer. My mum was being slowly drugged so that she wouldn't realise what was going on and could be manipulated, and maybe to make her so dizzy she might fall again, this time with worse consequences. And tonight, someone tried to kill her. And killed George. Who would do such a terrible thing?

I lie down on the narrow bench that serves as a bed in the police cell and rest my head on the thin pillow. None of this makes sense. I remember how I thought that George might be after Mum's money. Yet he is the one who was killed.

I must have dropped off to sleep through sheer exhaustion because the next thing I know is that the cell door is open and the policewoman is talking to me. 'You're free to go, love,' she says.

I rub my eyes and sit up. 'Have you caught who killed George, and has been drugging my mum?'

'We're questioning someone at the moment.'

'Who?'

'We can't tell you yet. Your stepsister is waiting outside for you.'

'Alison?' I get to my feet. *What is Alison doing here? And where's Nick?*

The policewoman leads me out then Alison comes rushing over to me.

'Lizzie. How are you?' She hugs me. 'This is all so awful. I'm so sorry.'

I'm overwhelmed by her compassion for me when the man she regarded as her father has been killed.

'Your mum's okay, thank goodness. She'll be home tomorrow.'

'And Nick?'

'We thought it was best if I talked to you first.'

I don't like the 'we'. As if they're a partnership instead of us.

I look at her warily. 'What's going on, Alison? Who have they arrested?'

Her eyes meet mine and something in them makes me steel myself for the answer.

Please don't let it be Nick.

There's a long pause before she says, 'Kenny.'

74

ALISON

Three hours ago

Kenny. The last person anyone would suspect. I walk into Sheila's house and notice that his bags are packed and guilt is all over his face.

'Why did you kill Dad?' I ask.

He looks at me in surprise, and I can see the pain in his eyes, which are red-rimmed from crying. He and George were really close. 'It was an accident,' he stammers. 'It was Judith I wanted dead. But he startled me. Dad was no innocent, you know. We planned all this together. Right from the start.'

I keep my voice soft, calm. I want to encourage him to tell me everything. 'You and Dad planned to kill Judith for her money, then were going to frame Lizzie? Why? Is it because of what happened to your mum?'

I don't say 'Mum', I know that Kenny hates that. When he found out that Carol wasn't my real mum he forbade me from ever calling her mum in his presence again. 'It's your fault she died. You've got no right to call her Mum,' he'd say. Never in front of Dad and Sheila though. He was all sickly charm in front of them. Kenny the good egg who would help anyone. Only I knew the real Kenny, but even I didn't think he would stoop this low.

The grief is replaced by anger and his eyes are like hard black pebbles. 'It was Dad's idea to find a rich widow to marry, he was in a lot of debt. We both were. We were going to fleece her and share the proceeds.' He is almost gloating. 'I suggested to Dad that he join the Agatha Christie Facebook group, women would trust him more if they thought they had a shared interest. I didn't know who Judith was at first, but when she accepted Dad's friend request we saw her photos and I recognised one of a younger Lizzie. That's when I got the idea to make it look like Lizzie was trying to harm Judith. I wanted to make her pay.'

I try not to show any reaction to this. I want him to keep talking. 'So you were lacing Judith's food and drink with antihistamines?'

'Yeah. Me and Dad were both doing it, neither of us was there all the time so it deflected suspicion from us. It was a bonus when Lizzie thought it was you.' He chuckles, and a shiver runs down my spine. He's mad. I've long suspected that he was unhinged but never imagined he'd go this far.

'Is that why she went dizzy and fell down the stairs on their wedding night?'

Kenny shakes his head. 'No, that was low blood pressure. Dad put an extra blood pressure tablet in her pill box, so that she'd think she hadn't taken it. The double dose made her blood pressure crash.'

I recall Dad coming down the stairs with Judith's tablets, telling her she'd forgotten to take them. Even on their wedding day he was planning to harm her. I can't believe he could have been so cruel. 'That's horrible. How could you two do this to an innocent woman?' I really like Judith, she is kind, friendly, warm. I'd been so pleased that she and Dad had got married, and all the time it was just an evil scheme to get money out of her. And worse.

'We didn't set out to kill her, just make her confused so that she wouldn't realise what was going on and then we could take control of all her finances. The silly cow insisted on keeping her funds separate when she and Dad got married, so we had to do something. We took her will and personal documents, then when she was drugged up Dad got her to sign for a loan against the house, she didn't even know what she was doing. I transferred some money from her company into my account. It was all going okay, but bloody Lizzie wouldn't leave things alone.'

'You started the fire?'

'No, that was Dad. He wanted it to look like Lizzie did it. We needed her out of the way, she was getting too suspicious.'

No wonder Dad was on the scene so quickly, putting the fire out.

'So what happened today? Why did you kill George?'

Kenny wipes the back of his hand across his eyes. 'I didn't! I love Dad. It was an accident. He came in on me when I was about to smother Judith with a cushion. It would have been a painless death. He was furious because he'd said no one was to die. Well, his other plans weren't working, were they, and we both needed money desperately. If Dad hadn't come in, I would have put the cushion back and it would have looked like a natural death.'

'What about Lizzie, were you going to kill her too?'

He shook his head. 'No, death's too easy. I wanted her to suffer for what she did. I wanted her to feel what it was like to lose a parent. Like I had to when I was only a kid.' He fixes his eyes on me. 'And don't tell me you suffered too. She wasn't your real mum.'

He really did want to get revenge on Lizzie, I think with a chill. Lizzie was right all along, someone was trying to harm Judith, and tormenting her. I wish I'd believed her sooner. I knew Kenny had been deeply affected by Mum's death, but I thought he had dealt with it by now. I never dreamed he would do anything like this. Not until he crept behind me at the back of the garages and hit me on the head. At first I'd thought it was Nick, wanting to stop me telling Lizzie and Judith about his part in George's death, but as I lay in hospital, thinking it over, I realised that it was Kenny.

'Why did you attack me? Was it to frame Nick?'

He laughs. 'It was all part of the plan to make Lizzie doubt him, and leave him. I wanted her to lose everything, like I did. And she's easy to wind up. A couple of bad reviews, a jar of peanut butter in the cupboard – I borrowed Judith's keys for that and to slip the receipt in Nick's pocket. It was so easy to make her – and Nick – think she was losing her mind. It was fun to play around with her head a bit. Serves her right.'

I remember something else. 'Did you try to blackmail Nick too? How did you know what happened to Arthur?'

'I overheard you two talking about it, so thought I'd put the squeezers on. And seeing as it looks like Nick was being black-mailed, it's even more credible that he would take the company funds. I've covered my tracks and made sure it all leads to Nick so he can take the rap for it.' He picks up his bag. 'Now get out of my way.'

'You're going nowhere,' I tell him.

His face contorts with fury. 'Don't try and stop me! This is all down to you,' he roars, pushing me against the wall. 'My mum died because of you! You shouldn't have sat by Lizzie when you knew she was eating peanut butter. And then you took ages getting the EpiPen, it was as if you wanted her to die! And now my dad is dead too! You've destroyed my family.'

Shit, he really is deranged! He's killed his own father and I'm pretty sure he'll have no reservations about killing me too.

His hands are either side of my head, pinning me to the wall. 'You started all this off. You're the cause of it all.' Spittle forms on his mouth and some lands on my cheek. I want to rub it off but I can't get away.

'Now get out of my way!' He grabs my shoulders and flings me away from the door.

As I sink to the floor I hear the door push open and a voice shout out, 'Police. Drop that bag and put your hands in the air.'

75

LIZZIE

We're back at Mum's house because Alison wants to talk to us in private. Jodie is at ours looking after the kids, she's been marvellous taking them to school and collecting them again, and Mum is still in hospital under observation. Me and Nick listen dumbfounded as Alison tells us that Kenny killed George, had tried to kill my mum, and how George had deliberately targeted Mum for her money, and robbed her. Even though I'd suspected something was going on, I can barely believe what Alison is telling me. I feel physically sick at the danger my mum was in. I had never suspected Kenny. He was this friendly big brother figure, popping in with cakes and treats, always helpful and smiling.

'So Kenny and George were in this together?' Nick asks in astonishment.

'They were both doctoring her drinks and food with antihistamines to make her confused so that she wouldn't realise what was going on and they could take control of all her finances. George got her to sign some papers to take out a loan on the house, and to transfer all her assets to him if she died.' Alison swallows before continuing. 'Then George realised Kenny was taking things further and was planning on killing Judith so that they could have her insurance money, and her house. He was deeply in debt from gambling, and the men he owed the money to weren't prepared to wait much longer. George walked in and found him about to smother Judith with a cushion and tried to stop him. In the ensuing fight Kenny grabbed the lamp and hit George on the head.'

I can't believe what Kenny has done. I look again at the bruise on Alison's face where Kenny had thrown her to the floor. 'You shouldn't have gone to tackle him by yourself. You could have been killed.'

'I'd arranged for the police to come, I just hoped that they got there in time. And they did.' She turns to Nick. 'Kenny also took money from the company accounts and made it look like it was Nick.'

The shocks keep coming and I'm battered by it all. And poor Mum, she knows none of this yet. I feel sick to realise it was all a lie. George didn't love Mum. All he wanted was her money. And he was working with Kenny to fleece her. He'd forged Mum's signature for a loan, and he also altered the will so everything went to him when she died. She is going to be devastated when she finds out.

'Kenny has now changed his story to say that George was about to smother Mum and he stopped him,' Alison goes on, 'but I had my phone on record in my pocket, so we have proof – although I'm not sure if it's admissible in court – and it was Kenny's DNA on the cushion.'

'I knew it,' I whisper. 'I knew Mum was in danger. I wasn't paranoid.'

Nick and Alison both exchange a look.

'There's something else I have to tell you,' Alison says. 'It was Kenny blackmailing you, Nick. The police found the message on his other phone.'

'What?' I stammer, turning questioningly to Nick. 'You never told me that you were being blackmailed.'

Alison gets up. 'I think this is something you two need to talk about privately. I'm going to see how Sheila is. I'll leave you to it.' Her gaze falls on me, solemn, apologetic. 'I want you to know that I'm really sorry about all this, Lizzie. I wish I'd realised sooner what was going on. And I'm sorry for my part in what Nick is about to tell you. I never wanted any of it to happen.'

This sounds serious. I swallow. Are they going off together? Was I right about that too? Is that what Kenny was blackmailing Nick about? Threatening to tell me if Nick didn't pay up.

76

LIZZIE

'What is it?' I demand after Alison has left. 'Are you in love with Alison? Are you leaving me?' The idea of a life without Nick is devastating and I mentally prepare myself for his confirmation that my world as I know it is about to end. But he shakes his head vehemently.

'No, Lizzie. Of course not. I'd never leave you. I love you.' His voice breaks and he swallows. 'But I haven't told you the whole truth about the night your dad died.'

What? I lean forward and focus on him, remembering the text I received which mysteriously disappeared. 'What do you mean?'

I listen, stunned and confused, as Nick haltingly explains that he knew the extension cord was faulty but had been distracted by Alison as he was about to put a warning label on it. 'I'm so sorry, Liz. If I had put a label on it, your dad would never have tried to plug the photocopier into the socket.' He twists his hands together agitatedly. 'But in my defence it was Friday night and I thought no one would be in work until Monday. And your dad was supposed to be working away so I had no idea he would come back to the office.' His eyes are on my face, gauging my response. 'I'm so sorry. He was breathing, Lizzie, and we called the ambulance straight away. It was a heart attack that killed him.'

Shock courses through me. Shock and anger. 'So while you were having sex with Alison at the office, my dad came back and tried to use the photocopier? The one you knew was faulty, but you were so desperate to have it off with Alison you couldn't spare five minutes to put a warning sticker on it? And you didn't mention that anyone else was there when my dad suffered that electric shock.' Rage is flaming inside me. 'Not only did you flout health and safety procedures, but you also lied to us, lied to the police. And you've kept up the lie for years!'

'Arthur was alive when Alison left, she had a flight to catch. So when he died I kept her out of it, she was in France by then.' He reaches out for me but I pull away. I don't want to be near him right now. He's lied to me ever since he came into my life. Did I ever really know him? 'More like you didn't want any questions asked because you knew that you could be charged for not adhering to health and safety restrictions! You knew that you were responsible for my dad's death. That if you hadn't been so bloody eager to have sex with Alison, Dad would still be alive.' Sobs break out, noisy, gut-wrenching sobs. I put my hands over my mouth as tears spill out of my eyes and step back as Nick tries to comfort me. 'Get away from me! Keep your hands off me!'

His face creases and he shakes his head again. 'It wasn't like that. You've got to believe me. I've carried this for years, Liz. I tried to make it up to you and your mum, worked hard to make the company a success.'

I remember how he came to our house straight away, told us about Dad's accident, comforted us both. How he kept coming around. Was that to appease his guilt? So no one would wonder why he was there so late that night and why the electric socket hadn't been marked as faulty. 'Is that why you married me? Because of guilt?' I demand between sobs.

'No!' he protests. 'I swear. I love you. I loved you from the moment I saw you.'

I don't believe him. And I don't think I can forgive him. He's kept this a secret for years. And I can't help wondering if he didn't take advantage of the situation. Married me so he could get hold of Dad's company.

'That text, you deleted it, didn't you?' I demand. 'You wanted me to think I'd imagined it.' I know by the look of shame on his face that I've guessed right.

'Look, Lizzie, let's go home. You're exhausted, you've been through a lot. You need time to digest this, but please believe me that it was a tragic accident. I was in a panic, scared of what had happened, of what would happen. So yes, I lied a little. And once I started that lie I had to keep it up. What good would have come from telling anyone? And yes, I admit that I deleted the text but only because I was scared of losing you.' He steps towards me, imploring. 'I love you, Lizzie. I've always loved you. I'll do anything to put this right.'

I can't deal with this. Not after everything that's happened. My mum was almost murdered, she's still in hospital, we both almost died in a fire. Now Nick, my rock, has confessed to being a liar and responsible for my dad's death.

'You can never put it right!' I scream at him. 'My dad is dead because of you. I don't want you anywhere near me. I want you to pack your things and go. I don't want you in the house.'

'Leave you and the kids? I can't do that! Look, Lizzie, I know you're upset but we can work through this. You need me. The kids need me.'

There he goes, scared I can't cope without him. That I'm going to fall apart and do something. Well, I'm not. I wasn't imagining things all this time, was I? Someone was out to get

Mum. Someone did sneak into our house. Nick was hiding things and playing with my mind. I was right all the time. That knowledge makes me stronger. I'd doubted myself but now I don't. This has knocked me for six, yes, but I'll cope. Me and Mum will cope together just like we did when Dad died.

I shake my head. 'I can't bear you to be near me. When Mum comes out of hospital today I'll bring her back to mine. We'll look after each other.'

'The kids. You can't stop me from seeing the kids.'

I reach right down into my soul for strength. 'I want you to get out of the house and give me space so that I can deal with this. Surely you owe me that?'

His shoulders slump, his whole body sinks like a deflated balloon. He nods slowly. 'If that's what you want.'

AUGUST

77

LIZZIE

The summer has gone by in a bit of a blur. Mum struggled to take in everything that happened, that George and Kenny had planned to defraud her. Her only small comfort was that George had stopped Kenny from killing her, so she has convinced herself that he loved her after all, but she finds it hard to grieve George's death after everything he did.

'How could I have got it so wrong?' she whispers to me. 'They all seemed such a nice family.'

'People aren't always who we think they are, Mum. It's not your fault that you were so trusting.'

'You warned me that I was rushing into things and you were right.' Tears spill down her face, and I hold her tight. I haven't told her about Nick's carelessness causing Dad's death. I can't bring myself to add to her grief. She's struggling enough as it is. Physically she's getting stronger, thank goodness. She can manage the stairs, now, and is sleeping in Grace's room, while Grace sleeps with me.

I've told everyone that Nick is working away. Even Jodie doesn't know the truth and I always tell her everything, but not this time. This is so big that I'm scared to share it, because once it's out there I can't take it back, and I don't know what the consequences will be for Nick. Can he be charged with negligence or even manslaughter? Do I want him to go to prison for it? My mind is in turmoil and the only one I can speak to is Alison.

I don't feel any anger towards her because she didn't know about the electric socket being faulty and when she caught her flight Dad was still alive. And he would still be alive today if the shock hadn't given him a heart attack.

Alison is still here, living in Mum's house, tidying it all up and overseeing the redecorating the insurance company have arranged to be done because of the fire. She is really supportive to me, talks to me for ages on the phone when I can't sleep, comes over to help with Mum and the kids. I know she's in touch with Nick too, she told me so, but I don't mind. I know there's nothing between them. I wonder if there's also nothing left between me and Nick too.

My emotions have turned from raging fury to devastation and then acceptance. I realise that Dad's death was an accident and that Nick did his best to save him and look after us. I understand why he was scared to tell the truth. Like I was when George's wife died. But I was a child then, I wasn't responsible for my actions. Nick, though, was an adult. And I can't shake the feeling that Nick only married me out of guilt.

The kids are at school and Mum is asleep, so I sit out in my Zen garden, drinking in the calmness and tranquillity. I remember how Nick worked all weekend to create this for me while I was at Mum's, too consumed by guilt and anxiety to get out of bed. I gaze around at the carefully chosen statues, the plants, the bench I am sitting on. I've always loved it here. It exudes peace and love.

Nick's love. He didn't have to build this for me, I acknowledge. He didn't have to do any of the things he did. He didn't have to come and look after us, arrange the funeral, keep seeing me. Marry me. No one knew what had happened that day except Nick and Alison, and she had gone to live abroad.

Nick could have walked away from it all, got another job. No one would have ever known. Instead he stayed. Tried to make things right. Because he's a good man who made a mistake. A mistake that probably eats him up like mine did to me.

I don't know if he married me out of guilt, I guess I'll never know. But he loves me now. I can feel it as I sit here surrounded by the proof of his love. I can see it in his eyes when he speaks to me, I can feel it when he touches me. And I love him too. I don't want to live without him. I have to forgive him, like I've finally forgiven myself.

I pick up my phone and send him a text. Then I go back indoors to Mum.

We're in the kitchen having a cup of tea when I hear the front door open.

Nick comes into the kitchen and his eyes meet mine. He looks tired, drawn and like he's lost a bit of weight. He holds out his arms hesitantly.

I get up, walk over to him and into his embrace. He wraps his arms around me and I rest my head on his chest. 'I love you, Lizzie. Never forget that,' he whispers.

'I love you too,' I say.

We'll get through this. Just like we've got through everything else. One mistake doesn't define us, it makes us stronger. We will find a way to heal and move forward. What defines us is the love we have for each other, the bond we built, the family we have together.

A LETTER FROM KAREN

Dear Reader,

Thank you so much for choosing to read *The Stepsister's Secret*. If you enjoyed it and want to keep up to date with all my latest releases, just sign up at the following link. Your email address will never be shared and you can unsubscribe at any time.

www.bookouture.com/karen-king

I always think of my psychological suspense books as being the dark side of relationships, where instead of a happy ever after, things go wrong. A wedding can be such a happy occasion, when two different families merge into one big one, but it can also be the time when old grudges are revisited and secrets exposed. In *The Stepsister's Secret* the bringing together of the families exposes terrible secrets from the past, and the story is a mixture of guilt, revenge, secrets and greed. Lizzie is concerned that her mum, Judith, has fallen too hard and too fast for the charming George, who seems to adore her. Then she discovers that George's daughter is connected to an awful event in Lizzie's past that has traumatised her to this day, an event that she has never told anyone the whole truth about. But she isn't the only one who has a secret and within days the fractures in the family are exposed and lives are in danger. Is Lizzie's stepsister Alison to blame or is someone else behind it all?

I hope you loved *The Stepsister's Secret*, and if you did, I would be very grateful if you could write a review. I'd love to hear what you think, and it makes such a difference helping new readers to discover one of my books for the first time.

I love hearing from my readers – you can get in touch through social media or my website.

Thanks,

Karen

www.karenkingauthor.com

instagram.com/karenkingauthor
facebook.com/KarenKingAuthor
x.com/KarenKingAuthor

ACKNOWLEDGEMENTS

There are a lot of things that go on in the background when writing a book, and a lot of people who help with the process. I would like to thank all the Bookouture editing team for their expertise and support, and particular thanks to my amazing editor, Rhianna Louise, for her invaluable input and constructive advice. A special thanks to Aaron Munday for creating such a stunning cover. And to the fabulous social media team who go above and beyond in supporting and promoting our work and making the Bookouture Author Lounge such an enjoyable place to be. You guys are amazing! Also to the other Bookouture authors who are always willing to offer support, encouragement and advice. I'm so grateful to be part of such a lovely, supportive team. Thanks also to the Facebook groups of The Savvy Writers' Snug and Trauma Fiction for answering my research questions.

I'm indebted to all the bloggers and authors who support me, review my books and give me space on their blog tours. I am lucky to know so many incredible people in the book world and appreciate you all.

Massive thanks to my lovely husband, Dave, for all the love and laughter you bring to my life, answering my numerous questions and reading through my final manuscript to help me catch those troublesome typos. And to my family and friends who all support me so much.

Finally, a heartfelt thanks to you, my readers, for buying

and reviewing my books, and for your wonderful messages telling me how much you've enjoyed reading them. Without your support there would be no more books. Thank you. Xx

PUBLISHING TEAM

Turning a manuscript into a book requires the efforts of many people. The publishing team at Bookouture would like to acknowledge everyone who contributed to this publication.

Audio
Alba Proko

Commercial
Lauren Morrissette
Hannah Richmond
Imogen Allport

Data and analysis
Mark Alder
Mohamed Bussuri

Editorial
Rhianna Louise
Ria Clare

Copyeditor
Janette Currie

Proofreader
Jennifer Davies

Marketing
Alex Crow
Melanie Price
Occy Carr
Cíara Rosney
Martyna Młynarska

Operations and distribution
Marina Valles
Joe Morris

Production
Hannah Snetsinger
Mandy Kullar
Nadia Michael
Charlotte Hegley

Publicity
Kim Nash
Noelle Holten
Jess Readett
Sarah Hardy

Rights and contracts
Peta Nightingale
Richard King
Saidah Graham

RAISING READERS
Books Build Bright Futures

Dear Reader,

We'd love your attention for one more page to tell you about the crisis in children's reading, and what we can all do.

Studies have shown that reading for fun is the **single biggest predictor of a child's future life chances** – more than family circumstance, parents' educational background or income. It improves academic results, mental health, wealth, communication skills, ambition and happiness.

The number of children reading for fun is in rapid decline. Young people have a lot of competition for their time, and a worryingly high number do not have a single book at home.

Hachette works extensively with schools, libraries and literacy charities, but here are some ways we can all raise more readers:

- Reading to children for just 10 minutes a day makes a difference
- Don't give up if children aren't regular readers – there will be books for them!

- Visit bookshops and libraries to get recommendations
- Encourage them to listen to audiobooks
- Support school libraries
- Give books as gifts

There's a lot more information about how to encourage children to read on our websites: **www.RaisingReaders.co.uk** and **www.JoinRaisingReaders.com**.

Thank you for reading.

Made in the USA
Las Vegas, NV
17 February 2026

42038374R00184